BLOODFIRE

By Helen Harper

BOOK ONE OF THE BLOOD DESTINY SERIES

2ND EDITION

BOOK COVER DESIGN BY YOCLA DESIGNS

Chapter One

I ran steadily along the length of the beach, just on the edge of the salt foam and odd straggle of seaweed. A few seagulls were keening overhead and the sky was a cloudless azure blue with the light gaze of the morning sun scattered across the ground. My feet pounded into the soft sand, making light indentations that would soon be swept away by the unstoppable force of the sea. It was just the elements and me. Feeling the exhilaration of the moment, I sped up to a sprint until I felt as if I was flying. My heart thudded at a fast yet steady beat and I sucked in the salty air, filling my lungs before exhaling loudly.

Mack.

Go away.

Mack.

Piss off.

MACKENZIE!

I finally slowed and answered. *What?*

I'm going to check on the eastern perimeter. There have been rumours circling in the village about some strange noises. Will you come with me?

I hesitated, considering whether to put John off or not. It had been quiet lately and the few incidents we'd investigated had turned out to be nothing more than harmless local wildlife. I debated internally for a short moment; I could always stay out here and finish my run instead. Then I gave myself a brief rueful smile - who was I kidding?

Mackenzie?

I grumbled unconvincingly back at John's vaguely irritated nudge.

Way Directive 22, Mack.

Totalitarian dictatorship more like, I snorted mentally back at him. *I'm on my way.*

The alpha's word is law. There was more than a hint of self-deprecation apparent in his Voice before he broke off the mental link.

Thinking to myself that John was lucky that I was always a stickler for the rules – well, some of them at least - I moved away from the shore and headed into the forest, jogging through the trees. Dry pine needles crunched satisfyingly under my feet. I leapt over a few moss covered rocks and headed towards the east. Although the keep's grounds were officially around ten acres, we considered all of Cornwall our playing ground, at least up until the border with Devon where another pack took over. The eastern perimeter he had referred to wasn't that far away, however, just the far side of Bodmin moor. A few years ago we'd been in a bit of trouble around the moor because some bright spark with a digital camera had snapped Alexander in his animal form. He was just a kid so fortunately hadn't matured to full size yet – and the photo was blurry enough to cause doubt and dissension amongst those who saw it - but the gutter press had a field day waving it around and extravagantly spreading tales about the 'Beast'.

They'd had a similar problem since the Eighties in neighbouring Exmoor. Apparently, when the Marines were initially sent in to track it down, the commanding officer, who was never able to catch what he thought was just a dumb animal, had commented on that beast's 'almost human intelligence'. Hah! Still, with Alexander, we'd been lucky that there had been a particularly thorny problem in London at the time involving some water-wights terrorising pleasure boats on the Thames, or the Brethren, the shapeshifters' equivalent to the Royal Family and the government all rolled into one, would have come storming down. Instead they sent down some mages who waved sticks around for a few days, warning everyone that if the very public rumours continued then Cornish heads would roll. Or so I heard. John had me hide in the basement the entire time, however fortunately it didn't last too long. I suspected that Cornwall was considered too parochial for the Brethren to bother themselves about, even with such a shocking breach of protocol. Although word was that when they went to Exmoor after the first beast sightings, they had ripped the offending shifter apart, scattering his body parts across the whole of the United Kingdom as a warning.

I jogged along a small brook until it curved upstream towards the hills, then hopped over it and headed towards where I knew John would be. I finally found him crouched in a clearing, not far from the edges of the moor.

"You sound like an elephant running through those trees," he complained.

I put my hands on my hips and raised an eyebrow. "Is that the thanks I get for interrupting my run to come and investigate the over-energetic dalliances of some bunny rabbits?"

"That was one time." He straightened up. His salt and pepper beard and bald head, along with the laughter lines around his eyes, hinted at the wisdom and experience contained within that smart mind of his. John had been alpha in Cornwall for thirty-two years, and was universally liked and respected by the pack, but that didn't mean that I couldn't still have a little fun.

"So what is it this time? Don't tell me, I've got it, a sheep has gotten lost on the moor and its bleating is terrifying the farmers."

He held out his palm. There was a small shiny black object resting in the middle. "I wish that's what it was," he said grimly. "Take a look at this."

I picked it up from his hand and rolled it through my fingers. It was almost entirely weightless, and very smooth, and there was also something else. I held it up to my ear and heard an odd chiming sound.

John looked at me sharply. "You can hear it?"

"Sure," I said surprised.

"Describe it to me."

"You mean you can't hear it?" I was puzzled. Compared to my own hearing, John could hear a leaf drop from fifty paces away. "It's like bells. Only not, it's more continuous than that. Like a never-ending echo of a chime."

He pursed his lips, clearly unhappy. "It's a wichtlein's stone."

"A mine fairy's? They knock three times and a miner drops dead?"

"You've been reading too many fairy tales. Wichtleins do sometimes hang around old mines and tease the men that work there, but more often than not they are true harbingers of evil. I don't think one has been seen in the British Isles for more than a century."

"What do you mean 'true harbinger of evil'? What kind of evil? Vampire evil? Shadow men evil?'

"Try large scale death and destruction evil."

"Oh." I paused. "So not bunny rabbits then." I felt a brief shiver of heat inside me.

John held out his hand and I dropped the stone back into his lined palm.

"So what's next?"

His brow furrowed further and he looked at me with troubled eyes. I had a nasty feeling I knew what he was going to say next and felt a brief nervous tremor.

He sighed heavily. "I'll have to file a report with the Brethren."

Damnit. Up till now, for at least as long as I'd been old enough to be aware of how the pack was run, any reports John had sent to the Brethren had been *after* any Otherworldly messes had already been cleared up, and the details had been purely informative and retrospective. In other words requiring no further action. This reeked of a mess that was about to begin instead – and for me that spelled danger, especially if the Brethren were going to gallop on down to 'save' us.

I eyeballed John with a mixture of hope and skepticism. "Really? We can deal with death and destruction without them."

Unfortunately his voice was flat. "No. Something on this kind of scale is something they need to know about."

"Will they come here? Do I need to leave?" I asked quietly, curling my nails painfully into my palms.

He didn't pause before answering, which I suppose was slightly reassuring. "I shouldn't think you'll need to. Even if they arrive with a delegation to see our little pack, we can mask you well enough – of course as long as you're not in a position where you'd be expected to shift. Julia's been improving the lotion since the Brummie delegation were here last autumn. With that on even the Lord Alpha himself won't be able to smell a hint of your humanity."

I felt an immense wave of relief. As far as I was concerned, this was my home, even if the Brethren would strongly disagree. And probably summarily execute me for daring to think otherwise. Because I was human - and humans were not permitted to even know about the Brethren or the mere existence of shapeshifters, let alone live with them for seventeen years.

As for the lotion, shifters have an animalistic sense of smell. The first time another pack's members had visited us, years before when I was just a kid, Julia had set to work creating the potion that now, on occasion, we used to hide my all too human scent. She'd been getting better and better at it. Fortunately the fact that I spent all my time with my pack meant that the worst of my so-called human stench was already covered by sheer transference, while the lotion did all the rest. I had been meaning to ask what was in it for years but had always thought better of it. Sometimes ignorance was bliss.

John looked at me steadily. "I won't let you be put in any danger."

I forced a laugh. "I can look after myself. More than most shifters can."

"The Brethren aren't like most shifters. In Cornwall we're generally an amiable and peaceable bunch who fight off the odd wild bunny."

I smiled despite myself.

He continued, "Don't dismiss what you've already heard about them. They're different. But also don't forget that they're strong and unforgiving because they have to be. Without the Brethren keeping the local packs like us in check there are those shifters who would," he paused for a heartbeat, "cause trouble."

Actually I knew of a few who'd cause more than trouble. "But you're the alpha here. Can't the local alphas keep the trouble-makers in their packs in check?" I was aware that there was an irritating whiny note to my voice but I seemed unable to prevent it. John's voice, in return, remained calm and steady.

"A lot of my power comes from the fact that I can draw on the Brethren when I need to. And alphas can be trouble-makers too," he added with a slight smile.

I nodded slightly, trying not to let the nervous panic rise any further. I usually tried to forget that there were big bad things out there like the Brethren. It wasn't good for my health to think about the what ifs. Like what if the Brethren discovered who I was and killed me? What if they killed the whole pack for harbouring me? What if my mother hadn't compelled the Cornish pack to take me in? What if she was still alive? What if…

Nope. It didn't do any good.

"Anyway," John continued, "from what I hear the new Lord Alpha is eager to stamp his authority across the Kingdom. He's already made several visits to different packs and I have no doubt that sooner or later he'll make his way to us whether we wish it or not." He watched me carefully. "It might be better to get it out of the way while we can still maintain some control over the situation."

I snorted. "Whatever," and quickly changed the subject back to the wichtlein's stone. Bureaucratic protocol might demand that we had to inform our Lords and Masters about it, but I was curious as to whether 'large-scale death and destruction' was really going to happen, or if it was just scare-mongering. "How seriously should I take this rock?"

John's expression was suddenly completely humourless. "As to that, I'd say as seriously as possible. The ways and actions of the Otherworld are rarely without good reason." He held the little black stone between his finger and thumb and gazed at it quietly for a moment before placing it inside his shirt pocket and buttoning it over.

I frowned. If John was treating the situation that gravely then it definitely merited my more earnest attention. "I'll stay here and scout the area, and see what I can find."

"Are you armed?"

I had my usual throwing daggers taped to my arms. And, of course, there was my blood. "I'm good."

"Okay, then. I need you back at the keep by sunrise though or I'll send Anton out looking for you."

I threw John an evil look. Anton and I were not exactly mates. He laughed lightly and, picking up his broad rimmed hat that he'd left at the side of the clearing, turned towards the keep.

I watched his retreating back for a moment and then started looking around, belatedly realising that I hadn't thought to ask him about the rumours he'd heard that had made him come here in the first place. Scuffing the dirt in a few places that looked as if it might have been disturbed, I wondered if the gossip had been related to the stone. It certainly made a strange noise but it would never have been loud enough to attract anyone's attention from far away, and the village itself was at least ten kilometres from here. Maybe the wichtlein that had left its little offering in the first place had been of the loud variety. I shrugged and continued looking carefully around me. Despite my best efforts, I couldn't find any more shiny stones though, or traces of anything else. I paused for a moment, trying to use my Spidey senses but clearly I was either no superhero or there was nothing to be found. However, my gaze fell to the area on my right, which was dark despite the afternoon sunshine, and contained dense undergrowth that could be hiding all manner of things. Hopefully not actual spiders.

I forced my way through and sniffed the air. It was heavy and musty but felt natural. I ploughed ahead. Peering through the tangle of creepers and trees, it seemed as if there was something up ahead. Certainly not anything alive, or even undead, but there was something there that looked as if it didn't belong. I squinted, but couldn't work out what it was from this distance. I guessed I'd just have to push through the maze of prickly gorse bushes to find out then. This would have been easier if I'd been wearing jeans instead of my running shorts.

I took a deep breath and gingerly stepped past the first clump, wincing slightly as the sharp thorns scored the skin on my thighs. I gritted my teeth and carried on, hoping this was going to be worth it. By the time I reached the other side of the thigh-high bushes, although I'd already gotten used to the mild irritation of the pain, beads of blood were forming down the front of my legs. Cursing John, wichtleins and the world in general under my breath, I looked up and realised that what I'd spotted was a length of black cloth. Odd. I checked around it, in case it was a trap of some sort, but it appeared to be merely hanging on its own from the branch of a gnarly oak tree. I tugged it a few times but it was fairly stubborn so I yanked harder, falling backwards into the gorse as it came free.

"Shit!" I swore loudly, and even looked around to make sure that no-one had seen my fall. I wouldn't have put it past some of the pack to have set all this up just to have a laugh at my expense. Grimacing in pain as the thorns pulled away from my skin, I forced myself up and looked at my prize.

It was about three yards long with a skein of silver thread running through each side. It was unlikely that a Cornish local had left this behind, given its thorny location and heavy feel. I raised it to my nose and sniffed, before choking as the unmistakable stench of death hit my nostrils. Definitely not a local then. Unlikely to be a pack member playing a practical joke either – their sensitive sense of smell would have made it difficult to even get close to the material. Yet there was obviously something Otherworldly about it.

I searched around again for any other traces of anything, but came up short. There were no signs of a trail to be seen. I certainly wasn't a tracker of John's standards but I was fairly competent despite my lack of shifter super-senses. However, there was nothing; in fact it was as if the cloth had just dropped dramatically from the sky. The mystery deepens, I thought cryptically. Still, perhaps John might be able to shed more light on it. After all, for all I knew, wichtleins were merely keen fashionistas along with casually dropping ominous rocky notes of doom for random passersby.

Looking up, I realised that the afternoon was turning into dusk, with the blue sky darkening over just a tinge. I glanced back at the gorse, the only way out, and sighed. Better get going, I figured. After this, I didn't think I'd be wearing any pretty skirts for a while. Well, to be fair, I didn't actually own any skirts, or dresses, but that didn't mean I didn't want the choice to wear them if I wanted to - without looking as if I'd travelled through a meat grinder at least.

It took me some time to get back through the thorny bushes and return to the clearing. I had another quick look around, just in case I'd missed something, but there was nothing there. Trying to avoid touching it with my bare skin, I put the black cloth over my shoulder, and headed westwards for the keep. The light-hearted feeling I'd had earlier that day during my run had completely dissipated. The potential Brethren visit notwithstanding, John was clearly taking this whole omen very seriously. I made a mental note to check the keep's library later for any information about wichtleins. It was possible I could dig up something useful on the Othernet too.

I wasn't far from home when Tom, my sparring buddy, bounced up to me. His tortoiseshell hair glinted in the fading daylight and his smile matched his sunny appearance. "Hey Red! Where have you been all day? And what is that awful smell? Have you been digging up old graves again?"

"Out for a run, then I helped John with some poking around in the forest. I found this on my way." I pointed at the cloth from where the offending reek was coming. He couldn't help himself from leaning over closer and inhaling deeply, then recoiled away from me in disgust. Tom was the kind of guy who'd fart under the duvet then be compelled to lift up the cover to sniff.

"Eeugh! Let me guess, you were down a rabid rabbit hole and came across the shroud of Bugs Bunny?"

Clearly, my recent exploits had not passed without comment across the pack. I considered telling him the truth but figured that if John hadn't mentioned it to the others yet then it was probably not my place to say. "Something like that," I said dismissively, waving a hand airily in front of me. Tom shrugged and grinned, moving around to my non-death cloth wrapped side and placing an easy arm across my shoulder.

We walked companionably towards the large grey castle-like building. Even after living here for years, I still felt a little thrill whenever I saw it looming towards me. Cornwall's history was steeped in Celtic myths and rumour had it that our keep was built on the ruin of a centuries old Celtic castle. It certainly wasn't a fairy tale castle with turrets and steeples, but its solid squatness was both welcoming and reassuring. The grand oak gate at its entrance bore marks of various violent fights and incursions from the past, either from the shifters who'd lived there in years gone by, or from even earlier inhabitants, and the rippling imperfections in the various visible glass windows hinted at its lack of modernity. Behind the keep, out of sight, was Julia's little herb garden in which she grew any manner of weeds to feed her various concoctions, while in front lay a long drive covered in pale pink shale which had the unnerving habit of jumping up by themselves and chipping a long line of visitors' gleaming car paint. However, regardless of anything, it was my home and I loved it.

Julia was just inside the door when we entered, pinning something up onto the noticeboard. She was a tiny woman with grey hair, slightly older than John and a whole lot scarier. She'd lived with the Cornwall pack her entire life and treated everyone as if they were naughty children. She fixed me with a death stare. "Mackenzie Smith, don't you dare come into the keep with that…thing. It smells like Hades."

I lightly touched the cloth on my shoulder without thinking and then recoiled slightly at the shudder its touch gave me. "I need to show it to John," I protested.

"I don't care. It is not entering this building and defiling our living space. Besides, John has already gone out." She sniffed delicately and continued to glare at me until I rolled my eyes in acquiescence and began to back out.

To be fair to her, despite the keep's vaguely menacing appearance outside and shabby interior within, it was well-kept with a seemingly ever-lasting lemon fresh smell. I had long suspected that she hired brownies to clean it at nights, but had never been able to catch any of them to prove it. As Tom virtually sprinted up the stairs to get out of her way, I flounced outside and headed for an unused shed beside the north face of the keep, tying the cloth securely to a post inside before stomping ungratefully back in. She was waiting for me in the hall.

"When will he back?" What I really wanted to know was whether he'd called the Brethren yet and if they were really coming to our little corner to investigate.

"He said he'd be some time dear, but that he'd probably return by supper."

I scowled in annoyance. Now that I'd removed the evil smelling object from her notice, she'd reverted to calling me dear again. Julia called everyone dear. I knew she wasn't trying to be patronising but any endearments of any sort wound me up. Duck, hen, chick, even Red as Tom insisted on calling me, all annoyed me. Mack was fine. If you were Julia or John, you could get away with Mackenzie, but woe betide anyone else who tried that one. My red hair wasn't the only fiery thing about me. I was pretty sure that from the moment of my arrival at the keep, the whole pack had been aware of my volatile temper. And it wasn't entirely my own fault that I'd fly off the handle at times. Despite my mother's last words to keep my bloodfire a secret, I'd mentioned it to Betsy, a werelynx shifter the same age as me, when we'd pricked each other's fingers at age nine and sworn a blood pact of friendship to each other. I think at the time I'd just been happy to have finally found a friend. She'd vowed – and still to this day continued to assert the same, I might add - that she'd felt the fire inside my blood when we'd pressed our pinkies together. And, naturally, a scant three hours later the whole pack knew that I had a strange heat inside me that shaped my emotions and often directed my actions. I was pretty sure that most pack members were under the impression that it was a particular side effect of being a puny red-haired human, and my limited experience outside the shifter world meant that I couldn't genuinely say otherwise. Certainly, since that day, I'd learned never to entirely trust Betsy with a secret again. John, for his part, had merely raised an eyebrow and gently suggested that I made sure the fire didn't burn me out. Ha bloody ha.

I murmured something back at Julia and headed for the kitchen, hoping I could find something to eat and avoid having to sit down and pretend to enjoy Johannes', the resident pack chef's, cooking with the rest of the pack later on. Betsy herself was in there washing a plate. She arched an eyebrow at me.

"You smell....interesting, Mack." She looked behind me. "Is Tom with you?"

I shrugged. "He was but he disappeared when Julia started harping on at me."

She looked oddly disappointed for a second before returning to the sink. "Are you coming to the Hanging Bull for a jar tonight?"

I opened the fridge and dug inside for some bread and a hunk of cheese before sitting down at the large scarred wooden table. "Nah. I want to hit the library and check out a few things."

"Your young policeman might be there."

"He's not 'my' anything." I started sawing at the creamy cheese. I'd had a very brief affair with the local copper. His name was, and I'm not joking here, Nick. It hadn't lasted long. I'd had the feeling that he was looking for a little wife to keep the home fires burning while he saved the village of Trevathorn and its environs from dangerous washing line thieves and the local drunks. That was never going to be me. In fact, as nice as he was, I rather felt that I'd had a lucky escape.

I finished making my sandwich and started chewing it down. Unfortunately, Johannes took that moment to enter the kitchen. He saw me eating and gave me a baleful look.

"I...er...I'll be here for dinner, Johannes, I just need a little snack," I said hastily.

He humphed grumpily and began peeling potatoes. "Dinna think that you can pull tha wool o'er my eyes, dahling."

"I'm not! I've been out all day, didn't have lunch. I wouldn't miss your cooking for the world," I swore, hating myself for the lie - and Johannes for the endearment.

Betsy choked back a guffaw. "Just make sure you give her double portions to make up for that lost lunch, J." She leaned over to him and gave him a peck on the cheek. I forced a smile. It'd serve me right, I supposed. She winked at me on the way out and I pulled a face at her in return.

Once the door closed behind her, I rested my head on my hands and cocked an eye up at Johannes. I knew that while his cooking might not tempt my palate, he was a fount of knowledge and, unlike Betsy, wouldn't go opening his mouth to the others. I debated whether to pump him for more details on this afternoon's revelations or not. It might save me a few hours of digging around in the library. "What do you know about wichtleins, J?"

He looked up, somewhat appeased that I was asking him for information. "Scary bleeders those ones, " he said slowly. "Seen one 'ave ye?"

I shook my head. "Just a…rumour."

He sat down across from me. "Wichtleins ur trouble. Mah grandfaither saw one once, doon the mines. Knocked three times befaur disappearing. He hud enough guid sense in 'im tae get the hell oot of Dodge. Less than ten minutes efter the roof collapsed 'n twenty three men were kill't."

That gibed with what I'd originally thought. "So they stay underground?"

"For the maist part. If'n ye see one on the surface thae, ye'd better skedaddle. 'parently they on'y dae that when thair's summat big abrewin."

"What about tokens? Do they usually leave signs behind them?"

"Thay like tha mines and th'underground so often stanes."

"Stanes?" I was momentarily puzzled.

"Aye, lass. Wee hard pebbles."

Oh, *stones*. Now I got it.

Johannes regarded me gravely. "Stanes as smooth as silk and black as a witch's heart. Find on o' them and running for the hills willna do you ony guid. Cos then yer card's marked."

But I hadn't found the stone – John had. I pursed my lips, worried. Perhaps I should go after him just in case. I knew he could take care of himself but a harbinger of doom directed at him in particular was not good news.

I thought of one more thing. "What about bits of material?"

"Material? Nae that Ah've heard, lass." He leaned back and folded his arms and frowned at me with a serious expression on his weathered face. "You teck care of yersel' min'?"

I nodded. I appreciated that he hadn't asked my why I was suddenly so interested in wichtleins but the gnawing worry for John ate at me. "I don't think I'll be eating dinner after all, J."

Concern flickered in his eyes. "Aye, mebbe best not, love."

I stood up to leave. "It's Mack."

He looked puzzled. "Eh?"

"Never mind."

I headed for the door, checking the straps on my arms that held my daggers as I left. I did briefly consider picking up a bow and some silver tipped arrows as well. The shifters wouldn't go near silver, but it didn't affect me and was a powerful weapon against anything not wholly of this world. Though chances were I'd make a mistake and end up hitting John himself instead. I was a mean shot, but I knew enough of the vagaries of prophecies of doom to know that they were as likely to come about by your attempted actions to stop them as anything else. Perhaps it had been clear that the wichtlein's token wasn't intended for John though and I'd just missed it. He was at least as knowledgeable as Johannes, and would surely know how the stone worked, and therefore would have acted more appropriately concerned for himself if he'd believed that he was the target. He'd certainly been aware enough to appreciate that it was to be taken seriously. I mean, after all, he was calling the Brethren in for goodness' sake. He wasn't anyone's fool.

Yet despite taking the sudden appearance of the stone seriously, John hadn't appeared that worried about his own safety this afternoon. He'd been laughing and joking around, in fact. I paused. Or had he? I tried to think whether it had been both of us laughing about the repeated bunny adventures or whether it had just been me. Damnit.

I stopped to grab my trusty hunters' backpack and leather jacket to stave off the cold night air on my way out. Hearing Julia moving about on the first floor, I called up the stairs to her. "Julia?"

There were a few thumps and I could hear someone cursing. Her head eventually peered down from above the shiny first floor banister. "Yes, dear?"

"Something's wrong. Where did John say he was going to?"

My question hung in the air for a heartbeat and something flickered in her face. Fear?

"He didn't say." There was another moment's silence before she cleared her throat. "Should I muster the troops?" Her voice was quiet.

I thought about it for a second. Perhaps I was just being paranoid. But if I wasn't and John was really in danger then he'd need all the help we could give him. I'd rather look like an idiot and have him safe than risk the fact that he might be hurt. Shifters might regenerate cells and heal at phenomenal speeds, but they were still more than capable of being mortally wounded.

I flicked a serious glance at her. "That might be best. I'm going to head for the beach by the old cottages. Get the others to fan out from here and see if they can find him. "

Julia lifted back her head and roared. It was unbelievable that such a small woman could create such a racket. Almost immediately the sounds of shifters running for the hall could be heard. I couldn't wait even for them though. The fire inside me was already rising with every moment that passed. I shrugged on my jacket, swung the pack on my shoulder and left.

Bloodfire

Chapter Two

Practically speaking, there was a limit to the number of places that John could have gone. We'd been east that afternoon so he wouldn't be there again now. Having little patience with the local humans, he generally avoided the village so that was probably out. North of the keep was the road and south was the forest, then the coast. It was usually the case that any nasties around would try to avoid being inadvertently run over by a heavy goods lorry so stayed in the opposite direction. And where there were nasties, that's where I'd find John so south it was. I kept my mental fingers crossed that I was just over-reacting but made sure that I stayed fully alert and engaged, and that my daggers were easily accessible and wouldn't snag on my clothing when I needed them most.

One of the inexplicable skills that I had, and could boast about to, er, no-one, were a few parlour mind tricks. I could hear and respond to the alpha's Voice in the same way that a real shifter could, which admittedly might just be a side-effect of living with the pack for most of my life, much in the same way that women's periods aligned themselves if they lived together in close quarters for a long period of time. It was just too bad the Voice didn't work both ways, in my case or in the shifters' cases. Unfortunately only alphas could initiate mind to mind conversation and although I shouldn't by rights be able to hear him because I wasn't a shifter, the rules for me were the same. I couldn't contact him, he could only contact me.

But I also did have superior tracking skills – for a human at least – and was often able to sense when I wasn't alone. At this particular point in time it was all I could use because, without the shifters' superior sense of smell, I had little else to rely upon to find John as quickly as I could. Still, I was pretty sure that at this moment there was nothing out there hiding in the darkness and shadows.

Carefully checking the enveloping darkness around me as I went, I jogged steadily down through the worn forest path. I heard other shifters call out to each other in their animal voices from some way behind me. So far, nothing. The overhanging branches of a nearby tree caught my hair and pulled at it, catching some of the strands and yanking my head back. I cursed and stopped briefly to untangle myself when my gaze caught something gleaming on the leaf-strewn ground. I bent down to take a closer look before using the cuff of my jacket to scoop it up. It fell into my palm and heat started to rise in the pit of my belly. A wichtlein stone. Was this the one John had found earlier or was this one destined for me? I rolled it into my hand. It felt the same as John's one, but I had no way of knowing whether that was usual or whether it really was the same one. I was about to bring it up to my ear to test it for the chiming sound when I realised it felt unpleasantly damp. I picked it up gingerly between my thumb and forefinger and brought it closer. It looked like blood. I sniffed cautiously, then reached into my backpack without taking it off my shoulder and rummaged through its contents blindly. I kept my eyes trained on the stone.

My hand finally found what I was looking for when it curved round a cold metal canister. It never to hurt to come fully prepared. I pulled out the hydrogen peroxide, twisting it so the nozzle faced the stone, and sprayed a tiny portion onto the black surface. As soon as the chemical hit the shiny surface it began to foam. It was definitely blood. The curling heat inside me rose higher and my insides felt as if they were starting to burn. The feeling of panic matched the bloodfire but I did my best to push them both back down. Neither would help me right now. I put the stone carefully into a side pouch where it wouldn't get lost.

The moon continued to shine steadily down, casting shadows amongst the heavy trees. I could hear the distant hooting of a night owl out searching for prey and the skitter of a small animal somewhere nearby. I ignored them all and concentrated on the signs I could see at my feet. There was something else there. Reaching into my pack again, I found my torch, and clicked it on to look closer.

He had been this way. John was light on his feet and left little trace of his presence but I knew him well and knew this area. He'd disturbed the bush to my right, brushing past it as he ran. And judging by the distance between his steps, he'd been running fast, as if something had been after him. I frowned and arced the torch over the area, first close by then further along the path. There was something up ahead. Stepping forward, I tried separately to sense what it might be, but I was no shifter and came up short. Fuck. Where had he gone?

I pushed on the hydrogen peroxide nozzle again and began to spray liberally on the ground in front of me, hoping it wouldn't work. All I could smell was the damp, musk night air, with the deep smell of the earth rising up. I peered down squinting and holding my breath. The peroxide foamed in a few spots. More blood. It didn't mean it was John's though, it could belong to any kind of wild animal. It might even be days old. Despite these thoughts, the ever–present fire inside of me began to heat up even more and I could feel the flames licking up the sides of my stomach.

Mackenzie?

I almost jumped for joy before realising that something was different.

Was that…? *Julia?*

Yes. It's me. Defeat laced her words.

I felt my legs buckle under me. Only alphas could use the Voice to communicate and if Julia had found hers that meant that John's was gone. That John was gone. I gulped in air and felt the pain blossom through me. From the other side of the forest, a keening howl followed by caterwauling began. They were swiftly joined by others as the pack hunters came together in sudden horrifying grief. I couldn't breathe and fell forward onto my hands, barely registering the damp moss beneath my palms. One huge sucking sob sprang from my mouth. It couldn't be true, it just couldn't.

No.

I forced myself up. The bloodfire wouldn't allow this. He might still be okay.

I pushed forward with the torch in front of me like a ward, spraying as I went, moving faster and trying to ignore the hard knot of tears forming inside my chest. The foaming was getting heavier and the tracks were becoming clearer. It was definitely John's trail; I was beginning to recognize the heavy gait that slightly favoured his left knee. But if he was bleeding and in danger, why hadn't he shifted? Then he could have fought, he could have regenerated...

Until I saw it for my own eyes, I wasn't going to believe he was dead.

A cobweb brushed my cheek but I didn't even bother to lift my hand to shake it off. The trail was leading down towards the beach and away from the keep. Whatever had been chasing him, if anything had been chasing him, this creature that left no trail, he'd made sure that we were not going to be targeted by it too. He was a weretiger though. He was powerful enough to beat off almost any of the Otherworld creatures that ever made it through to Cornwall. It didn't make sense. I gritted my teeth and kept going, up over the final rise that led to the dunes.

And that was when I finally smelled the iron rich stain of blood myself. It had to be in a large enough quantity for my weak human nose to pick it up. I took another step and saw him. Or rather what was left of him.

His hat lay in a pool of blood that glistened darkly and wetly in the gloom. What I first thought were creepers reaching out from his belly I sickeningly realized were his intestines trailing away from him for what seemed an impossible distance. John's usually bright eyes were open, glassy and staring. A milky caul had already begun to form over his pupils. His mouth was open wide, and for one horrible moment I thought that he was laughing at me. It wasn't a laugh though. It was a scream.

I collapsed then and there, unable to move. The torch, and hydrogen peroxide canister dropped from my hands. I felt rather than heard something come up behind me and shove me roughly out of the way. I barely registered the shape of a bear taking a step forward then clumsily falling back. Part of me realised that it was Anton but it barely registered. Others came up from behind but none of them moved past the border of blood. Finally a pair of arms grabbed me from the ground and pulled me up and back. My feet dragged on the ground. Everything went dull and the air itself seemed to pause. There was silence while the world slowly spun into a black nothing.

*

When I came to, I was lying some distance away from the body. John's body. I could still smell the salty drying blood. I gagged and retched, sitting up to empty my stomach of the earlier half-digested cheese sandwich. Before I'd even finished, a hand cuffed me round the side of my face spinning me back to the ground.

A nearby wolf snarled.

Anton's face swam towards me. He must have shifted back to human. "What...the...fuck...did...you...do?" His dark eyes fixed on me unwaveringly. He cuffed me with his other hand.

The wolf snarled and knocked into him, forcing him to stagger slightly to the side. It stood in front of me, fangs bared, growling.

"She might be your fucking friend, Tom, but she knows something about this." He stepped forward again, trying to get past Tom's wolf form. Tom snapped at him warningly. "You don't get to do this, you piece of mange. I knew we couldn't ever trust a human," Anton spat. Another figure joined his, backing him up by assuming an attack position. Their eyes were both covered with a yellow sheen.

I leaned on Tom and pulled myself up to my feet. I looked at the three of them, completely numb. A wave of freshly decaying flesh hit my nostrils again, but this time I felt almost clinically detached from it. "There was a stone. A wichtlein stone. He found it today over in the east. That was the last place I saw him."

"Fucking ape! You're lying through your teeth!"

"It's the truth," I said dully.

Betsy padded over to me and sniffed. She gave a feline nod of her head acknowledging the truth of my words and padded softly away. Julia's Voice flared over all of us. *You all need to return to the keep. I'm sending a few others out with a bodybag. They'll get all...they'll get John and bring him home. It's not safe for the rest of you to be out.*

Anton growled.

This is not under negotiation. You will do as I say.

I vaguely realized that her Voice didn't quite have the ring of compulsion that a true initiated alpha's would have. Even Anton seemed to understand what disobeying her would mean for the pack, however, and drew back. "This isn't over, human," he spat again.

I just looked at him, unable to respond. I turned back to the keep and started to walk.

Chapter Three

"Red? Red? Mack?" A hand shook my shoulder roughly. "Mackenzie!"

My eyes moved up towards Tom. Part of me noted the panic and fear in his eyes before I looked back down again at the flagged floor of the great hall. I could barely remember getting here.

A hand slammed into the side of my face, slapping my cheek with a stinging crack and half knocking me off the chair. What the…? "Get a grip of yourself, dear. This isn't helping."

I raised my eyes to Julia and stood up, kicking the chair behind me, eyes blazing and blood firing. I took a threatening step towards her and she smiled dispassionately. "That's better. Now tell us what you know, Mackenzie. Focus."

I shook my head to dissipate the slight ringing in my ear and stopped, slowly looking around the hall. Everyone was there, the whole Cornish pack. Some looked frightened, others angry. It seemed as if all their eyes were turned to me, waiting for some kind of explanation.

Focus. Focus the fire.

I took all my grief and anguish and locked them away deep inside, allowing my bloodfire to flicker and bring me back to life. If only it could be that easy with John. Taking a deep breath, I told them all what had occurred that day, trying not to leave any detail out.

"We have no proof that any of this is true," Anton growled once I'd finished.

"We have the cloth," said Julia, smoothly, "Alexander has been looking over it outside but has found nothing remarkable about it other than the smell of death. And Larch has confirmed the time of death was around 7pm. Mackenzie was still here in the keep then. In fact everyone was here in the keep then because it was almost dinner."

"So whoever did this to John wasn't one of us," Tom mused.

"Yes," nodded Julia. "At least we don't have to go through the rigmarole of needlessly accusing each other." She looked at Anton as she said this. He held her gaze for a beat before looking away and I knew then, beyond a shadow of a doubt, that Julia was the only person who was right to be alpha.

"So what's next?" asked Betsy. She scratched at her neck awkwardly and looked scared. "Are we all targets?"

I picked up the chair I'd kicked and calmly set it back on the ground, before looking round at each and every shifter. "What's next is I find out who, or what, did this, and then I garrotte them. I'm going back to the site."

Julia took a step forward, asserting her authority. "No-one is going anywhere until we know it's safe."

Anger sparked inside me. "I'll go where I fucking well please. I'm not letting that thing, whatever it was, that killed John spend even one more minute alive than necessary."

"You will do as I say. Until we know what we are after, we cannot afford to let this happen again." She reached out and gently touched my shoulder. I fought the urge to not pull away. "You will get your revenge, Mackenzie. As will we all."

"Amen to that," murmured Tom.

From somewhere inside the keep the phone rang. Julia seemed to slump ever so slightly. "That'll be the Brethren. I called them and left a message as soon as John was found." She tightened her grip on me for just a second and then left to answer it.

I sat back down. I couldn't avoid the Brethren now, no matter what happened. The Way stated that whenever a pack alpha passed away, the Brethren had to be present to ensure that the transfer of power to another was without incident. Way Directive number forty-three. Apparently, in years gone by, there had been bloody battles between potential successors, with candidates being mysteriously bumped off at appropriate – or, depending on whose side you were on, inappropriate - moments. The rites and formalities to properly acknowledge a new alpha traditionally took three days. I could only hope that the Brethren wouldn't stick around for longer to investigate into John's death. I could probably fool them for a short period of time with Julia's lotion but I doubted I'd be able to keep up the pretense for any length of time, especially when sooner or later I'd be expected to shift. But I was damned if I was going to be run out of my home before I found out who had murdered the only father figure I'd ever had. One plus side was that they had a new Lord Alpha, because Xander Brandy, who'd been alpha up until recently and by all accounts was a vicious bloodthirsty werebear, had retired. I wasn't exactly a celebrity follower but even I'd have had to have been hiding under a rock to avoid noticing the chatter on the Othernet about it. I didn't know much about who his replacement was, in fact it seemed few did, but a newbie might be easier to fool.

For several minutes, nobody made a sound. Shifters were, as a rule, pragmatic about death. When you spent your time chasing after nasties, killing them yourself and often seeing your friends killed by them too, you tended to become somewhat inure to nature's most reliable outcome. But we hadn't had a death by unnatural causes for almost 13 years, which was virtually unheard of in the shifter world, and the fact that it was John, the alpha, made it doubly hard for everyone. Eventually one of the younger shifters broke the brooding weight and unearthly stillness by reaching over to her friend and hugging her. It was if she had released everyone. Suddenly there were tears and exclamations and hugs happening all over the hall. Tom pulled me to him and wrapped his arms tight around me, then Betsy, then Johannes, then almost everyone. It felt briefly cathartic, and while I knew that for most of the shifters it genuinely was, it didn't waver my resolve to hunt down and kill whatever had done this as soon as was humanly possible.

Eventually Julia returned. As soon as her presence was registered, everyone stilled and looked at her in unhappy anticipation. "They will be here by noon tomorrow. Their delegation will stay for the requisite three days, during which time they will also investigate

John's passing and the manner of it." Her voice was quiet but it completely filled the space. "They will perform the rites to appoint a new alpha and release any pack members who wish to depart, as is the Way."

"Will they stay for longer if they can't find John's killer straightaway?" someone asked.

I felt a frightened heat rise at the thought being voiced aloud.

"Not unless there is evidence of further imminent danger," she said.

Bloody lazy arses, I thought, contrarily. One of their own alphas had been murdered and they wouldn't see the investigation through to its conclusion because they couldn't be bothered taking the time themselves. I knew that was what I wanted but, still, it irked.

"Take this time to come to terms with tonight's events and to decide what your personal plans are, whether to stay with the Cornish pack or to move on. Make sure you choose the right path for you, because once it's made there will be no going back."

The Way stated that pack members were tied to their alphas for better or worse, no matter what happened. However, once an alpha passed away, members were free to choose other packs. It happened from time to time. Johannes in fact had joined us from another pack when his alpha had died several years ago. It occasionally meant that packs were weakened considerably from within in more ways than one, but the Brethren apparently kept a close eye on the situation and would allow a small number of humans to be turned and recruited if it was deemed absolutely necessary. They generally frowned upon it happening too often, as that put all shifters at greater risk of discovery. Potential newbies were chosen very carefully and I'd heard it was a particularly bureaucratic process, even though those who turned down the option were spelled by mages to forget they'd ever come into contact with shapeshifters. In fact, it had only happened three times in the last decade. After all, pack members did not, as a rule, have any trouble reproducing all on their own. It was extraordinarily rare that shapeshifters left without joining another pack, of course, as then they would be deemed as rogue. In those situations, the Brethren would get all uppity and track down said shifter to prevent them from doing anything that might be considered unsavoury or even dangerous.

Julia continued. "We may need intervention at some point with the local law enforcement. Mackenzie?"

"If they come sniffing around, I'll deal with them." One of the advantages of having a policeman as an ex-boyfriend I supposed.

"Good. I will need to talk to you about the – other issue too."

Anton laughed coldly. "You mean the fact that she's human? We'll all be dead if the Brethren find out."

"Which they won't," she said, without looking at him. "The geas still stands. Not just for Mackenzie's sake but for all our sakes. The Brethren's ways are an unknown quantity to me."

I had to batten down the urge not to stick my tongue out at him, as if she had been particularly

37

protecting just me when I really knew it was about everyone. I held no illusions that even though most of them liked me, their lives would be simpler and safer without me. They had all been bound and forbidden to speak of me as a human to any outsider, even another shifter, after my arrival when I was just a kid. And it was pretty much universally believed that, if I was discovered, they would all be put to death. No-one really knew that much about how the Brethren would actually react though. Probably because no human had ever been stupid enough to stick around shifters for any length of time without being eventually turned – not that the Cornwall pack hadn't already tried to turn me. I was clearly defective in some way if even a lycanthropic bite wouldn't do its stuff.

Regardless of any of that, it was usually only the alpha who travelled to London every trimester to meet and talk to the bigwigs so it was only John who'd ever known that much about them. He'd give them reports on the pack's well-being and activities, and receive his orders which could range from, 'Keep doing what you're doing' to 'Destroy any fairy circles you see' to 'Scary things are heading your way so kill them all.' Julia had been to visit them only a few times, usually for particularly glamorous and important social celebrations, while I didn't think any of the rest of us plebs had ever even been close to them. Elitist scum. The girls spent inordinate amounts of time following the Othernet gossip about some of the more visible Brethren members, oohing and aahing about the ongoing fights, relationships and power struggles, but I'd never really been able to muster up the will to care.

I should probably change that now, I figured. Know thy enemy.

Julia crooked her little finger at me. "Come." For now, I followed.

*

The office was a small cramped space piled high with papers and odds and ends. It led into John's study on one end and the great hall on the other. I was never entirely sure what it was really supposed to be used for. Whenever there was paperwork to be filed, usually whenever there was a kill order fulfilled or an incident deemed serious enough to be written up, then one of the pack would be designated as secretary. I saw it as demeaning and worthless to spend any time at all cooped up writing about crap that had already happened but I was well aware that were plenty of shifters who enjoyed the quiet – and the mind-numbing safety - of the four walls. I picked up a loose sheet that had found its way onto the floor which said something about Directive 98 of the Way being breached without probable cause. I almost laughed. Directive 98 referred to 'wearing clothes unbecoming an officer of the pack'. Given that shifters transformed naked, I had a hard time working out how any clothes could be more shocking than seeing it all hang out all the time anyway. There were 232 Directives in total. Clearly, someone somewhere had absolutely no sense of humour and no life. Then it occurred to me that the fact that I knew all the Directives inside and out probably meant that it was me.

Julia pulled up an ancient swivel chair that had bits of grey stuffing sticking out of the back of it and sat down heavily. For a few minutes she didn't say anything at all. I laid the paper down on the cluttered wooden desk and waited.

Finally she spoke. "We need you here and we want you here, Mackenzie. Don't ever forget that. This is not just about the geas or about the Brethren. It's about us too."

I was taken aback at the honesty in her eyes and suddenly found myself blinking furiously.

'Don't get me wrong," she continued, "you're antagonistic and temperamental. You don't follow orders and you can't be compelled. And whatever it is you've got inside you that flares up causes me great concern. God only knows how you can do some of the things that you can do. But I would trust you with my life, and the pack's lives, and I know they feel the same. I also know that there is nothing you wouldn't do for us."

"Anton might argue with you on that one."

"He's young. He'll get over that chip on his shoulder soon enough. My point is," she leaned forward, "that I am not protecting you because I'm being forced to as a result of some spell. You might not be a shifter but you are still one of us. Not only that but we need you to find out what happened to John, just as soon as we know it's safe to do so and we have all the information we need. I love everyone in this pack but I have no illusions that we don't have many able fighters. And you appear to have certain skills and abilities that are closed to us. So we need you emotionally and physically."

I struggled to find my voice. "I...I...need you too. I need all of you."

She picked at the arm of the chair. "I know, dear. Which is why we need to make very sure that the Brethren don't have any reason to pay you any attention whatsoever. I can gloss over your part in John's final hours and I'm confident that we've improved on the scent lotion from last time. As long as you regularly apply it every six to eight hours, no-one will smell human on you. We need you to act nondescript, however. Become grey."

"Huh?" I was momentarily confused. The emotions that her words had stirred, coupled with the almost overwhelming grief that I was only just managing to keep a lid on, were muddling my thoughts.

"I mean fade in with wallpaper. Dye your hair so it's not longer the colour of fire. And, speaking of fire, keep that down inside of you as well. Wear dull clothes. Don't discuss shifting. Don't discuss anything, in fact. It's only for three days and then they won't bother us again."

I thought about what she'd said before, that they might stay longer if there was danger. "What if it's longer? What if they decide to stay?"

"We will give them no reason to do so. I will assure them that we are capable of finding John's killer ourselves. We certainly have a history of being independent and capable – and remember a lot of that is down to your skill in keeping us safe. That will stand us in good stead. The pack will be good and keep the geas, although expect a certain level of starstruck idiocy when the Brethren first arrive." She paused for a moment and changed her tone. "Are you going to be all right, Mackenzie?"

I fixed her with a confident look. "Yes, no problem." I was all business-like now. Go me. "They're not going to dazzle me and I can do all those other things. Head down, be unobtrusive, don't discuss anything with anyone."

"Are you going to be all right in dealing with John?"

She meant dealing with his death. I swallowed and paused for a heartbeat before taking a deep breath and answering. "Yes. Because I have to be." My voice rang clear and I knew it was true. I'd do him no favours by curling up somewhere in a corner and weeping.

Julia stared at me for a moment, her eyes unblinking. Then she nodded as if to herself. "Okay then." She stood up and stretched, catlike despite her age. "I am going to take a long bath. There's lotion in the cupboard." She jerked her head to the closet next to the study door. "They'll be here at noon tomorrow – be ready."

I nodded. Julia left quietly but I remained standing there for a second or too, mulling over what she had said. I didn't want the Brethren to come. But then I hadn't wanted John to die either. I just had to swallow it down and last the distance. It couldn't be that hard. With that resolve in my mind, I opened the closet and found the unmarked lotion bottles. I took them all. If I was going to do this, then I was going to do it properly. It was time to get ready.

Chapter Four

By midday the next day my unshakeable resolve was weakening. I was hot and irritated. My scalp felt itchy from the dye and every time I turned my head I could smell the shifter lotion reeking from my skin. Of course I didn't dislike shifter smells – after living with them for so long I rarely even noticed any difference between their scent and mine, not that it was an unpleasant difference – but I wasn't used to smelling them on myself.

We were all standing in the hall. It was a large room immediately off the great oak front door. Shabby portraits of alphas from decades past adorned the walls, along with a couple of twee chocolate box landscapes. Underneath the paintings were panels of varnished yet undecorated wood and on the floor were slabs of smoothed grey stone. I tried to push aside the reminder of why we had all been there in the same place just last night, feeling myself still perilously close to great hiccupping tears that I was pretty confident would never stop if I let them start. Standing towards the back, I shifted my weight from one foot to the other. I had chosen my spot very carefully so I could keep myself relatively hidden from the gaze of the incoming Brethren. I was too sensible to aim for the very back – that's where the trouble-makers usually headed and I was sure that those standing there would be noted immediately for no other reason than that they were hanging back. But I still wasn't happy.

The tension in the room was palpable. I tried to breathe through my mouth to avoid being assailed by the stench of weak fear that was emanating from those around me. It was so obvious that even I could smell it. By my side I could feel Tom shifting from foot to foot. I hissed at him in irritation and he stilled for a heartbeat before returning to his nervous shuffle.

"It's been almost an hour," he moaned. "Why aren't they here yet?"

"Perhaps they've been held up because they haven't finished eating all their young yet," I snapped.

"Oh dear," came a soft voice sheathed in steel from behind me. "I hardly think that attitude is going to impress the Brethren, Mackenzie."

"And why the fuck would I want to impress them, Anton?"

The voice laughed, gratingly. "I give you two hours before they see you for the rabid animal you are and put you out of your misery. Oh, but wait, you're not an animal, are you? You're..." The voice deliberately stopped just there, daring me to fill in the blank myself.

I spun around, left hand clenched while my right reached into my sleeve for my dagger.

Cease.

I brushed away the voice inside my head and began to slide it out of its sheath. In front of me, Anton's blue eyes sparked, daring me to continue.

Mackenzie Smith. You are drawing attention to yourself.

I stilled, realizing that other heads were starting to turn my way.

"Red, are you crazy?" Tom's hand snatched at my wrist although his body remained facing the front. "Do you want them to notice you?"

"They're not here yet."

"And what happens when they arrive and you've got your hands wrapped around his throat?" Tom nodded his head in Anton's direction. "You don't want to give them any reason to single you out."

Anton's eyebrows raised tauntingly.

Mackenzie. The boy is right. Remember what we spoke about. You know what would happen if…

I pushed the voice out, slamming shut the mental gates, and turned back to face the dais. Unable to help myself, I glanced in Julia's direction. The older woman gazed back impassively, no sign on her face that she was upset that she'd been shut out from my thoughts. I grimaced and forced my hand to move back down to my side. My fingernails dug into my palms. I could hear Anton laughing from behind me.

Not a good start. And it hadn't actually even started yet.

Anton had the same geas about revealing my true nature placed on him as the rest of my pack, and couldn't say a direct word about it, but that didn't mean he wouldn't find other ways of forcing my hand and making me show who I really was. I didn't know why my presence caused him to feel so much animosity but I'd given up trying to change his mind about me years ago. I was certainly never going to be anything but human, not unless a vamp decided to snack on me, and even then that might not work. John had offered me the chance to be turned into a shifter when I reached my majority of eighteen. I had jumped at the chance, naturally. It had meant that I would finally, truly, belong. He'd bitten me and waited for the cells in his saliva to work their way through my body. Unfortunately something inexplicable had prevented the lycanthropic cells from taking hold – just another reason for Anton to jibe at me for being different. The result of the bite had merely been several days of unbelievable agony. And of course by the end of it I was still frustratingly human. However, if I kept my cool, and didn't let my bloodfire get out of control, Anton wouldn't be able to do anything about it. Piece of cake.

Tom's eyes slid towards me. I nodded slowly and he exhaled, his hand releasing my arm.

My usual bright red hair was now a mousy brown and I was wearing a uniform of generic jeans and t-shirt. Nothing that would draw any attention to me whatsoever, unlike several of the pack members who had taken the opportunity to dress dramatically. As far as I was concerned, though, as soon as this rigmarole of a ceremony was over, I could forget the Brethren ever existed. Until then all my attempts to hide in plain sight would be for nothing if I couldn't get a grip on my temper.

I slowly uncurled my fingers and forced myself to relax. Perhaps they weren't coming after all I pondered, half hoping - and half chafing at the thought that they had so little regard for my pack that they couldn't even show up on time. Didn't they understand what we'd all just been through? I almost growled. Even without the group's fear of what would happen to them all if my true identity was discovered, and the deep-seated grief that marked John's passing, they were all on tenterhooks about the imminent arrival. Would the Brethren like them? Would the Brethren find out who killed John? Would the Brethren save the world? Would we be honoured enough to be allowed to wait hands and feet on them? I snorted, making Tom look worriedly over at me again. I ignored him. Screw the Brethren. Part of me wished that I was long gone and so wouldn't have to witness the pathetic displays of my pack, my surrogate family, straining at the bit to do anything to please the sodding Brethren. Idiots.

I'd confirmed that none of them other than Julia had ever had cause to come in contact with the Brethren before now – well, let's face it, we lived in a backwater town in Cornwall for chrissakes, nothing had ever happened before that would have warranted the Brethren's attention – but the crème de la crème of the shapeshifters' reputation still preceded them. They were known to be bloody, ruthless and entirely without mercy for anyone who didn't meet their exacting standards. And still, the pack sighed over them as if they were gallant heroes galloping in to save the day.

And, as it was, I'd have to stay throughout the ceremony, so that the shifters who had taken me in when I was all alone wouldn't be faced with any hard questions, or harder punishments because they were one 'shifter' short. We couldn't afford to have the heroes looking for me as a suspect for John's murder when the real culprit was still out there. In three days' time I'd be free to find the bastard myself. I wondered if the Brethren were so arrogant to think that they would solve it that quickly and with that much ease, or if they just didn't care and didn't want to spend any more time away from the bright lights of London than was absolutely necessary. It didn't matter. Whoever was responsible for John's murder was going to die a slow and agonising death at my hand. Added to which, my late night conversation with Julia preyed on my mind. I wanted desperately to believe that she was telling the truth and that they all actually did indeed need me.

A sound came from outside and the waiting pack straightened their shoulders and puffed out their chests as if they were one. I did the complete opposite and tried to hunch down. The wooden doors at the right of the hall swung open and twenty or so people, all dressed from head to toe in designer black, came casually striding in.

As if they owned the place, I thought, gritting my teeth and hunching down lower.

The Brethren stopped and lined up in front of us. All of their hands were resting lightly on weapons that hung from their belts. Even from my lowered position I could see the glint of steel. Flexing their authority, no doubt. I looked fixedly down at the floor instead.

A tall gray haired man stepped forward, eyes sweeping over all of us. The room was so quiet that I fancied I'd be able to hear Anton's balls finally dropping behind me. I risked a glance up at their new leader. He wasn't what I'd expected. No obvious outpourings of power or charisma. He didn't look weak physically but neither would I have thought that I

couldn't beat him in a fair fight. This was just a guy –
and an old guy at that. I studied him carefully. There
was certainly an air of grace and elegance surrounding
him and he held himself with confidence and the
suggestion of strength but still…I didn't see it. Maybe
it was a shapeshifter thing.

He started to speak. "The Brethren brings
condolences for the loss of the Cornish pack's alpha.
We know that he was a good leader who kept the Way
and held you together. Do not fear that we will not
uncover the truth of what happened." His slate gray
eyes slid over the room. "His death was untimely and –
unexpected."

I blinked at the sudden unexpected rise of tears
and my throat constricted and felt tight. John had kept
us safe, all of us safe. He had never treated me
differently, despite my non-shifter status, and had even
spent a ridiculous amount of time training me to fight
so that I could hold my own against the rest of the
pack should they suddenly decide that having a puny
human amongst them was them was too much insult
to bear. And there were some who thought that way –
Anton behind me for one.

A memory rose unbidden of my ten year self and
John outside the keep.

I had been crouched down, throwing dagger in
hand, shaking in fear.

"Mackenzie Smith, if you give into fear then it
will rule you. Take the fear and turn it into focus. Use
that focus wisely. Feel for the creature and prepare
your mind."

We had been hunting a small wyvern that had been terrorising local farms. The Cornish pack was generally peaceable and didn't engage in much fighting (well, very few people or even Otherworldly things came to sleepy Cornwall to fight) but John had insisted that this was the time I put my training to the test in the real world. I had straightened up slowly and targeted my thoughts towards the clump of trees at the far end of the field. No fear.

A huffing sound had vibrated towards us. I had blocked out everything else and focused on the noise, willing the wyvern to leave the safety of the brush and come out.

"That's it," came John's voice. "You WILL do this."

I remember gripping the dagger tighter and taking a step forward, probing the trees with my eyes until I spotted a sudden movement on my far left. I took a step forward, and then another. Without warning the wyvern had burst out of the copse and flown like a dagger towards me, staying low to the mossy ground. I kept hold of the fear and, as the creature swooped close, I swung up, gripped onto its leathery neck and hung on with one arm. The wyvern had screeched in rage and dragged me up. It had veered one way then another, trying to shake me off before a taloned claw came swiping round to scrape me off. I had raised my leg and snap kicked the claws out of the way. I felt hot inside and knew that the fire, if I let it, would burn out of control. With my free hand I felt for the soft space in between the beast's shoulder blades and sank the dagger in. Of course once the wyvern tail-spun down I had belatedly realised that I was far too high and that hitting the ground was going to be very hard and very painful.

"Focus the fear and fan the flames," I had whispered to myself, before letting go of the wyvern's neck at the last minute and rolling to the side to avoid being squished.

My technique had been sloppy and careless but John had run towards me with a huge grin splitting his face. He'd gathered me up in a bear hug.

"See? See? I knew you could do it. You might not be a shifter, girl, but you have got skills, and power. You're amazing." His eyes had shone down at me with pride and I had realised in that moment that nothing else mattered. I had killed the wyvern and he was proud. It didn't matter that I was human, I could focus my mind with more skill than most shifters and I had taken down the little dragon when half of the pack would have been too scared to try. I belonged.

Later we had stripped down the carcass together and burnt it. I still had a tooth from the creature's mouth in the small chest where I kept my meager valuables. John had not let me fail at anything – but now he was dead and I had failed him.

Not without some effort, I zoned back into the present and realised that the gray eyed man was still talking. "These are dangerous times and you are without an alpha. For thirty years we have left you in peace. We respect the Cornish pack and the work that you do keeping this corner of the country safe, however we also offer you an opportunity to brighten these sad days. We will aid you by conducting the ceremony and appointing a new alpha, as is our responsibility. We will hold evaluations and interviews with every single pack member to ensure the appropriate alpha is chosen.

"And we also extend you an invitation. The best and the brightest among you may join us, come to London and become part of the Brethren, the shape-shifter elite. We have spaces for new recruits. This is your opportunity to join in the battle to keep all of this world, not just Cornwall, safe from all harm."

A tremor of excitement and fear ran through the assembly. Well that was interesting. Not only would the individual pack members be able to leave and join other packs around the country but they now could also become part of the so-called elite. I knew that just as there would be many shrinking from this challenge, just as many would rise to it and demand it. My brow furrowed. No doubt the Brethren were really just looking for cannon fodder. I felt my hackles rise while forcing myself to acknowledge that this could be a good thing. As much as I might despise them for their reported brutality and aggression, the Brethren could be doing me a massive personal favour. A new alpha would keep my geas in place, and the Brethren's recruitment drive would surely allow me to see off the likes of all those troublesome shifters who still couldn't accept me. And who were probably champing at the bit to show off anyway. I was still contentedly sure that Julia would be named alpha – otherwise why else would her Voice now be working?

Without false modesty I knew that, despite my human shortcomings, Julia was right and the pack benefited from at least some of my skills. I might not able to shift but I was pretty much the best they had in any fight, to the extent that since I'd turned into a teenager and gone into defense full time they hadn't lost any shifter to anyone or anything. Apart from John. I grimaced and shoved that thought away before it overwhelmed me.

Beside me, I could hear Tom panting like a puppy, patently desperate for approval. I wouldn't have been surprised if he jumped up then and there screaming, "Pick me! Pick me!" Never mind, I'd manage to convince him otherwise later.

Forgetting that I was supposed to be keeping my head down, I scanned the ranks of the other Brethren shifters. I was curious now about what their feelings were about taking in some of their distant country bumpkin cousins. My eyes travelled down the line. There was a bored looking blonde haired woman with a stance that suggested predator –wolf perhaps – then a slight dark man who was obviously a fox judging by the calculating cunning in his eyes, then there was…uh-oh.

The next shifter was looking right at me. Green gold predatory eyes gazed into mine expressionlessly. I snapped my eyes back to the floor and stopped breathing.

I'm no-one, no-one worthy of attention, I whispered silently, trying to quash the rising panic. I couldn't endanger the rest of the pack by being discovered. Every sinew in my body screamed but I forced myself to keep my eyes and head trained on the ground.

Don't look up. Don't look up. Don't look up. Seconds passed. Minutes.

"Hey," Tom nudged me. "What are you doing? Let's go."

I slowly raised my head and abruptly realised that the introductory assembly was over. The Brethren, including scary green eyes, were leaving to be directed to the guest quarters and the rest of the pack who hadn't rushed off to play the part of ingratiating hosts were milling about in little huddles, no doubt discussing just who the 'best and brightest' would be. I breathed a sigh of relief. It was okay, I'd passed. Now all I had to do was keep out of their way for the next three days and I'd be free.

Chapter Five

Back in the dorm, I paced around, trying to release some of my earlier anxiety. I wondered if I'd able to sneak out and do some hunting without any of the Brethren noticing. Probably not. I picked up a pillow from a nearby bed instead and pushed it against the wall, started pummelling it , the speed and weight of my fists keeping it in place. 3 days. That was just 72 hours – in fact make that 70 now. I could do this.

A throat cleared behind me. "Julia, won't be pleased if you destroy her soft furnishings."

"I'm not destroying anything, Tom."

A few stray feathers fell from the edge of the now burst pillow. I cursed and let it drop, turning round.

"It's okay," he said, reassuringly. "The masking worked – they didn't smell you."

"Sure, as long as I don't plan on bathing any time soon and keep slathering myself every 6 – 8 hours, then I'll be absolutely fine." I retorted sarcastically.

Tom came closer. "You will be great. They'll do the rites, choose the alpha, ask for leavers and then it'll all be over."

"He'll still be dead." I looked at Tom and breathed out. "Sorry. I just…."

"I know." He reached out and tucked a loose strand of hair behind my hair and changed the subject. "I miss the red."

"Yeah, me too."

I was pretty sure I could never be called vain but I did love my hair. I patted its new colour self-consciously.

Mackenzie.

Julia's voice popped into my head.

I need you to meet me by the tree.

I'm on my way. I sent back immediately before turning to Tom. "I have to go."

"Practise with me later?" His eyes held mine pleadingly.

"You want to join the Brethren." It wasn't a question.

"They're not all bad, Mackenzie."

"They're brutes."

"Please?" He blinked at me with large brown puppy dog eyes.

Oh, for goodness' sake. I sighed and nodded. "I'll meet you at the usual place after dark. Around 8pm?"

Tom nodded at me and I spun around to leave the dorm. I padded down the draughty corridor to the stairs thinking for the millionth time how handy it would be to be able to shift into something warm and fuzzy. John had refused to install central heating, insisting that Cornwall's warmer climate and woolly jumpers were enough. I shivered. My beloved keep was old and in dire need of a makeover. The stone steps leading down to the ground floor were at least covered with a shabby red carpet that had definitely seen better days. Some insulation was better than none, I supposed. John had said the keep had charm and character; I had retorted that Stonehenge had character but that it didn't make me want to live there. I tugged at my ponytail and sighed. I missed him. I closed my eyes and briefly pinched the bridge of my nose, causing me to stupidly miss the hole in the carpet on the next step. My foot slipped and, before I knew it, I was sliding down the rest of the stairs on my arse, coming to land in a rather undignified heap at the bottom.

"Graceful as always, Mackenzie," drawled Anton.

I glanced up and saw to my horror that he was standing there with two of the Brethren, the bored looking blonde and another, who were both looking down at me with slightly disgusted expressions. Shit. Shifters didn't fall, they had too much balance and grace for that.

I cleared my throat too loudly, muttering something inane about ungainly new shoes designed for humans, and pulled myself to my feet. I aimed for the front door trying to pretend that my left hip wasn't completely killing me and tugged at the handle to get out. I could hear Anton's voice behind me. "Of course, not all our pack will impress you…."

I slammed the door shut behind me and stalked out before realising that stalking hurt too much and a pathetic looking limp was much more necessary. That had been a careless move.

Several gleaming – and expensive – cars sat in the driveway. At the front was a sleek black sporty car and, just visible and bending down next to it, running his hands over the paintwork, was the green eyed Brethren bloke. I tried not to smirk as I realised that his showy pride and joy had clearly been scratched by one of the unreliable pieces of gravel that covered the ground of the drive. His back stiffened as he sensed my presence and started to rotate round to look at me so I quickly turned away and began walking smartly to the meeting point before he could start talking. I got lucky and he stayed silent, but I could feel his eyes on my back until I turned the tree-lined corner towards the green.

By the time I reached the old oak tree where I used to practise archery, dusk was approaching. I could just make out Julia's figure in the dim light.

"I'm sorry it took me so long, I…er…" I didn't want to disappoint her with tales of my already clumsy human behavior.

"Enough. It's not important," she said dismissively. "Whatever you've done so far can no doubt be explained away."

How did she do that? I could feel myself redden in embarrassment; after all it wasn't my fault that the carpet needed replacing.

Julia ignored my blush. "We've got more pressing matters to discuss," she continued. "I wasn't expecting the Lord Alpha himself to be here."

"You mean the gray haired guy? He didn't seem that bad actually, " I commented, swinging myself on to a low branch.

"Fool," she hissed unexpectedly. I almost preferred dear. Almost. "He's not the Brethren's alpha, that's just what they want you to think. He's merely their spokesperson. I thought you'd have picked up on where the real power was coming from."

I suddenly had a horrible sinking feeling in the pit of my stomach. "Ummm…green eyes?" I offered tentatively, hoping I was wrong.

"Green eyes of the devil, hair as black as coal mined from hell, and physical strength to match his strategic skills."

"Oh." I'd only noticed his eyes. My hackles rose. "So he thinks that he'll trick us by pretending to just be a minion?"

Julia sighed. "It's a smart move. He can find out more about us if we're not jumping to attention every time he walks past. Besides which, regardless of the attempts at blurry paparazzi shots on the Othernet, he appears to dislike the limelight."

"We're not his enemy, Julia, he doesn't need to dislike us," I pointed out.

"He doesn't know that. There was a lot of resistance when he took over as Lord. And he's only been in that position since August - he's ridiculously strong, and not just physically, but there are a lot of the Brethren who still don't feel that they can trust him."

I dismissed the subject. "It doesn't matter. I'll stay out of all their way and he'll never notice me." Of course that meant trying to ignore the fact that he'd noticed me during the welcome ceremony.

"You can't," she said flatly. "He's demanding that every single pack member's skills are tested and that he personally oversees each evaluation. I can't gainsay him. No doubt there will also be interrogations to find out who is responsible for John's death."

"But everyone's whereabouts have been accounted for!" I burst out, suddenly angry. The embers of flame inside me that had been quashed since the terrible meeting in the hall were starting to flicker. "What right does he have to come in here and do this?

59

We don't need to be evaluated to know what our skills are. And what right does he have to take pack members away to London? Why the fuck should we do anything they ask?"

"Because no matter what your opinions may be, Mackenzie, they are the alpha pack, and he is their alpha leader. Without the Brethren we would not exist. They support us financially and allow us to live here with minimum interruption in the safety of Cornwall."

I scoffed. "If it was safe here in Cornwall then John would still be alive. Besides, why is this the first time they have come here in thirty years? They didn't care about us before."

"For which we should be thankful, dear."

I could feel the flames continue to rise, scorching my insides and daring me to let them out. I forced myself to control them and looked at Julia right in the eyes. "Are you going to let them just take our people away?"

Julia sighed. "You know as well as I do that those who leave will want to do so. The old ties to the pack have gone with John's death"

I wasn't going to give up and was breathing harder at the effort of banking the fire. "Why are they going through this pretense of choosing our new alpha? We all know it's you already!"

"We've been through this. The rituals are what keep us together, and this is one of the most important. If I want to be a strong leader, then I need to be seen to be following the Way."

"It's stupid," I muttered childishly.

"It's the Way."

Julia folded her hands together implacably and looked at me. "At the risk of repeating myself, you need to rein in that temper if we are to get through this."

I was immediately apologetic and could instantly feel the fire falling back down to a smoulder. "I know. I'm sorry." I suddenly thought, and not for the first time, that I should have left when I became 18 and couldn't be turned. This wasn't fair on any of them, even bloody Anton.

"This is your home." She reached and touched me softly on the arm and then reiterated her point from the previous night. "We need you too."

I looked down at her face. Her repeated reassurance didn't change the truth of the thought, however. If I wasn't here then there would be no danger to them. I should have gone years ago, even if I had nowhere to go to.

"Here's what you'll do. Continue with the lotion. Do NOT bathe. When you are called to interview, act meek and weak. When you are asked to fight in an evaluation, then do so poorly. We do not need them to pay you any attention whatsoever. If they ask you to shift, tell them you're embarrassed because you're only a werehamster and of no use to anyone anyway."

" A were hams…!" I spluttered.

"It was the easiest scent to replicate. It's not completely accurate but werehamsters are rare enough that I think you'll manage to pass further inspection. Above all, do NOT lose your temper."

I jumped off the branch. "Okay, " I said quietly. "What about John's killer?"

"Once this is done and they've gone, then we deal with that. Who knows, they might even find the culprit themselves. They are the Brethren for a reason, after all."

I scoffed again. "They might be strong but that doesn't make them smart."

"Don't underestimate them," Julia said with a steely expression. "Especially the Lord Alpha."

"I won't. But John's killer is going to be mine." I looked at her steadily. "68 hours to go."

*

After leaving Julia, I wended my way to Trevathorn, the local village, skirting the keep just in case any of the Brethren decided to take in some of the night air. The village lights were on and I could hear the hum and murmur of voices from the Hanging Bull as I passed. Most of Trevathorn's inhabitants were under the impression that we were some sort of cult – probably a fair assumption actually – but as long as we didn't trouble them too much, they left us alone. Shifters had been in the keep for at least the last couple of hundred years so even the most fiercely Cornish of the locals would nod if we passed them in the street, accepting us as part of the scenery. I occasionally wondered if they suspected the truth but, if that was the case, they never let on. Nick had certainly never said anything about the pack, other than to murmur a few easily dodged questions about why I lived with them.

I didn't wear a watch but I was conversant enough with the night's sky to know that I was early and had time to kill before meeting Tom. I paused briefly, just past the door of the pub, before turning back and heading in. John had said that the locals had initially alerted him to the clearing where he'd found the wichtlein's little stone so perhaps I could dig something else up.

Inside the pub, the lights were warm and welcoming. There were a few people at the tables along the edges while Adam and the Ants bopped out from the ancient eighties' heavy jukebox. I nodded hello at a few familiar faces before perching on one of the barstools and ordering a diet Coke. I chatted to the barman while he poured my drink and tried to think furiously of a way to bring up strange noises and black pebbles without being too obvious.

"Is this seat taken?" A smooth voice uttered behind me.

It was Nick. Excellent – if anyone knew about anything strange happening, it'd be him. I turned and smiled, probably a mite too brightly by the sudden wary look on his face. I had to admit that he was looking good, blond hair smoothed back and a light tan that would be unusual in any other part of England bar Cornwall. I patted the stool next to me and gestured for him to sit down. He grinned at me, flashing a display of even white teeth and highlighting the little dimple at the side of his cheek. There was no denying that he was very cute, and that many girls would consider themselves lucky to have his attentions, but he was just so…old-fashioned.

"Hitting the hard stuff, are you Mack?" he asked.

"I'm working out with Tom in a bit," I answered, taking a swig of Coke and crunching down satisfyingly on a cube of ice.

He frowned slightly. When we'd been dating, he'd never quite been able to believe that Tom and I were just friends. I didn't really care.

"What the hell have you done with your hair anyway?"

"I fancied a change," I said airily. He didn't look very convinced so I moved swiftly on. "So how are things in the land of the crime-stoppers?" I took a sip of the Coke and hoped that was enough of an opener to get him talking.

"Same old, same old," Nick said with half a grin, "although there was a shocking case of burglary this morning."

"And....?"

"And nothing. It was probably just kids. Perkins was broken into but nothing much was taken."

Perkins was the local hardware store. It sold an array of DIY tools and kitchen implements. Probably nothing that a supernatural creature that left no tracks would be involved in. Not unless they had a penchant for home/cave/backwater portal improvements at least.

I feigned interest to keep him happy. "So what was taken?"

"A bag of coal and an electric screwdriver." He leaned back on the stool and folded his almond brown arms.

"Riiight," I said slowly.

"Like I said, probably just kids." He smiled. The wariness in his eyes had gone and been replaced by a slightly over-eager expression that vaguely alarmed me. We'd parted on good terms but I wasn't keen to have to quash any lasting hopes he might have that I was the woman of his dreams.

"Well, whatever keeps you busy, I suppose." I gulped down the rest of my drink. Clearly there wasn't anything to be gained from staying any longer.

"Leaving so soon?" he asked, the smile leaving his eyes.

"Like I said, I need to meet Tom." I stood up.

"You should be careful out there, Mack. By the sounds of things there are a lot wild animals around at the moment."

I paused briefly, half turning towards him.

"Didn't you hear the racket last night? It sounded as if we'd been invaded by London Zoo."

That would have been the pack, when John's death was discovered. Nothing new for me there then. I pulled out a screwed up five pound note from my back pocket and left it on the bar, motioning to the barman to pay for Nick's drink too. "Well, if I see any polar bears walking around with electric screwdrivers, then you'll be the first person I'll call."

"Do," he replied, with a cheesy wink.

I sighed inwardly and headed back out.

Trevathorn was a pretty place with window-boxes and cobbled streets but it was not exactly a teeming metropolis. After ten minutes of brisk walking from the door of the Hanging Bull, I was leaving the outskirts behind me and was in sight of the beach. The roar of the waves and salt in the air beckoned me and I quickened my step. I had briefly considered standing Tom up and going back to the site of John's death to see what else I could dig up but I recognised that with the Brethren around that probably wouldn't be smart. They had to have people out there already.

I stepped up to a jog, skirting the tough grass that scattered the path to the dunes. The moon remained high in the sky, throwing shadows across the landscape, although fortunately it would not be full again for another fortnight. By the time I rounded the top of the dunes, Tom was already on the sand, waiting. I slowed and took my time walking down towards him. Falling down once a day thanks to my seemingly inborn clumsiness was more than enough, thank you very much, and the sandy slopes were steep enough to warrant at least some care. The tide was out, leaving strands of seaweed and ocean detritus behind it. A small crab scuttled out of the way of my feet as the sand levelled out. Tom stood patiently, watching my approach.

I gave him a mock salute and, wordlessly, he handed me one of two wooden staffs before widening his stance in preparation. I ran my hands down its unvarnished length and it occurred to me that I was in need of some sparring. I had a lot of aggression still pent up inside. I wiggled an eyebrow at Tom, ducking just time to miss being hit by his first swipe. I retaliated with a crouching sweep that knocked him off his feet but he leapt up with more agility than he'd shown in recent sessions.

"Been practising much?" I inquired lightly.

He didn't answer and instead began circling me. His left flank was open so I jabbed him under his ribs and was rewarded with a faint ooph. He tried to even the score with a swipe but I pulled back just in time so that his staff found nothing but the wind. He immediately recovered, spinning the wooden pole adeptly in his hands and then lunging forward with an underarm attack that caught my clenched knuckles. I hissed slightly in surprised pain and retaliated.

We continued for some time, with no sounds to be heard other than our breath, the knocking of wood as the staffs connected and the rumble of the sea. I was beginning to feel my muscles tingle with pleasure at the exercise and a faint sheen of sweat graced both our foreheads, when he suddenly grinned and threw away his staff, pulling off his t-shirt and sweats. I took a step back and watched, ready.

He bowed his head and tensed, beginning his shift. It amazed me every time how an 80 kilogram man could become such a huge animal. Where did the extra weight come from? Shifters didn't transform into normal looking animals – even the smaller weres, the rodents and such-like, became larger than their human forms. And again, most definitely not for the first time, I wished I had my own shift.

Tom's bones creaked and his skull elongated outwards. His muscles rippled and the hair follicles around his chest and legs extended till he was shaking out his coat on all fours, with fangs bared and yellow eyes gleaming. Tom was a wolf. Generic, I know, but he had both speed and strength and wasn't afraid to hold back.

He leapt at me without any further warning and I rolled to the side on the soft sand just in time, springing back onto my feet and turning to face him again. His haunches tensed and he tried to feint left but the tension in his body had given him away. This time I used the staff to snag him under his belly and twist him onto his back. He whined slightly before staggering back to his feet. I paused for a second, just to check, but his tail gave a brief wag. Good, I wasn't ready to go home just yet; the fire in my blood was only just starting to flicker.

He manoeuvred around so that I ended up with my back to the ocean. Clever boy, now he had the high ground. He rose up on his hind legs and snapped at my face so I was forced to take a step back. Then, without warning, he barrelled into my midsection and knocked me off my feet, landing on top of me on the sand. I could swear I saw a glint in his eye.

"Tom, if this is when you decide to shift back to a naked man, I will not be happy," I mockingly warned. He was a friend, but most definitely without those kind of benefits.

He licked my cheek and went for my throat. His canines scraped the skin on my neck before I managed to twist and pull out my knife while using the staff to knock him to the sand and pin him down. I smiled.

Tom blinked slowly, a sign of defeat, so I let him go. He shook himself out and shifted back to speak. "One day, I'm going to beat you at this, Mack."

"I have no doubt," I murmured turning my head slightly to give his some privacy to get dressed. "You need to watch your left side before you shift though.

You keep leaving yourself open and you need to work on your body tension. I know what move you're going to pull five minutes before you do it."

"Are you using mind tricks again?"

"I don't need to, your body does all the talking."

"I'll practise in the gym when we get back." He had an almost deranged glint in his eye.

"Tom, about the Brethren."

"Don't. I know you're going to try to talk me out of it, but don't you see I have to try? John is gone, there's no reason to stay."

"It's because John is gone that you have to stay," I snapped. "We need shifters who can guard against whatever got him."

"Mack, if you couldn't track it and John couldn't survive it, I don't think I'll do much good."

"And what good do you think you'll do in London, then? You're my friend, Tom, I need you here," I said softly.

He jerked. "I asked you not to try to change my mind. Not everything in this world can be done to suit you, Mack. I want to go and if they'll take me then I'm leaving." He walked away up the dunes.

I frowned after him. Well, that could have gone better. I probably shouldn't have tried to guilt him with the whole 'I'm your friend, don't leave me' part - that wasn't fair. I just didn't want to lose him to the big bad because I wasn't sure that he'd be able to hold his own. Perhaps I was just being patronising and over-protective, but he probably was my closest friend. If I wasn't going to look after his best interests, then who would?

I sighed and picked up the discarded staff. As I stood back up I felt a prickle on the back of my neck, as if someone was watching. Tensing, I searched the line of trees. Way Directive 3: All shifter activity must be kept hidden. The locals never bothered coming out this far, especially at this time of night, but it would be just my luck that a stray tourist out for a midnight stroll would decide to head my way. I tried to pierce the night gloom, searching for a hint of anything sentient, but came up with nothing out of the ordinary and eventually shrugged at my own paranoia. The tension of having the Brethren here was clearly playing tricks with my mind.

I turned to face the sea and gazed out at its expanse, emptying my mind for a brief moment. The gentle swish of the waves rhythmically beat against the beach and I closed my eyes for a second, breathing deeply. Then I turned back towards the heavy dunes and headed for home.

Chapter Six

It was late by the time I got back and the keep was quiet. Some floorboards on the third floor where the Brethren were housed creaked, but everyone else seemed to be asleep. I slipped into the dorm and lay down on my bed. I figured I'd go for a shower in a minute before I remembered that I wasn't allowed to. Ick. Soft snores came from several of the other pack girls - I was pretty certain that with all of the heartache and worry of the last few days I personally wasn't going to get any sleep any time soon. Although shifters would stay awake for the entire full moon period, reveling in the extra power it gave them, they tended to keep a fairly normal sleep pattern the rest of the time. Usually it suited me perfectly because I truly loved my narrow bed, unfortunately right now it was just irritating that everyone else was in dreamland. Yup, tossing and turning would be the best I could hope for.

I closed my eyes and almost immediately slept a dreamless sleep.

Seven hours later the sun was streaming into the dorm room and hitting my face. I moaned and turned over, sticking the pillow over my head. I could hear the voices of the other girls chattering. It was a blessed relief to hear some normality after the hushed tones of the last twenty-four hours.

"Is he single?" Lynda wanted to know.

Ally giggled. "He'd better be! Oooh, that body, wouldn't you just love to feel it wrapped around you."

One of them threw a stuffed cow at me. Shifter girls might be tougher than most human ones but they definitely loved their cuddly toys. "Mack, what do you think of the alpha?" It was Betsy. Whatever I said to her would be round the pack before I'd brushed my teeth. I didn't answer and kept the pillow firmly closed over my head.

"Mack, apparently he's not the one who was talking last night – that was Staines, the Brethren's Head of Strategic Deployment or something. The Lord Alpha is the gorgeous one with the black hair." Ally laughed again.

"Did you clock those muscles?" One of the others loudly shrieked. I winced at the noise.

"I heard that when he took over as Lord Alpha, he had sixteen challenges to the leadership, and that he beat each one without even breaking a sweat. And that he's really shaking things up in London – wants to stop a lot of the old traditional ways and bring the Brethren into the twenty-first century."

I may not have known a lot about our de facto leaders but I was pretty sure that the old guard wouldn't be too keen on that.

"Well, Alexander said that apparently even the vamps are afraid of what he's going to do next. That when one of their Masters went round to welcome him as the new Lord Alpha, he didn't even bother to answer the door."

Ally piped up again. "I read last night on the Othernet that he has dozens of girls just gagging to be with him, not just because he's in charge now, but because he's very, very skilled in pleasure as well as pain." She almost purred this last comment. I snorted aloud, which was a mistake, because it drew their attention back to me.

"Mack! What do you think of him?" Betsy repeated; clearly she wasn't going to let me get away from this.

"Obviously I need to stay away from him as much as possible," I said, finally pushing my pillow out of the way and turning over. I sat up and tried to eyeball her into submission.

"Oh yeah," she answered, somewhat deflated, before pausing briefly to give me a funny look and asking, "Why are you rolling your eyes like that?"

I scowled.

"Do you think they'll really kill us all for breaking the Way and letting you stay?" asked Lynda tremulously.

"It's not as if we had a choice," said Betsy, firmly. "That witch made us take her. And she was only a little kid, we couldn't have turned her away."

That 'witch' was my mother. I bit my tongue hard. And I wasn't a little kid who needed protecting any more.

Ally spoke up. "Well, it was John who forced us not to say a word to anyone. We couldn't go against our alpha, could we?"

"Yes, but John's dead," stated Betsy with a grim face. "We're not under any real compulsion now."

Silence filled the room. I had wondered when they'd start realising that. In fact I was surprised that Anton and his cronies hadn't made more of it yet. Perhaps I'd misjudged them and they'd keep their mouths shut after all. I checked my watch. 56 hours to go — hardly any time at all for twenty-four shapeshifters to have to keep their mouths shut. I looked back at Betsy and glared at her again. She gazed back at me innocently before sending me a grin and a wink.

Ally padded over to my bed and bent down, hugging me unexpectedly. "We love you really, Mack, and not just because of your snappy dress sense."

"Yeah," added Betsy, grin still in place. "Even if the Lord Alpha himself got on his knees and pleaded directly to us with that weak-at-the-knees face, that flowing hair that you'd just love to run your fingers through, those bulging biceps that would wrap themselves around…"

I threw the stuffed cow back at her. Betsy neatly dodged it, without moving her feet, and laughed warmly. "Even then, Mack, even then we wouldn't betray you. You're as much a part of the pack as the rest of us."

I tried to appear tough by growling, "Yeah, well, that's just what I'd expect." The effect was somewhat ruined when a single tear traitorously escaped and ran down my cheek. Bloody girls.

There was a sharp knock at the door then Julia came in, dressed unexpectedly in a navy business suit. She sent me a warning look, which I tried and failed to interpret. "The Brethren have set appointments for each of you to be evaluated and then interviewed. There are sheets posted downstairs. You need to check your times and, for God's sake, don't be late."

Lynda giggled again, her earlier trepidation seemingly forgotten. "Are the interviews private ones with the alpha?"

"No," Julia said. "He'll oversee all the evaluations but only some of us are lucky enough to have the privilege of being interviewed by him." She looked meaningfully at me. Shit.

"I don't want to go to London, and I don't want to be alpha," interjected Julie, "Can I skip the evaluations?" Bless her.

"It's their prerogative to test every pack member. I imagine they're curious as to why we've sustained so few serious injuries over the years."

Betsy looked at me. "I guess our resident human is good for something."

I pulled back the duvet and swung my legs out of bed. "Just remember that when I go down at the first punch this morning."

*

After re-applying the shifter scented lotion and getting dressed, I headed down to the hall. The evaluation schedule was stuck on the noticeboard, next to an old ragged poster advertising the spring social. I checked for my name and noted that I was down to fight Theresa, a weresquirrel, at 10.30am. Tom was listed against Anton fifteen minutes later. I breathed a sigh of relief - he had no hope against that canny bastard. The interviews were scheduled for the afternoon. No problem. At all. Honest.

I headed for the canteen and took my place in the short queue for breakfast. Johannes, who had come to us from the pack up in Berwick about five years ago when his alpha had dropped dead of an early heart attack, had clearly been at work. I dolloped burnt bacon, scrambled eggs and some slightly charred toast on my plate. Someone came up next to me and started to do the same. I glanced sideways and realised it was one of the Brethren. I tried not to hold my breath.

"Mmmm, crispy bacon," she said.

I was about to retort something in Johannes' defense when I realised that she was being genuine. Odd – even those who normally liked their bacon crispy found Johannes' offerings hard to handle.

She piled several pieces on her plate and smiled at me from under a dark fringe. "I'm Lucy." And then added, just in case I wasn't sure, "I'm with the Brethren."

"Mack. Cornwall pack."

"Woman of few poetic words there, Mack. We don't bite, you know." She laughed suddenly, "Well, not this early in the morning anyway."

I'd withhold judgement on that one till they left without discovering my true nature. "I'm sure you're all very cuddly."

Lucy snickered again. "Relax. We're just curious about you. We visit the countryside packs whenever they need help with a particularly vicious Otherworlder or arbitration with an in-pack dispute. We've never had to come here before and you've never needed us. It's….unusual."

She was trying to be friendly, not combative. I took a deep breath and tried to match her relaxed attitude. "Not much happens around here. Not like London, I guess."

"Yeah, beating up vampires and city-slicker daemons while dodging the Ministry of Mages is a whole lot of fun." She added some black pudding to her plate while I winced in anticipation of her ruined tastebuds. "I'm sorry about your alpha. It seemed like he was a good guy."

'He was," I replied, swallowing down the unexpected lump in my throat. "When I find out what killed him, I'll rip its guts out."

Lucy looked at me curiously and paused for a second before asking, "So what are you?"

I knew what she meant but I wasn't going to go down that road unless I really needed to. The ways of actual werehamsters were a mystery to me and I didn't want to get caught out. Deliberately misunderstanding her question, I replied, "Hungry," and turned to sit down at a nearby table. Now that I've covered a few niceties you can go away, I willed silently, looking down at my unappetising plate and hoping she'd get the message.

Unfortunately Lucy wasn't going to give up that easily. She sat down opposite me and began shoveling food into her mouth. I stared in fascination, before picking up my knife and fork and gingerly taking a few bites myself.

"You know what I mean," she said insistently between mouthfuls. "What's your shift?"

"I don't like to talk about it." With any luck she'd think that I was a small weak were that I was slightly ashamed of. Like a hamster. Then I belatedly remembered that I'd said I was going to rip the guts out of whatever had slaughtered John. Oops.

"Huh." She looked somewhat nonplussed for a second before continuing, "Well, I'm a honey badger." That explained the voracious appetite then. I was relieved it appeared that she wasn't going to push me any further to reveal my own shift. "It's a pleasure to find out so much about you, Mack 'I don't like to talk about it'." She took another mouthful and began chewing hard on a piece of bacon.

"I'm sorry. I'm just nervous." I didn't want to play the meek and weak card, and I clearly wasn't much good at it. Lucy seemed like a decent shifter who I'd normally get along well with, despite her Brethren affiliations. Then I thought briefly of Julia's instructions and realised that if I was to survive this then I had no choice. "You all just look so strong and…masterful." Oh god, kill me now. She flicked her eyes at me briefly, with a faintly amused expression on her face, before returning her attention to her plate.

I took a few more bites and was about to speak again when a bell sounded. Lucy immediately stood up, suddenly all business instead of focused on her food. "The evaluations are about to begin." She looked at me assessingly. "I wonder how you'll do?"

I coughed, staying in my seat. "I'm…er…not much of a fighter."

"It's not just fighting skills that we're after."

Yeah, you are looking for anyone who'll help you force your control over every shifter in the country, I thought irritably. "I like it here in Cornwall." I scratched awkwardly at my neck, then realised what I was doing and pulled my hand down to my side.

"I can understand that." She pulled slightly at her black shirt, smoothing it down. "I think there are a few of your comrades who want to leave though. Come on, this is going to be fun." Her eyes gleamed with a spark of gleeful anticipation.

I sighed and stood up too. Better get it out of the way, I supposed.

*

The whole pack was assembled in the gymnasium by the time I arrived with Lucy. It was utterly ridiculous that everyone was being made to participate in the evaluations, like we were some kind of performing seals here just for the Brethren's benefit. It was equally galling to see how excited some of them were with various typical shifter tics manifesting themselves. Was that Tom actually pawing the ground? I tried to catch his eye but he didn't look up. He must still be pissed off with me. I looked up at the gallery and noted Staines, the blonde and the Lord Alpha but didn't see any others. They were huddled together in some kind of confab. Whatever. Lucy noted my survey and murmured that the remainder of the visiting Brethren were out investigating the area where John had been killed. As if they'd find anything, I thought. There were no tracks and no traces of anything. That didn't mean I wouldn't still find out myself what it was that had ripped him apart like that so gorily. I wasn't stupid enough to not acknowledge that the Brethren would have skills aplenty but I knew I was simply more invested in finding his murderer than they were.

I took my place at the side with the rest of pack while Lucy headed up to the gallery.

Staines began to speak, his voice filling the space. "Tomorrow evening we will confirm the new alpha of the Cornish pack. In the meantime, in accordance with the Way, we shall evaluate all members' skills to help determine who that shall be."

I rolled my eyes at the obvious procrastination. It was still going to be Julia. The evaluations were just the Brethren's way of reminding us that they were in control.

Staines consulted a sheet. "Nina and Betsy, take your places."

The two girls stepped forward, looking visibly nervous. "Begin," said Staines.

They circled each other warily. Neither had weapons, in accordance with the rules of the evaluations, but they could shift if they wished. I pegged Betsy as the winner. She had more tenacity about her than Nina. It was Nina who made the first move though, pouncing towards Betsy with a feline swipe. She caught her on the side of the head and Betsy took a staggered step back. Score one to Nina.

I looked up at the gallery again. The blonde was making notes while Staines frowned down at the fight. Lucy at least looked down more encouragingly. The Lord Alpha was next to them, arms folded. This was the first chance I'd had to study him properly. His hair was pure black, as Julia had mentioned, and he retained a golden all over tan that didn't look like it came out of a bottle. And, as advertised, his physique was…impressive, I had to admit grudgingly. He towered over the other two, filling the space. I could see what Julie had meant about having those arms wrapped around you and doubted that he ever had any trouble getting a girlfriend. I was equally sure that if he was your enemy he'd squash you without breaking a sweat or giving it a second thought. I wondered what his were actually was and shivered involuntarily.

On the gym floor, Nina squealed and I returned my attention to the fight. Betsy had her by the hair and on her knees. I smiled, before remembering that I shouldn't know anything about fighting or appreciate a strong display of it in any way. Meek. Weak. Meek. Weak. Betsy looked up at the gallery for approval and the Lord Alpha nodded. With that the fight was over. The blonde took a few more notes then the next pairing began.

The evaluations went by with unhappy swiftness. I could see that virtually everyone's techniques lacked flair or skill but couldn't decide if I was pleased or disappointed that there was no-one to impress the Brethren. Once Johannes' and Fergal's evaluation was over – Fergal won as Johannes' fighting was about as impressive as his cooking – Staines called me and Theresa and we took to the floor. Our eyes locked briefly. Theresa knew that she would beat me with ease for the first time in her life but that she also had to make it look like a genuine win, rather than that I was throwing the fight. I wondered if it annoyed her but figured probably not. She was a warm-hearted were-squirrel who I was pretty sure was content with her lot in Cornwall, not least because she had a huge crush on Johannes. Those two were going to be doing some serious mating before too long. Maybe she'd help him out in the kitchen then and we might get some edible food. One could always live in hope.

I didn't want to draw attention to myself by too obviously not trying so I took a step forward, making sure that I was completely open to a counter attack, and swung clumsily at Theresa. I managed a glancing blow off her shoulder while she retaliated with a fist to my face. The fire inside me started to rise but I managed to immediately dampen it down. It didn't hurt much but I made a show of wincing dramatically before trying to feebly kick her off her feet. She sidestepped me neatly and launched out her arm. It wasn't a great shot but I let it flip me onto my back and lay there for a second, giving her the win. Fast and painless. I peeked at the rest of the pack who had been following the fight closely. Anton had a smirk on his face but the rest kept their expressions clear. Good. I was pretty sure there was a glint of approval in Julia's eyes as well.

Theresa was looking up at the Brethren for confirmation so I followed her gaze. The Lord Alpha looked irritated so I aimed for embarrassment and shrugged as if there was nothing I could have done. The blonde murmured something to him and he nodded briefly at Theresa. She extended me her hand and pulled me up to my feet.

On our way back to the sidelines, with our backs to the gallery, I mouthed thanks at her. She grinned at me and I exhaled softly. With the evaluation done there was just the interview to get through and then it would almost be over.

Anton leaned over to me when I re-took my place, "Watch me make your boyfriend howl in agony." He swaggered towards Tom in the middle of the floor.

I counted to ten and gritted my teeth. It didn't work so instead I envisaged breaking his nose with my fist. That was better.

Tom had already shifted into his wolf form by the time that Anton reached him. I could feel the rest of the pack murmuring around me. He was the first one to make such a blatant show of intention about doing well in front of the Brethren. Anton grinned ferally but stayed human. By not shifting he was also signaling that he was more powerful than Tom and didn't need any supernatural aid to win. For the first time in my life I found myself hoping the arrogant prick would be successful. Tom snarled at him and they began.

Anton danced around Tom's shape with light steps, teasing him by bluffing forward then stepping back. Even as a wolf I could sense Tom's frustration. He snapped his teeth a few times but didn't connect. Without warning, and in a blur of motion, Anton karate-chopped Tom's back and then danced away again. Tom didn't go down but he was clearly winded. He snapped again at Anton and launched himself at him so that they both ended up in a tussle on the floor. Anton managed a few jabs at Tom's underbelly but it seemed as if Tom was gaining the upper-hand because all of a sudden he drew blood from Anton's arm. I cursed silently. I'd expected more from Anton. Tom could have ended it there and then but he pulled back and Anton bounced back to his feet. They eyed each other up. Tom's body tensed and I could tell he was going to go for Anton's left. Unfortunately for Tom, so did Anton. As soon as he made his move, Anton spun round and scissor kicked. Tom collapsed and it was over. Anton swept a mocking bow in front of the crowd and despite my relief that Tom had lost I still wanted to knock that smile off his face. Meek. Weak. Meek. Weak. I continued to recite in my head.

The remaining evaluations passed without incident. Julia beat her opponent with ease and, other than Anton's performance, no-one else had appeared particularly skillful, I felt proud that my pack had acquitted themselves without any real disasters. The few bites I'd had for breakfast had done little to appease my appetite and I was actually starting to look forward to some lunch. Because of the evaluations and his own forced participation, Johannes had ordered in some outside catering. Excellent.

I started to move towards the door but Theresa caught my hand and shook her head warningly. Oh right. We hadn't been 'dismissed' yet. It was as if we were bloody kids in a kindergarten. Staines' head was bowed as the alpha spoke to him. He looked puzzled but nodded anyway and took a step forward.

"Thank you for your efforts. We applaud the pack of Cornwall for their skills. To complete the evaluations, there will be a re-match. Fighting again will be Anton and," he looked over his shoulder at the blonde's notes, "Mackenzie."

Bugger. Bugger. Shit. Bugger. Why make us perform twice? I'd given them no cause to do this. The assembled pack on the gym floor murmured uncomfortably. Walking back to the centre of the gym floor, and trying not to look too pissed off, I decided that the Brethren just wanted to see the 'weakest' pack member humiliated further. Well, fine. I'd let them humiliate me by allowing Anton to beat me and then I could pretend to slink away and lick my wounds. The wankers.

The pack members around me were clearly concerned and tense but I smiled graciously as if this had been expected and stepped forward to the marked out circle. Anton did the same. He licked his lips in anticipation. Yeah, suck it up, fuckwit because you'd never beat me under any real terms.

Mackenzie... Julia sounded worried.

Don't worry, I'll deal with this.

Anton pulled off his shirt and raised his eyebrows at me before undoing the drawstring of his trousers. I was taken aback for a second. He was actually going to shift. He opened his hands out to me invitingly as if asking me to shift also. This time it wasn't about an acknowledgement of power: he was trying to force the Brethren to realise what I was. Bastard. I smiled calmly back at him and shook my head. God alone knew what the Brethren thought about my actions after my dismal performance earlier. I'd have to think of a reason for not shifting later on.

Anton was a black bear, which meant he packed a hell of a wallop in his shifter form. This was going to hurt. And once the Brethren left, I'd make him pay. I straightened my shoulders. "Let's do this."

He transformed within a heartbeat and raised up on his hind quarters with a triumphant roar. I took a step back and tried to look scared. Be meek, be weak.

He moved down to all fours and pounded towards me. I stood my ground and waited. He got closer and reached out with one heavy claw. I felt my body spinning through the air and twisted so that the fall wouldn't hurt me too much. I would have stayed there and hoped that it was enough but he came at me again, teeth sinking into my side, their points piercing through into the soft flesh. The pain was excruciating. He shook me a few times then flung me against the wall, which I hit with a thud. I lurched to my feet.

From across the room I heard Tom's voice snarl something at Anton. Bloodfire pulsed in my skull, forcing its heat to rise through me, while I could vaguely sense Julia trying to use her Voice on Anton. With her status not yet confirmed as alpha, however, there was nothing she could do to compel him. For some reason, compulsion powers didn't exist until after the confirmation ceremony.

He came again. I dully wondered again how I was going to explain not shifting and regenerating when he hit me full on, knocking out my breath. He raised a paw, extended his claws and scraped them down my cheek before bringing the same claws to his mouth and sucking off the blood. My blood. I felt the fire coursing through my entire system. Anton's face looked oddly surprised for a second then he did the same with the other cheek before lifting up his entire paw preparing to strike. Through the haze of pain, I registered the power that he was preparing to put behind this blow and it occurred to me that this was his plan. He'd kill me with sanction and solve forever the problem of the little human. It hadn't dawned on him that after I died the Brethren would investigate why I'd not shifted and they'd work out I was human. Then they'd kill everyone.

The rage built up inside me and the flames took over. He was playing with the pack's lives. I sprang to my feet in one movement, ignoring the sudden streak of dizziness. He was not going to do this. Anger took over me and flooded my system but I knew with cold clarity what to do. The fire won. I sprinted back to the wall, aiming just to the left of his crouched body and ran three steps up before using it as a springboard to spin off. I was too fast and Anton had no time to turn. I put my hands round his thick neck and twisted, snapping it in one movement. My bloodfire roared in approval and he collapsed to the ground.

He was a shifter. He'd recover. I wiped a smear away from my cheek and turned and walked painfully out of the room.

Helen Harper

88

Chapter Seven

I limped towards the stairs. My side, where Anton had bitten me, was seeping with blood and I was pretty sure that I had a couple of cracked ribs. I was hardly aiding my own cause at this particular point in time. I dreaded to think about the state of my face after his claws had drawn blood from my cheeks.

Tom came running up to me. Clearly he'd decided that he was talking to me now. "Shit, Mack, I can't believe that just happened." He took my arm. "Let me help you."

"Fuck off, Tom."

He reared back, hurt, and I sighed at him in exasperation. "I'm meant to be a shifter, remember? I have supernatural strength and healing powers. I don't need help in getting to my own room."

"Oh, right. Yeah." I could see his brain working through the implications of my non-shifter abilities. "What are you going to say to them when you don't heal?"

"I haven't worked that out yet."

Mackenzie, they're heading your way.

No prizes for guessing who 'they' were. I cursed and tried to straighten. Pretty lights danced in front of my eyes for a second and I was filled with nausea. Now would not, however, be a good time to faint. Staines and the alpha came striding out of the gymnasium with the blonde and Lucy tagging behind. I wondered idly if that was because they were female and knew their place. The bloodfire returned momentarily at the thought, allowing me to regain some of my equilibrium.

"Ms Mackenzie," said Staines. "That was an...interesting fight."

"I'm thrilled that you found it so entertaining," I responded drily.

The Lord Alpha stepped forward, golden green eyes intent. "I'm curious as to why you put up such a poor showing in your first bout, given that you were able to dispatch the bear so summarily." His voice was smooth and deep, faintly accented with an indefinable Celtic burr.

I felt rather weak at the knees but I was sure that it was just from the pain and slight concussion. I swallowed. "Errr..."

He came even closer so that I was forced to crane my neck to meet his gaze. "Could it be," he purred, "that you are trying to avoid being invited to London?"

"Yes! That's it. Definitely," I said, jumping on the excuse.

"And why is that exactly?" His voice was laced with steel.

I took a step back, hating myself for it but worried that the lotion might not be enough to mask my scent at these close quarters. I looked at Tom for inspiration. He jauntily hooked an arm through mine and beamed effusively at the alpha. "She just can't bear to be without me," he said, and stroked my hair lovingly. I tried not to jerk away and stuck a smile on my face.

The Alpha's eyes went cold. "I see. Well, you'd better shift so you can start healing properly."

I cast around for an excuse. "I'm…ummm…..I'm….. in mourning. I have taken a vow not to shift until our alpha's murderer is brought to justice." I silently apologised to John for the lie but kind of also applauded myself for my genius.

"Indeed." A muscle pulsed in his cheek. "What happens when it's the full moon then? If his killer has not been found by that point, I mean."

"I possess unbelievable self-control," I lied and tried to smile at him disarmingly, although my head took that moment to suddenly start pounding with pain again so it came out more like a maniacal grimace.

He looked down at me unfathomably. I wondered if swooning onto his broad chest would be considered poor self-control. Probably should try and avoid it, I thought.

"Well, I'd better get this gorgeous girl back to her, I mean, our room, so that we can get her fixed up for this afternoon," said Tom, rather breezily, although I could hear the note of underlying tension in his voice, before he carefully swung me round to head back for the stairs.

"Take care now," the Alpha murmured at our backs.

I knew that he was still watching with the others so I tried very hard to pull myself up the stairs without crying out. Tom did a good job of pretending to be a gentleman rather than just providing the support I needed so that I wouldn't fall and somehow we made it up to the landing and round the corner.

"Was that the best idea?" I wheezed.

"What?" he said innocently.

"Saying that we're mated. And that we're sharing a room."

"I didn't actually say that," he pointed out. "He merely inferred it."

"You said that we shared a room."

"Oh, that. Well, maybe it's best I did. You shouldn't be left alone in your condition. Besides what was that about not shifting because you're in mourning?"

"It was the best I could come up with at the time. I thought it was rather good." I clutched at his arm as we rounded another corner. "You do realise that you've lied to the alpha of all alphas and you're screwed if he takes you to London? He'll use the Voice and you'll be compelled to tell him whatever he wants. He'll work out in about five seconds flat that you were lying just now."

"That's not going to happen now Anton's beaten me, though is it?" Tom answered quietly.

"I'm sorry," I said.

"No, you're not. But it's okay." He pushed open a door to one of the unused couples' rooms. "Let's use this one." I sagged against him in relief and stumbled inside. He closed the door behind him and sat me down on the bed.

"I'll need to get some first aid materials. And some clean clothes." He looked at me. "Can you wait here on your own?"

I nodded back at him and lay down, closing my eyes.

Two minutes later, the door opened again. Go away.

A brisk voice filled the space. "Mackenzie? Are you okay?"

I lifted myself up with a struggle and saw Julia. "Hey," I said weakly, before sinking back down. "I'm fine."

"That was stupid," she muttered.

"I had no choice!" I protested.

"I was thinking of Anton, but you could have handled it better too."

"How?" I asked, rising up again. "How could I have survived what he was doing? If I'd died and they'd found out I was human...," I didn't need to finish my sentence.

"After that display, I think the human part remains to be seen," she said softly. "All you've done is proven to them that you're the strongest, fastest member of the pack. They'll invite you to London."

I grunted. "Well, I don't have to go. Apparently I'm in love with Tom and we can't bear to be separated."

Julia laughed, surprising me. "I don't think he's your type, dear."

"What am I going to do, Julia?" I felt flooded with despair. "I can't heal, I can't shift, I smell funny...they're going to work it out sooner or later."

"They won't. This mourning idea of yours might work."

"Oh, you heard about that then."

"Yes. And anyway, there's only a day and a half to go and then they'll be gone." She turned to leave.

"Julia? Have they found out anything at all about John?"

A flicker of grief crossed her face. "No. It's as you said. There's no trace of anything. They have arranged for a mage to visit the scene and scan it though."

Alarmed, I sat up higher still, ignoring the shooting pain in my side. "A mage? But they'll know straightaway that I'm not a shifter!"

"And won't care. Mages are paid to do a job and that's what they do, no more and no less. As long as you don't get in his or her way, they won't say anything."

"How terribly mercenary," I murmured.

"It's the way of the world, dear. I'll pass some of my yarrow ointment to Tom when I see him. It will help with the healing and make this afternoon easier."

Oh yes, great, I still had the Spanish inquisition this afternoon. Zippideedoodah.

"Use damp cloths to get the worst of the blood off then re-apply the lotion. You're probably safe to bathe after the interview, as long as you don't go near them again for a few hours."

"Yes, ma'am!" I snapped off a sloppy salute.

Julia sighed deeply. "Take care, Mackenzie."

Tom returned not long after Julia's departure. Fortunately, he'd remembered to bring some scissors to cut off my clothes, along with some brutally strong painkillers. I briefly considered saving my modesty and trying to dress the wound myself but I knew that it'd be more sensible to just accept his offer of help. He was actually surprisingly gentle, carefully peeling away my blood-soaked t-shirt to reach the ugly wounds within. He dabbed at them with the cloth that he'd brought, soaking up the worst of the leaking blood, and then used Julia's ointment as an antiseptic and healing agent.

As he was binding my ribs up carefully with a bandage, Betsy entered. She didn't look particularly happy to see me lolling around half naked with Tom, in fact there was a dangerous flash of something in her eyes. I'd taken enough painkillers to dull not only the pain but also my senses and wondered if I'd half-imagined it for a second. That was until she started speaking.

"What the fuck? You're an item? Since when?"

Oooookay, then.

Tom, naturally, was oblivious. "It's just for the Brethren."

"Fuck the Brethren!" Betsy spat.

I couldn't have agreed more.

"And what the hell were you doing in that fight with Anton?" She fixed him with a hard glare and put her hands on her hips. "Do you want to go to London?"

"It would be amazing, wouldn't it?" Tom sighed expansively.

I didn't think I'd ever seen Betsy that upset, not even when her favourite soap character was axed in a horrific ball of fiery death storyline. I gaped at her. She was already in the throes of shifting with her spine elongating and pockets of fur springing out on her bare arms.

"Jaysus! You're tying that bandage all wrong!" There was a definite note of hysteria in her voice now. "Get out!"

"Huh?"

"Get out!" She pulled him to his feet and practically threw him out the door. I looked at her with shocked surprise and was about to start speaking but she silenced me with a growl and went to work on the bandage. Tom and Betsy – wonders would never cease. An uncontrollable urge to giggle overtook me. I tried to smother it and ended up snorting in a most unladylike fashion. She slapped me on my uninjured side.

"Don't, just don't, even go there, Mack."

I snorted some more, now hiccupping a little too. She gave me a death stare until I managed to subside and she spoke. "Don't think I'm letting you off with this either, Mack. When you heal, and the Brethren have gone, and we're all safe, I'm going to kill you too."

I hugged her fiercely. She seemed surprised to begin with but then hugged me back. "I mean it. You are going to be one dead human."

"Whatever you say, Bets."

She humphed for a few seconds before pulling back. "Now put some clothes on. We're going to show those arseholes that one little fight isn't going to knock you down."

*

At least this time I managed to avoid the hole in the carpet on my way down the stairs. It was a painful trek to the canteen, however, despite being doped up to my eyeballs on painkillers. Even without shifting, pack members would heal quicker than your regular run of the mill human like me so I'd still have to do a fair degree of pretending not to be in mind-numbingly awful pain, despite my mourning excuse. Tom admitted that he felt bad that he'd shifted during his fight with Anton, otherwise he'd have jumped on my bandwagon to give my reason more validity. It was a nice idea, but I figured that if the truth did come out, the rest of my pack would have a better chance if they could simply pin the blame on the unshakeable geas. Voluntarily helping to cover up a human beyond the spell's required bounds would be a different matter

Everyone, apart from Anton, was in the airy canteen by the time we arrived. There was a brief lull in the conversation when I walked in, some eyes reflecting approval while others showed distaste and even a tinge of fear. Whether that was because of the danger my actions had created, or because of the danger of me myself, I didn't know and didn't care to wonder. I also didn't dare look over at the Brethren's table to see what was in their eyes. Aiming for a nonchalant air, I tried to move towards the nearest empty chair without looking like I was in pain. It really wasn't very easy at all and my head was woozy by the time I made it. Betsy pulled up a chair beside me and chattered away as if there was nothing remarkable at all going on. Bit by bit, everyone else returned to their lunch.

Unfortunately I realised rather belatedly that the outside catering Johannes had called had set up a buffet. Excellent. More walking. More standing. More pain. I reached down under the table and began pulling out one of the screws from the side leg. It took me some time, and poor Betsy was struggling to find

Helen Harper

enough inanities to blather about to cover me, but I eventually managed it. Palming the screw, I nodded at her and we stood up. I dug the screw sharply into the palm of my hand. The returning sharp pain was an antidote to the constant drug dulled ache, and would keep my senses alert long enough to make it to the buffet table and back again without fainting. As I walked I pushed it in further, breaking the skin and drawing blood. When we passed the Brethren's table I thought I saw the Lord Alpha inhale sharply, but there was no way on earth that he'd be able to smell a few drops of fresh blood right now after all the many drops that had just been spilt in the gym. Then I panicked that the lotion must have rubbed off during Tom's medical ministrations and that I hadn't re-applied it again properly and my humanity was starting to seep through. However I must have imagined it because he returned to his plate, with a brief flash of brilliant white teeth visible as he bit into a slice of crusty bread.

I picked up a plate and lay it down on the side so I could manage the buffet without letting go of the screw in my palm. With one hand, I randomly selected bits of food to fill it up. I desperately needed to eat but my earlier anticipation of dining on something other than Johannes' food had gone. Now I just needed the calories. Betsy was forking spoonfuls of what looked like a creamy curry on her plate next to me when Lucy, the Brethren girl from earlier, came up.

"So, not much of a fighter, then?" She inquired archly.

I blushed, annoying myself. "Ummm…it's complicated."

98

" I heard," she said, with a glance over her shoulder at Tom. "He's cute. "

I coughed slightly and continued putting food on my plate, in an awkward one-handed fashion.

"You must be hurting a bit after that, especially with not shifting. " She peered at me from under her bangs. "It might not be such a clever idea to do that, you know. Not shift. I mean, I get the idea of honouring your guy's death and all that, but if you're really sore..." her voice trailed off.

She had absolutely no idea. "It's fine," I muttered. "I'm fine."

"Yes, so fine that you're putting chocolate cake on top of your shepherd's pie."

I looked down at my plate. Oops. "I have a varied palate," I said shrugging, wishing she would just go away.

"Lucy," said a deep smooth voice, "can you go and check on the status of the mage's arrival?"

She snapped to attention and at once bobbed her head, light brown hair bouncing off her shoulders as she did so. The Lord Alpha. As if things couldn't get any worse. Lucy marched off smartly while he took a grape off a nearby plate and looked at me in much the same way that a cat would look at a mouse before pouncing on it and killing it. I squared my shoulders and craned my neck slightly to look back at him. I could just barely register Betsy's panic from over his shoulder but I kept my expression as calm as I could.

He popped the grape into his mouth and chewed slowly. Wasn't he going to say something? His green eyes held mine steadily but he remained silent. Damnit, I needed to think of something to say then. Weather?

"It's fortunate the rain held off," I said. God, I was an inane idiot sometimes.

He continued to look at me without speaking but I could swear there was a measure of amusement in his eyes now. I felt waves of power emanating from his still body and wondered briefly at the apparent fact that he'd had to fight for the Brethren leadership position. I tugged nervously at my ponytail. "I mean, then you'll be able to find the trail of whatever killed John without the scent being washed away."

He leaned closer into me and I caught a sudden whiff of a deep, clean and very masculine smell. I felt slightly woozy again and tightened my grip on the screw.

He finally said something. "Were you there?"

"Uh, where?" I barely resisted the urge to take a step back.

"At the beach. When his body was discovered."

I had no idea what to say. Should I say yes or try and lie? "Ummm…."

Betsy took that moment to rescue me by dropping her plate to the floor where it made an almighty crash and splattered food in twenty different directions. The Brethren Alpha turned around so quickly it made my head spin.

She giggled. "Oh, I'm so clumsy! It's just you made me nervous standing there. I had no idea that the Brethren were so powerful in person, and you the Lord Alpha as well." I could swear she batted her eyelashes just then. "Just what is your name?"

I walked away before I could hear the answer, gripping my plate tightly. I owed her more than one by now.

*

After lunch was over, the Brethren rose smoothly as if they were one and headed outside. Apparently this time they were all going to the scene of John's death to see it for themselves and then our interviews, or rather interrogations, would begin on their return. I was starting to feel more normal now that I had food in my belly, but I definitely thought that a bit of an afternoon siesta was called for. That way I could wake up in control, out of pain, and ready. The other pack members wandered off to do their own thing, while I made for the dorm. I supposed that I should technically go to the room that Tom and I 'shared', but I knew that my narrow bed in the dorm would make me more comfortable.

Two hours later I woke up again, feeling slightly groggy. The pain in my side was still ridiculously annoying but it was becoming more manageable. I didn't dare take any more painkillers just yet. I pulled on an old sweatshirt and went in search of some strong black coffee.

The keep itself was very quiet. I passed a couple of pack members who were moving quietly about their own business, but it was clear that most were outside somewhere and that the Brethren hadn't returned yet. All the better for me.

I hadn't been able to find my favourite chipped mug where I usually left it, so I tried to backtrack to where I'd last seen it. I was definitely something of a hoarder and didn't like to replace items unless it was absolutely necessary so I thought hard before realising that I must have put it down in the office when I went to check the weather on the Othernet. That had been before going out for my run on the morning of John's death. It seemed like a lifetime ago now.

I let myself into the small space, immediately seeing it propped precariously on top of a pile of papers. Letting out a small happy sigh of satisfaction I moved to pick it up, slipping past John's study door as I did so. I paused, as a thought suddenly struck me. It was just possible that there would be some information about the wichtlein and his thoughts on it on his computer. I'd never ever normally even consider broaching his sanctuary like that - but he was dead now and could hardly be hurt by my intrusion into his privacy. And I might dig up something that would help me find his killer.

I didn't give it another thought and walked deliberately back to the study door, wrenching it open with purpose. Even though the office door itself was closed, I took an involuntary glance backward to make sure no-one was watching and then stepped inside. I left the door slightly ajar behind me so that I could listen for any signs of the pack or the Brethren returning.

It was neat and tidy, and almost comforting in its familiarity. It was almost as if the essence of him still clung to the air. I didn't want to sit down in his old cracked red leather chair - that just seemed like too much of an intrusion - so I perched on his desk instead and booted up the computer.

It whirred to life and the screen lightened to the login page. Shit. I had absolutely no idea what John would have used for his password. I thought carefully and then tried typing in his birthday. The error screen popped up almost immediately. Then I tried pack, Cornwall, shapeshifter, even password, but none of them worked. My fingers drummed on the desk impatiently. John wasn't particularly tech savvy so I doubted he'd have picked something really secure like a string of random letters and numbers. Perhaps he'd left a note of the password lying around his desk. I started to lift up papers but there was nothing that jumped out. Still feeling slightly guilty at nosing around his personal belongings, I began opening up the desk drawers. The top one just contained an array of slightly chewed pens missing their lids, and the odd paperclip, while the next one down was filled to the brim with printouts of the pack's financial statements. The bottom drawer had a slight buzz around it as if it was warded.

I carefully lifted out one of the chewed pens and touched the tip of it to the lock on the bottom drawer. It started to singe slightly and melt. Okay, then, not that drawer just yet then. I looked around the rest of the office for guidance. There were shelves overflowing with every conceivable shifter how-to guide. Paperbacks on different Otherworld species, hardbacks on weapons and fighting techniques, even a large edition of Cooking With Aunt May, 'everyone's favourite lupine chef'. My side was starting to hurt again and I put my hand out to steady myself on the desk. Instead of the hard wood, however, my hand met with a heavy paperweight. John had always had it, for at least as long as I'd known him.

I picked it up to look at it further. It was made of Caithness glass and contained a pretty pattern inside of purple and red swirls. I was about to place it back down when I realised that the under-side felt oddly rough. Flipping it over, I saw that a small rune had been etched into it somehow. It looked Fae, but while I could speak a few basic words and sentences, I definitely didn't have the skill to decipher the rune itself. Unless…my eyes searched the bookshelf again. There! John had a dusty old Fae- Human dictionary sitting at one end. I pulled it off, struggling with its weight, and opened it. The rune had three markings on the side in the shape of three teardrops so I had a vague idea in which section to look in. Next to the teardrops was what looked like a little stringless harp. That helped. Faerie language was pictorial. Once you had an idea about what the separate pictures were, you could start to find out their meaning. I counted the brush strokes on the right hand side. Five. That meant that in the teardrop section, I had to flip to the five stroked subheading and then find the harp. I was too impatient and I almost tore through the pages to find the right part. I traced my finger down the listed runes before seeing it. Herensuge. Huh. That was Basque for dragon.

I leaned back towards the computer and typed it in. What the hell, it was worth a shot. To my delighted surprise, as soon as I hit return, the monitor chimed in happy agreement. I let out a long breath - I was in.

John's computer desktop was sparse. There were a few folders displayed so I clicked on one entitled Statistical Sightings, figuring that it might give me an indication about what Otherworld creatures had been spotted recently in the area. It opened up to a comprehensive table detailing the activities of various nasties going back to 2006. The figures were fairly even: in 2006 3 ogres, 17 trolls (I remembered there had been a particularly nasty bridge infestation that year), one Unseelie Fae encounter and a few others. In the next few years, there was little difference. However the last three months told a different story. It appeared that there had been more sightings and problems since March than we'd ever had before.

I pulled back slightly from my perch on the desk and absentmindedly rubbed my side. Things had been quieter lately, not busier. I'd spent my time routing out rabbits and foxes, not evil Otherworld creatures bent on destruction. The table even made mention of a Quinotaur, a five horned beast, that had been dispatched near the lake. I pouted slightly. Meeting new big and bad nasties made my day – why hadn't I heard anything about this one? Or all the others? I was convinced that if any other pack members had come across this number of creatures then they'd have been moaning in bitter complaint to everyone who came near. And whoever killed the Quinotaur would surely have boasted of their achievements to someone. I wondered if John had been doing all this himself, and sending the rest us off on wild goose chases instead. It was a phenomenal achievement if he had, but begged the question of why. Perhaps it was linked to the wichtlein's harbinger pebble. If things were so bad though, he'd surely have informed the Brethren before now. I felt really rather hurt that he might have been killing himself to keep Cornwall safe and hadn't asked me for help.

I moved the cursor to the menu and opened up the list of recent documents. There was one that he'd created just a scant few hours before his death. Looking at the time display, it must have been after he'd returned from the clearing. It didn't have a title but I double clicked the mouse to open it up anyway. There were just three words: black diamond stones – followed by a question mark. I had a bit of a question mark myself. What were black diamond stones? I silently cursed John for not leaving a clearer clue.

I scanned the bookshelves again, looking for something that might help and was about to pull down a precious gems and magical objects encyclopaedia when I suddenly heard voices and the slamming of doors from outside. Bugger it. Quickly closing down the computer, I stepped back into the outer office. I was just in time because Staines came suddenly striding in with the Lord Alpha. They were in mid conversation and didn't see me at first.

"My lord, we need to focus on the magic trail before anything else," Staines was saying.

The Alpha growled. "The mage can do that better than us. It's the tree markings that interest…" his voice trailed off as he saw me and his green eyes narrowed.

"Hi!" I said brightly. "Found it!" I held up my mug for display.

They both just stared at me silently. I cleared my throat. "Well, I'll get out your way then." I moved towards the door but the Alpha was blocking it. I looked up at him, waiting for him to move out my way. He folded his arms and continued to stare.

I felt a flicker of irritation from my bloodfire. This was my keep, not his. I moved to brush past him, registering the hard steely curve of his muscles as my arm touched his. He moved further back, blocking the doorway completely.

"Miss Mackenzie," he drawled softly.

My flames flickered higher. "Lord Alpha," I bit out.

He smiled predatorily. "You can call me Corrigan. Why are you here?"

"Because this is *my* pack's office and *my* coffee mug and I want to have *my* coffee." My eyes flashed, even as the small voice inside snapped at me to simper slightly and shut up, not anatagonise the man further.

He gazed implacably back. "I see. And how is that not shifting working out for you, Mackenzie? Feeling shaky yet?"

"Only from caffeine withdrawal," I snapped shaking the mug in the air as if to prove my point.

He stepped aside and gestured to the door with a flourish. "Then I will not impede your way any longer."

I humphed and stepped through. 'Impede' my way? Just let him try. For one horrifying second I thought I'd spoken aloud because from behind me I heard him speak again, with an iron tone to his voice. "Don't be late for our interview because you're guzzling the black stuff and jumping off the walls on a caffeine buzz. I do not appreciate tardiness."

Fuck off, I thought, and stalked off in the direction of the kitchen.

So his name was Corrigan. I scowled at myself and pushed the thought away. It was nothing to me what his name was. Arrogant fucker. I considered arriving late for the interview just to spite him but reminded myself that I was trying to portray meek and weak. I had clearly been massively unsuccessful so far. Closing my eyes and counting to ten, I tried to calm myself back down. I still had to do my best to pass under the Brethren's scrutiny, even if that would be difficult after my fight with Anton. Letting my temper and the bloodfire get the better of me would not help me or the pack.

By the time I reached the kitchen, my blood had settled back down to a simmer. Overhearing their conversation had at least given me some more clues to work with. I'd missed tree markings when I'd been out searching for John previously, probably because I'd been too focused on the ground trail. That was useful. The Brethren would be busy with the interviews until late evening so once my one with Corrigan was over I figured I could probably return to the scene of the crime unhindered.

I took a deep breath. This was going to be a long afternoon.

Bloodfire

Chapter Eight

Julia came and found me in the kitchen while I was sitting at the large wooden table with my hands curled around my now steaming mug of deliciously syrupy Java. I was lost in thought about what the tree markings might indicate.

"How's it going, dear?" She asked.

"Fine. Great." I said sarcastically. "John is still dead. The Brethren are still here and I have an interview with the Lord Alpha in fifteen minutes."

"Now is not the time to get worked up, Mackenzie. Keep your wits about you and we'll be fine."

I sighed and tucked a loose strand of hair behind my ear. "Yes, yes, I know."

Julia leaned towards me. "Do not fuck this up, Mackenzie."

I was startled by her swearing. "I won't. I'm just frustrated."

"And you'll get over it. There's just over a day to go then this will be over."

"29 hours." Not that I was counting or anything. I changed the subject. "Julia, did John mention anything to you about increased Otherworld activity?"

She shook her head, puzzled.

"What about a Quinotaur?"

She shook her head again. "He seemed quite tired but I put that down to being busy with the quarterly reports. He was out a lot though."

Yes, out doing the rest of our jobs for us. Anton took that moment to enter the kitchen. I noted with some satisfaction that he was moving stiffly but was still irritated that he could recover with such ease from an injury that would have killed most humans. He shot me a dirty look and went to the fridge.

"I think Anton and I need to have a little chat," said Julia calmly. She looked at me with her eyebrows raised. I took the hint and left, hoping that he'd get the chewing out he truly deserved. I should probably go and wait outside the office for my interview anyway. Arriving late would not help my cause.

*

When I got there, the blonde Brethren girl was outside with a clipboard, marking names off. She smiled at me briefly and I took a seat on a waiting chair. After a few minutes, Johannes emerged, smiling and shaking his head.

"He's some guy, yer alpha."

The blonde smiled again. "We're lucky to have him."

Oh, for God's sake. He was just another shifter. I rolled my eyes expressively and crossed my legs.

Miss Mackenzie. I am ready for you now.

I jumped. Shit, he could use the Voice on me. I hadn't anticipated that. I was about to make a sarky remark back to him when Betsy passed through my line of sight and glanced at me. I hesitated, remembering my brief.

As you wish, my lord. I answered back. Way Directive 32: Respect the hierarchy.

The girl put a check next to my name. "You'll do fine," she said. "He's really a nice guy."

Nice. Sure. He'd fought off sixteen leadership challenges and was in charge of the one group of people who could spell the doom of me and mine just because my mother had abandoned me here when I was kid. I gritted my teeth and curved up my lips to form a smile. "I'm just nervous," I said.

And actually I was. My palms were slightly damp and sweaty and I could feel a slight tremor in my knees. I must still be feeling the effects of the fight. As if in answer, my ribs took that moment to start throbbing with pain. I stood up. Best to get this over and done with.

Johannes gently touched my elbow as I went past. It was good to know that I had the pack on my side. Then I remembered Anton. Most of the pack at least. I pulled on the doorknob and went back into the office.

The majority of the paperwork from the desk had been cleared away. Corrigan was behind the desk, reading from a sheet of paper. I was rather surprised that he'd chosen not to use John's study. Staines was leaning against the wall and looking at me with a frown. I stood in front of them and waited. I wasn't sure if this part of their ploy – keep the underlings waiting to make them nervous, but actually it gave me a good chance to study my potential nemesis. His dark hair curled ever so slightly round the corner of his ears and at the nape of his neck, before disappearing into a pink striped shirt. He must be secure with his masculinity to wear pink, I figured. But then again his muscles were straining tautly at the material so I guessed that he had no worries in that direction. In fact he probably had a tailor to design his shirts that way in particular. I was equally amused to see that he was wearing a tie. Most visitors to Cornwall who arrive suited and booted get short shrift. We were not that kind of county. Interestingly, his fingernails were bitten down to the quick, which made me wonder if perhaps I should suggest a manicurist. Ally was particularly adept at French polishes. I smirked at the idea of the big bad tough Brethren Lord getting his pinky nail buffed and filed, which of course just made Staines frown even deeper at me. Yeah, whatever.

Eventually, Corrigan put the piece of paper down. He looked at Staines, who pushed himself off the wall and left through the door I'd come through. These two were not exactly fond of chit-chat. He motioned to a blue plastic chair that had been commandeered from the canteen and I sat down.

"So, Miss Mackenzie, we finally have some alone time to talk together." He smiled lazily at me, and I had the distinct impression of a predator sizing up its next meal.

I swallowed. Alone time? Oh hurray.

"I have to admit that I find you rather fascinating. One minute you are being knocked down by a tap from a little girl, and the next you are defeating a werebear in his own shift form."

I just looked at him. Two could play the silent game.

He stared at me for a moment before acknowledging my lack of response with a slight one shouldered shrug. I cast my eyes down, trying to play the part of submissive shifter. He continued. "And then of course there are your night time sparring matches on the beach."

My head snapped up. So there had been someone there watching after all. I wondered briefly why he'd been there and why I hadn't spotted him. If it had indeed been him, or just one of his minions tailing me. Corrigan smiled unpleasantly. I tried desperately to remember if either Tom or I had said anything incriminating while we were on the beach. I didn't think so but I couldn't be entirely sure. Memories are funny things; concentrate hard enough and you'll start remembering things that never even happened in the first place. My eyes narrowed slightly and I waited for his next move.

"So what is a shifter of your talents doing tucked away in sleepiest Cornwall, and why are you so desperate to stay here?" His green gold eyes bored into me.

That one, I could handle. "Er, well, I like the quiet," I said, "and then there's Tom, of course."

"Ah, yes, the boyfriend." He stood up and moved round to the other side of the desk. I tried to lean back to get away from him without leaving my chair. He frowned down at me. "Funny, I wouldn't have pegged the two of you as a couple."

"Do you think I'm not good enough for him?" I was aware of the note of rising annoyance in my voice. Careful, Mack, I warned myself.

"Not at all. I just wonder how someone like him could keep someone like you…interested."

Now what exactly did he mean by that? I looked directly into his eyes, challenging his stare. "Oh, I'm very interested," I said with a slow murmur.

The green in his eyes flashed for a second and he returned to the chair behind the desk.

I decided to aim for humility in a bid to get him to leave me alone. "Lord Corrigan, I don't want to waste your valuable time. I have no desire to leave Cornwall and believe that I have made that apparent to you already. Perhaps your time would be better spent with those shifters who would like to join in you in London."

He raised his eyebrows. "That may be but there are other matters that I would like to discuss." He was all business like now. "Tell me what you did on the day of your alpha's death."

"On the day of his murder, you mean."

Corrigan just looked back at me. I sighed and rubbed my eyes. "I went for a jog, then to the eastern perimeter. There had been some rumours about something there."

"And did you find anything?"

"No," I lied. I knew from my quick rummage around John's computer that he'd not written the wichtlein report before he'd died and, if I was going to make sure that the Brethren left promptly in a day and a half's time, then it was important that I gave them no further reasons to stick around. Besides which, I was going to find John's killer and wreak my own particular brand of justice on them. The last thing I needed was some jumped up overlords getting my way.

Corrigan's expression remained blank. "And then what?"

"I came back to the keep. When we realised that John hadn't returned, I went out with the others to find him. Then we did. Find him, I mean."

"I see." He raised a hand and pushed it through his dark hair, biceps rippling as he did so. "You're lying, Miss Mackenzie. Or certainly not telling me the whole truth."

Shit.

Tell me everything.

Oh god, he was trying to compel me with his Voice. It wouldn't work on me though so I had to be clever about this and make it seem like I was following orders. I opened my mind up carefully, letting an image of finding John's body then Anton pushing me aside flash up. I left off the part where Anton had referred to my humanity but allowed the idea that he'd accused me of being involved in John's murder seep through.

Corrigan nodded slowly. "Hmmm. So what is it between you and Anton? Perhaps he's a jilted lover?"

Hardly. He just couldn't stand the fact that I was human. "We just rub each other up the wrong way."

"I see," Corrigan said again. "So why does your *boy*friend," he emphasised the 'boy' part, "call you Red?"

Crapola. He'd heard that. I silently cursed Tom for his nickname. If I told Corrigan the truth, that I'd dyed my hair, he might suspect that there was more I was trying to hide. Think, Mack. "It's my favourite colour. I always wear it."

Corrigan's eyes slowly travelled down my seated body. I was wearing dark jeans and a black t-shirt.

"But, of course, I'm wearing dark colours now in mourning for John."

He tapped his fingers lightly on the worn desk. "Of course. You do seem to take this mourning aspect very seriously."

"I take his death very seriously." At least that part wasn't a lie.

There was a flicker of sympathy in his eyes. That annoyed me. I didn't need to know that the Lord Alpha had a nice side to him, no matter what the girl had said outside.

He changed tack. "You smell like a rat, or maybe a gerbil. I can't quite pinpoint it."

"I'm a hamster." Which was probably about as believable as the reason I'd offered up for Tom's stupid nickname. Shifters' personalities and abilities mimic their animal form. I could think of little that I'd manage to achieve so far that broadcasted a small furry compliant rodent.

He looked at me quietly for a moment or two but his expression gave nothing away. "Interesting. Werehamsters rarely have much fighting prowess. You, Miss Mackenzie, must be an anomaly."

I shrugged, trying to appear casual. He stared at me for another long moment before again tapping his fingers on the desk and saying, "Very well then. You are free to go."

Well, thank you very much, my lord. That hadn't been so bad, I thought, and stood up relieved, turning towards the door. I straightened my t-shirt and felt the tension leave my body. He wasn't so scary after all. My hand was turning the doorknob, however, when he cleared his throat and spoke again.

"Oh wait. One more thing, Miss Mackenzie." Great. "I'm curious as to what you bathe with."

Say what? I didn't turn around but my body stiffened. "I'm not quite sure what you mean, my lord."

"I mean, sweetheart, that you smell very odd. If you are a werehamster as you claim, then you're like none I've come across before. I can't quite put my finger on it but it's definitely an unusual scent that you carry around with you."

I wasn't sure if it was my fear that he was skirting towards the truth or the sweetheart comment that did it, but I whipped around without thinking, all cylinders firing. "I fail to see what matter what I wash with or how I bathe has to do with you." I snarled. "I've answered your sodding questions and played along. If you have nothing of any note to ask about then let me go."

So the kitten roars after all.

I opened my mouth to speak again then thought better of it and settled for glaring at him instead.

"Never mind," he answered airily. "I didn't realise it was such a touchy subject. Clearly there are depths to you that I need to plumb further. Some other time, I think, Miss Mackenzie."

I glared at him again and left. Goddamnit, I'd walked right into that one.

Outside, the blonde shifter was putting another mark on her clipboard. She beamed at me. "See, that wasn't so bad, now was it?"

Fuck off, Brethren girl. I forced a smile. By the time they all left, my cheeks were going to be aching. "It was great. He is indeed an impressive man."

"Isn't he, though." She sighed slightly and smoothed her hair self-consciously. "And he's single."

So sodding what? "Maybe you should ask him out on a date then."

She giggled slightly. I was somewhat surprised that the apparently stoic and somber Brethren members were capable of giggling. "Oh no, I could never do that. Lord Corrigan likes to do the chasing himself."

Screw Lord Corrigan. Which was actually probably what she wanted. I tried to smile at her again. "I have to go now."

"Okay then," she answered dreamily, no doubt imagining herself and Corrigan walking hand in hand down a deserted beach. I almost snarled again.

Julia was hovering around in the hall, looking over at me anxiously, so I flashed her a brilliant smile of fake reassurance before striding up to the dorms to change the dressing on my wound and get my backpack. Forget about Corrigan, I had clues to investigate and places to go and it was too late to change the fact that I'd stupidly snapped at him.

Once outside, I took a deep breath and filled my lungs. I figured I had a couple of hours before the rest of the interviews would be over. Plenty of time to see what I could find out about tree markings and to look for black diamond stones. I'd bound my side and my ribs tightly with bandages and taken a few more painkillers so I was pretty sure that I'd be able to conduct my investigations without the pain getting to me. I briefly considered finding Tom and asking him to come with me – and quizzing to find out how his interview had gone - but I didn't want to lose any valuable time and I was pretty certain that he wouldn't take kindly to me patently hoping he screwed it up, so I shifted the backpack on my shoulder instead and walked out towards the beach and the scene of John's death.

Despite my own ministrations, I didn't want to risk delaying the healing process by opening the gashes up on my side further, so I refrained from jogging and instead walked casually away from the keep. At least if anyone spotted me I could use the excuse that I was just out for a casual afternoon stroll to clear my head.

The path was lightened by sunbeams, in stark and bitter contrast to when I'd taken this route last time. A few birds chirped here and there. I noted my own tracks from the previous night, as well as a few others that were heavier and no doubt belonged to the Brethren. And John had said that *I* was like an elephant…I guess that's what living in the cement covered city did to your ability to tread lightly and leave little trace of your presence.

Scuffing over some of the more irritating trail marks as I went, I mulled over my interview with Corrigan, eventually deciding that he was just trying to get under my skin. If he'd really smelled anything human about me then he'd have squashed me like a bug without thinking twice. He had definitely just been fishing around. He probably tried to get a rise out of everyone he interviewed. I ignored the memory of the almost worshipful expression Johannes had had on his face after his interview. Anyway, Corrigan didn't matter – finding John's murderer did.

When I started to get closer to where John had died, I stopped focusing on the ground and started checking out the trees instead. I couldn't see anything yet that suggested the markings that Corrigan and Staines had been talking about it. I felt tendrils of dread curl around the pit of my stomach with each step that I took. I really didn't want to go there again. I wondered how much the pack had managed to clean up. Would there still be traces of his life blood there? Where it had seeped into the earth, taking the only real parent I'd ever known? I clenched my fists, nails curling into the palms of my hands. I couldn't let my grief escape. I needed to be strong and steely if I was going to avenge his death.

I still couldn't see anything on any of the trees. I circled a few of them, double checking, but there was nothing. What was I missing? By the time I reached the sandy spot where John had actually died, frustration was flooding in. Somehow the Brethren were seeing something I couldn't. I walked slowly up to the spot where his body had lain. There were a few indentations on the grass and in the sand but the blood was gone. I knelt down for a second and softly touched the ground.

"I miss you, John," I whispered softly. My words were whipped away by the wind. I blinked back a few tears and stood up again to look at the tree line behind me. That was when I noticed that the trees did indeed have markings on them. In a semi circle, facing the spot where he'd died, were one, two, three...seven trees together that had what looked like runes scoured into their bark. I felt some grim satisfaction at finding what I'd been looking for and strode over to the first one.

It was gouged deep into the flesh of the tree. Lifting my hand, I traced the outline of the rune, trying to work out what it was. These weren't Fae runes: there was something sharper and much more sinister about them than the rune I'd discovered on John's paperweight. I pulled out a small camera and snapped a photo of it. I still hadn't made it to the library or to the Othernet to dig up information on wichtleins. Now I had another reason to make sure I did. I went round each tree, taking a photo of each rune as I went. That there were seven runes on seven trees definitely meant something. Seven was a magical number that contained a lot of power within it.

I moved to the beach so I could stand on the dune and get a picture of all of the trees together. It was a struggle getting to the top of the sand with my injuries but I tensed my muscles, held my side and made it. I was about to take a photo again when something half-buried by the sand caught my eye. I crouched down and brushed away the sand. It was a ring of seven charred coals. All of a sudden several puzzle pieces started to click together and I hit the back of my hand against my forehead in exasperation. Of course. I cursed myself for being such an idiot.

Black diamond stones could easily refer to coal, and Nick had mentioned that someone had stolen a bag of coals from Perkins. And an electric screwdriver. I wondered for a minute whether the tree runes could have been made by a tool like that before realising that was ridiculous.

But at least now I knew where I had to go to next.

Chapter Nine

At this time of day, I knew I could expect to find Nick at the police station, probably filling out paperwork from that day's dealings with the crime underworld of Trevathorn. However, it was past five and I also knew that Perkins would be closing soon. I debated whether to visit the hardware store, or Nick, first. Remembering the glint in Nick's eyes when I saw him last, I decided that I would try the store first. Then I might be able to avoid talking to him altogether.

The village was busy at this time of day, with both locals and tourists bustling around. Most of them gave me a wide berth when they saw me striding towards them though. I guess my expression contained enough thunderous determination that they figured it was better to just get out of my way. It suited me fine. Tourists were irksome at the best of times, and I was not exactly in the mood for small talk with any of Trevathorn's inhabitants. My bloodfire was glowing in the pit of my stomach as I was forced to consider the idea that John had been deliberately targeted. Perhaps the wichtlein pebble wasn't so much a harbinger as a marker beacon, pointing him out to whichever big bad nasty had decided to chomp on him as a snack. The heat curled savagely around my lower intestines, threatening to take over at a moment's notice. I ignored it. This was a time to focus, as John would have said.

By the time I reached Perkins, it was almost half past five and I could see the eponymous owner,

Perkins himself, up at the glass door and flipping the little yellow sign from Open to Closed. Good. That meant I'd have peace and quiet to quiz him. I stepped up to the glass plate and rapped sharply. He gestured at the sign and his watch, shrugging expressively. I ignored this and rapped again.

He opened the door a couple of inches and poked his head out. "We're shut."

"I need to talk to you."

"And I need to go home and see my wife and kids." He tried shutting the door but I stuck my foot in the way.

"Please, Mr Perkins. It's important."

He sighed and appeared to consider the matter. It was not as if I was really going to give him the choice though. "Fine. But only for five minutes." He opened the door and let me in, then locked it behind me.

Perkins stood in the entrance, hand on his hips, and waggled his eyebrows questioningly. He was a small man, human of course, with a bald patch and slightly greying hair. He wore a red apron that proclaimed the words 'We're proud to work at Perkins!'

I opened my palms out, in a gesture of non-confrontation. "Can we sit down? I'd like to ask you a few questions about the robbery a few days ago."

He sighed expansively. "Why? Has the cult decided to become vigilantes now?"

At least he wasn't accusing us of breaking and entering. "No, but I think there might have been other similar break-ins in the area and I want to help out." I put on a pretty smile. "Please, Mr Perkins? I really do want to help."

He looked at me assessingly but I could see that he'd already given in. "It's probably more than the police are going to do, I suppose," he grumbled. "Here, come this way."

He took me into a little backroom where there was a small table and a couple of chairs. Along one side of the wall there was a sink, a little fridge and a kettle. "I suppose you'll be wanting tea, too?"

"How about coffee?" I asked, pushing my luck.

"Fine," he muttered, and set about getting two cups, flicking the switch on the kettle to on. Before too long, it was spitting steam so he poured the hot water onto a scoop of instant granules. I was a bit of a coffee purist and usually hated instant but I didn't think any further comments regarding his choice of brew would be useful at this point. I declined milk and sugar and he passed me the cup, sitting down at the table with me.

"So what exactly is it you want to know?"

I asked him how they got in.

"Broke the glass at the back." He pointed to a boarded up window behind me. "Figured it must have been kids 'cos it's so small."

I nodded briefly, thinking that it could have been anything of any size that could shift its shape to suit itself.

"Was anything other than the coal and the screwdriver taken?"

"Nothing," he answered. "Darn'dest thing as well, considering the till was right there. I'd not bothered emptying it that day because there wasn't much money in there, other than the float and a few odds and ends, but they didn't even try to open it." He shrugged and took a sip.

I mulled that over. "Were there any traces of anything else? Anything at all?"

He took his time answering. "Only the slime."

"The slime?" My life would have been a lot easier if Nick had mentioned slime when I'd talked to him before.

"Aye, smelly dark stuff. It was smeared along the shelf where the coals had been. There were a few drops of it on the floor too."

"I don't suppose you kept any of it?" I asked hopefully.

He looked at me like I was crazy. I supposed I probably was. "No," he answered slowly. "That police bloke, Nick whatsisface Jones, took some. Said he'd send it away for testing or something. I don't expect he really will, though."

Perkins' faith in the ineptitude of the police force was clearly unshakeable.

"He took the CCTV video as well."

I sat up. CCTV? That was interesting. And helpful. Although it did mean I'd now have to go and see Nick after all. I gulped down the rest of my coffee. "Mr Perkins, thank you so much for your time." I stuck out my hand and he took it.

"You're welcome. You culty people might be odd but at least you're polite."

I smiled at him slightly. "If I find out anything, I'll let you know."

Helen Harper

"It's hardly even worth me filing the insurance claim, girl, so I don't really know why you're bothering."

"It's the principle of the matter, Mr Perkins. We cannot allow incidents of this nature to take root in Trevathorn. It's a slippery slope, this kind of thing you know." God help me, now I was starting to sound like Julia. It worked though, because he grinned warmly at me before showing me out the front door and locking it firmly behind me again.

It was barely a hop, skip and a jump to the police station so I wandered over without any further delay. I could handle one horny copper. Once, inside I asked the duty sergeant to let me through to speak to Nick. He wasn't overly thrilled about it but called him up on the intercom to check first and then buzzed me through.

"Mack!" Nick stretched out his arms to greet me. "To what do I owe this wonderful pleasure?"

"I need a favour, Nick."

He shot me a sly smile. "For you, anything."

I gritted my teeth. "I'd like to see the CCTV you took from Perkins, and any report you managed to get from the lab about the slime."

His smile disappeared. "What do you want that for?"

"Trying to keep the streets of Trevathorn safe, Nick." I commented lightly.

He looked me for a long time, trying to judge how serious I was being. Eventually he spoke up. "I wouldn't do this for just anyone, you know."

I nodded, serious, but hopeful.

"The slime is still with the lab. How did you know about that anyway?"

I just shrugged and smiled demurely.

"Fine, whatever, don't tell me. And if the sarge finds out I showed you the CCTV, I could lose my job."

"Nick, I…"

He interrupted me. "Now, hold on. I didn't say no yet, did I? I'll show you it if you do something for me first."

"What do you want?"

"Have dinner with me. Tonight." There was a gleam in his eyes that slightly unnerved me.

"Nick, I'm sorry, but I'm just so busy at the moment…" I tried batting my eyelashes as Betsy had done at Corrigan at lunch although I had the distinct feeling that I looked like a fly had just flown into my eyeball instead.

"That's my price," he answered, and looked at me hopefully.

Fuck it. "Fine. I'll have dinner with you. But not tonight – can we make it next week, instead?"

"Okay, dinner next week but a drink in the Bull tonight after we're done," he countered.

I knew I wasn't going to win this one. "Okay. You're on."

"Come with me, then."

I followed him down the corridor into a small room that was already set up with an ancient TV monitor and DVD player. He gestured to a chair and I sat down. He sat next to me, stretching an arm behind the back of my chair, and clicked on the remote. The screen flickered to life and I could see the shop front of Perkins, the camera angled down to cover most of the shelves and the till.

"Around 2.30am, this happened," said Nick in a slightly bored voice.

A huge shadow loomed over the shop floor. It seemed to twist one way, then another. All of a sudden, the picture flicked to white snow.

"What? Bring it back!"

"That's all there is," he said with smug look on the face.

"You tricked me!" I thumped him on his arm.

"I did nothing of the sort. You asked to see the CCTV footage and I showed you the CCTV footage." He grinned at me.

"Oh, for fuck's sake," I muttered.

He looked down at his watch. "And would you look at that? It appears my shift is over, and you owe me a drink."

I rolled my eyes at him, irritated. "Fine, let's go."

"Ever the gracious lady, Mack." He took me by the arm. I grimaced, but let him lead me back down the corridor. He shrugged on a coat, said goodbye to the duty sergeant and we left.

The only other person in the Hanging Bull when we arrived was the barman. I ordered a beer as I was definitely going to need something alcoholic to avoid strangling Nick for making me do this. He pulled me over to a small table along the wall. "We can go into Penzance for our meal next week, if you like," he murmured.

"I'm sure that Trevathorn will do. We can go to the local café." I retorted.

"Trevathorn works for me," he said with a smile. "But the café food makes me ill so we'll have to go to my place. I'll cook." He winked at me. Oh good God.

I was about to answer him when a shadow fell across the table. I looked up and my heart suddenly sank into the pit of my stomach. It was Corrigan. He'd changed since earlier and was now wearing a dark turtleneck and a pair of jeans that stretched snugly over his thighs. I swallowed.

"Well, well, well," he said. "You're just breaking hearts everywhere you go, aren't you?"

Nick scowled at him and looked at me. "Who's this, Mack?"

"I'm her employer," said Corrigan, pulling up a stool and sitting down. The stool was too small for his body and he looked faintly ridiculous. I was still scared though.

"Where's John?" asked Nick.

"He's gone away on business," Corrigan said, keeping his eyes trained on me with a terrifying focus. "So, Mackenzie, does Tom know that you are out here meeting another man?"

Nick jerked. "Tom? Mack, you said that you and he had nothing going on."

I looked between the two of them. Hiding the truth from the Brethren alpha was definitely the preferable option. I sighed, hating myself a lot - and Corrigan more. "I'm sorry, Nick. I didn't want to hurt your feelings."

He jumped back. "And dinner next week? Were you going to come along and continue to lie to me?"

"Nick, I'm sorry, I…"

"Fuck off." He stood up, kicking his chair behind him, and walked out. The barman, polishing a glass a few feet away, raised an eyebrow at me. Corrigan stared stonily at him and he immediately coughed and muttered something about fetching a fresh keg from the back room, before darting away faster than I would have thought possible for a man of his size.

I looked at Corrigan, annoyed. He looked amused. "Playing around with a human behind a shifter's back, eh kitten? You're dangerous to know."

The fire inside me rose. "You idiot - he's the local policeman. I was trying to find out what he knew about John."

"And why would he know anything about John? He's just a human."

My reply died in my throat. Just a human. I looked at Corrigan, mute.

He laughed, oblivious. "I'll have to think of something that you would want from me so that I can get you to come round to my place for dinner too." There was a suggestive gleam in his eyes.

My mind went suddenly and abruptly - and completely - blank. I continued to stare at him.

His tanned hand covered mine. I tried to jerk back but he clamped it to the table. "You need to come with me," Corrigan said, with more than a hint of steel.

"I don't need to do anything," I replied, although this time without any fire. I was still confused by his last words. Between his proposition – had it even been a proposition? – and his dismissal of anyone human, my emotions were churning. I tugged at my hand and he thankfully let it go.

"The mage is here," he stated, calmly. "We need all of the pack back at the keep."

"So you came to get me yourself? Couldn't the Lord of all the Brethren find someone to run his petty errands for him?"

"Oh, believe me, kitten, I enjoyed doing this one on my own." His eyes continued to gleam and I was suddenly all too aware of his proximity. I scrambled to my feet.

"I thank you for your diligence," I said formally. "I'll see you back at the keep then."

I walked out of the pub, hoping that he wasn't going to follow. No such luck, however, as before I'd gone barely ten steps he was by my side. If he called me kitten again I was pretty sure that I'd have hands wrapped around his throat. Just as it seemed that I was getting somewhere by finding out more about who, or what, had killed John, the last person in the world I wanted to notice me had decided to make new friends. And I was definitely no-one's kitten.

"You're a rather prickly person, aren't you, Mack?"

I ignored him and tried to walk faster. At the very least I could do my best to get to the keep in double speed so that this couldn't be prolonged for any length of time.

"In fact you're the least pack-like shifter I've come across in some time. You appear to have a stubborn streak of independence that is – unusual - for our kind."

I stiffened. Was he going to suddenly dramatically reveal that he knew I wasn't a shifter after all?

"The thing is," he continued, "not only do you appear to be absolutely terrified every time I come near you, there appear to be some anomalies in your story."

Uh-oh. "What do you mean?" I could feel my heart suddenly beating louder and hoped that he couldn't hear it.

"You told me, very clearly I might add, that your nickname is Red because you wear red clothes."

"Yeah? What of it?" Go for nonchalant, I thought, that'll work.

"Your boyfriend, well the pack one at least, not the human, told me quite categorically that it was because it was a private joke between the two of you. That when you are, er, how shall I put this delicately? Intimate with him, you blush a particularly attractive pink colour."

Forget killing the Brethren alpha, I was going to kill Tom.

"And then, your charming little friend who fought first told me that it was because you have a fiery temper. Which doesn't surprise me in the least, I have to say. What does surprise me is that at the very least two members of this pack have lied to me. And I will not condone that sort of attitude. Now I could compel them – and you – to tell me the truth, but I'd rather have it voluntarily from you."

Now that all else had failed, I figured the truth was about all I had left. It might work, I supposed. "My hair is red. I dyed it. That's it."

"I see," he said slowly. "And why would you do that?"

I shrugged. "I wanted a change. Girl's prerogative."

"That still doesn't explain why your friends – and you – lied about it."

"It's, uh, a sore point, to be honest. I'd rather not talk about it."

I was tying myself up into circles. I was pretty sure I'd lied more in the last two days than I had in my entire life up till now. I couldn't think of any good reason as to why I'd dye my hair then lie about it.

"You can trust me," he murmured, voice silky smooth.

Think, Mack, think. "I've, um, always hated the colour." Sooo not true. "I was teased about it mercilessly when I was a kid and I've been trying to forget that I'm ginger. My friends understand that."

"To the point where they would lie to the Lord Alpha about it to protect your delicate sensibilities?"

"They're good friends," I replied shortly.

"So, let me see if I can get this straight. You've lied about your hair, you've lied about the wolf to the human, and the human to the wolf. Can anything that you say be trusted?"

I walked on stiffly. I was starting to get very scared indeed. "I've been under a lot of pressure lately. John was…he was…dear to me. If I've lied to anyone, it's only so I can find out what happened to him."

"I could compel you to tell me everything."

No you couldn't. "I suppose, you could, yes. That's much what I'd expect from the leader of the Brethren, use brute force to get what you want. Are you going to?"

"You don't seem to have much regard for us." He stared ahead. "It doesn't matter though, I have no doubt that you'll tell me the whole truth eventually, one way or another." There was a faint mocking edge to his voice.

"You are only here for another twenty four hours," I commented, tightly praying that he'd not changed his mind.

He laughed slightly. "Yes, but I somehow think our paths will cross again."

I bloody well hoped not.

Chapter Ten

By the time we got back to the keep, it was shrouded in darkness. I could hear the buzz of voices from inside, however. Corrigan beside me had thankfully lapsed into silence so I was free to work through my own thoughts. I wondered exactly what the mage was doing. I didn't know much about how magic worked, to be honest. I knew from my readings on the Othernet that it took years of training to be a mage, and that they often specialised in different areas, such as divination, alchemy, telekinesis or fore-telling. There was a mage academy located somewhere in Kent and powers were generally passed down generational lines. I had a vision in my head of a bald man with a long black cloak holding a glass ball, but perhaps I'd been watching too much Japanese anime lately. It briefly occurred to me that it might help the wizard if I mentioned the shadowy figure in Perkins but there was so little to really elaborate on that I decided to keep that little nugget to myself. He'd probably just end up getting in my way if I revealed what I'd already found out from good old-fashioned detective work. Of course that didn't mean I didn't want to know what he himself discovered while he was here.

When we reached the oak entrance door, Corrigan opened it and gestured at me. I was somewhat surprised that the ostensible leader of the shapeshifters was portraying himself as a gentleman – and somewhat nervous to have him at my back – but I entered anyway, with him close behind me. As soon as the door closed, Staines stepped up and whispered something in his ear and the two of them went off in the direction of the office. Everyone else was gathered in the hall.

Mackenzie, what on earth is going on? Why were you with Lord Corrigan?

Julia was looking at me with a rather alarmed expression at my suddenly departed companion.

He was just being annoying, I sent back silently. *Nothing to worry about.*

He might know that I was lying to him about some things but at least he definitely didn't suspect that I was human at least, I thought, remembering his utter dismissal of Nick. He had me pegged as a grumpy loner who was living in abject terror of him and the rest of the Brethren. I could live with that. As long as I chose to ignore his portentous comment about our paths crossing again that was.

I took my place in the crowd with the other pack members. Everyone seemed slightly excited and anxious again at the presence of the mage. I could sense a few glances my way and wished I could silently reassure the others the way that I'd reassured Julia. There were times that the limitations of shifters were gallingly unhelpful.

Tom moved up from the sidelines to be beside me. I shot him an evil look before whispering furiously, "You thought you'd tell Corrigan that I'm called Red because of the way I blush when we shag?"

At least he had the grace to look slightly embarrassed. "He put me on the spot. He wasn't even supposed to be doing my interview – it was the blonde chick. But he barged in during it and fired questions at me. I couldn't think straight. Something about the way his eyes look through you." He shivered slightly.

"What else did you tell him?" I put my hands on my hips, still annoyed.

"He wanted to know why we'd had so few injuries and deaths. I told him that we were just lucky. I wasn't entirely sure if he believed me."

"Well, I told him the truth so it's probably best if you stop lying to him."

Betsy's voice came up from behind me. "You told him you were human?" She said aghast.

"No, that I dyed my hair, stupid," I said. "I didn't have much choice after the things you two had told him."

"What were we supposed to say, Red?" Tom looked askance. "He's got this power and he looks at you and you want to tell him everything just to please him. And god knows we can't tell him the real truth."

"He doesn't suspect anything like that," I tugged on my ponytail. "He just seems to think that I'm the local lay with a penchant for inveterate lying. Anyway, from now on my hair is dyed because I hate my original colour. Oh, and I'm having an affair with Nick behind your back."

Betsy looked rather pleased at that one. I was about to say something that we'd both regret when the office door opened and Staines and Corrigan came out followed by a ridiculously young looking man with a shock of blond dreads. No wonder he'd agreed to come to Cornwall: our mage was a surfer dude.

Corrigan cleared his throat. "This is Alexander Floride, a mage from the city. We will travel to the site of John's death where he'll scan it for any signs of what might have occurred. We will find out who killed one of our own."

He wasn't yours, I thought sourly, he was ours.

The blond wizard stepped forward. "Hi there." He almost waved. Good lord, was this the best they could do? I realized that he was wearing a Nirvana t-shirt and ripped jeans. He wasn't even from this decade for god's sake.

"So, uh, yeah." He grinned a toothy smile. "I'm gonna hit the site, do some scrying and tell you what's what. S'all good."

I had to pinch myself to stop from rolling my eyes. I wondered idly if Corrigan was impressed.

Staines spoke up. "We need everyone who was present when his body was discovered to be with us so the scrying doesn't get mixed up. Get a coat and wait outside."

The pack sprang into action. I still couldn't move quickly because of my injury – and I noticed satisfyingly out of the corner of my eye that Anton couldn't either. Tom gallantly fetched my leather jacket and helped me put it on. It appeared that all of a sudden Cornwall was full of gentlemen. Wonders would never cease.

There were nineteen of us in total: Corrigan, Staines, the other Brethren members including Lucy, the mage, Anton, Tom, me and three other pack members. It felt like a goddamn school outing. I wouldn't have been surprised if Staines had pulled out a little flag and started waving it around for us all to follow. At least the crescent moon was shedding some light down around us. I'd heard that in the cities it never seemed to get properly dark because of all the lights, but that certainly wasn't the case in rural Cornwall.

We headed off down the path in single file. I could feel my bloodfire curl around me in tendrils of anticipation. Despite myself, and the mage's unlikely appearance, I was curious to see what he would do. I had to admit that I was starting to feel confident in my ability to pull off this pretending to be a shifter thing. I'd now had a couple of close encounters with the supposedly omnipotent Lord Shifty himself and I was sure that, despite knowing that I was scared of him and commenting on my un-packlike independence, he'd not actually suspected a smidgen of humanity about me. Add that to the fact that after my fight with Anton there was virtually no point in pretending to hide in the shadows anymore and I figured that I could get away with trying to sidle up to the mage and find out what he knew. Julia had already said that he had no interest in exposing me; the best plan was to initiate contact with him, get the human part out of the way and find out what he knew.

I stepped out into the undergrowth and quickened my step to catch up with him. He was sandwiched between two of the Brethren, who were marching along with straight backs and stiff shoulders as if they were in the army. Floride, by contrast, loped along with an easy gait and a hint of a swagger. I sneaked in beside him and ignored the hiss of annoyance from the Brethren shifter behind me.

"I'm Mack," I stuck my hand out and grinned at him.

"Uh, Alex," he replied, shaking my hand back. His palm was slightly sweaty and I resisted the urge to wipe my own on my jeans. He squinted at me more closely in the gloom. "Feck me, you're…."

"Wearing a nineties vintage leather jacket, I know," I smoothly interrupted before he said anything that would get me into trouble.

He tripped over a root that was curling its way across the path. "Ummm…yes, of course. I was just admiring the, er, tailoring."

"Then we both are of the same mind," I stated, rather pointedly.

He cast a slightly nervous glance at the back of the shifter ahead of him before shrugging and smiling. "I suppose we are, dude."

Dude? Jeez.

"So, how is this going to work, Alex?"

"You mean, um…"

"I mean the scrying, *dude*. How does the whole mojo mumbo go down?"

"Oh, uh, I draw on my power from the air's energy. It's a molecular thing. If a heebie-jeebie had anything to do with the guy's death, then I'll be able to spot it, scan it and trace it."

"Scan it? So you'll know what it was?"

"If there's enough of a trail, sure. I can raise up an image of the perp and project it."

"Are you ever wrong?"

"Never," he answered steadily. "As I said, if it wasn't human," he looked at me again as he said this, "and there's enough of its essence left behind, then I'll capture it. Its image, I mean," he added hastily, "I don't do actual capturing – I'll leave that to you beasty dudes. Or gals. Or whatever."

"Scared?"

"Sensible, dude, sensible."

He certainly seemed sure of his magic abilities, at least. I supposed that the proof was in the pudding and that I shouldn't judge him by appearances. He was at least doing me the favour of not judging me by my humanity, and was not trying to pretend he was in any way a physical match for a shifter. I appreciated the honesty and felt slightly humbled by my earlier attitude towards him.

"What do you think of our little shifter girl here then, Mr Mage?"

Anton. Shit.

"God, do you country types ever stop shooting the breeze?" The Brethren behind us interjected.

Anton turned and snarled at her. Well, it was good to know that we agreed on something. He turned back to me, eyes falling to my side where he'd bitten me earlier on in the evaluation fight.

"How are the wounds?" There was an odd lascivious gleam in his eyes. "Bleeding much?"

I scowled at him and Alex opened his mouth to say something when all of a sudden there was the sound of hundreds of birds flying up into the sky followed by a low rumbling thunder. The ground began to shake. From side to side, like an....

"Earthquake!" Someone shouted.

My brain dully registered the impossibility of natural earth tremors on Cornwall before launching into full self protective mode as the ground continued to sharply jerk from side to side, flinging Alex to the ground. The trees creaked alarmingly around us and there were sounds of others nearby becoming uprooted and crashing to the ground. I fell forward onto my hands and knees, and then quickly covered my head with my arms, the most vulnerable part of me should a great oak decide to plant itself on top of my body.

Up ahead one of the Brethren spontaneously shifted in a blur of ripped cloth and fur. I could hear growling and snapping from more behind me.

Be calm, floated Corrigan's Voice over everyone, using compulsion to erase the panic. At once the growling stopped but the rumbling and the shaking continued for what seemed like an age. I huddled into a ball, praying that the others back at the keep were alright. Eventually it seemed to stop.

Stay where you are. There may be aftershocks to come.

Alex staggered to his feet. I knew he wouldn't have heard Corrigan's warning and I yanked at his jeans to pull him down again. He shook me off and gasped, "That's not an earthquake."

"What do you…?" I realised suddenly that if it wasn't an earthquake, and he had used his powers to work that out, then it must be some sort of creature. It must be what had killed John. I stopped thinking, stood up with lightning speed, and ran. The adrenaline pumped through me, overcoming the pain in my side, and pelting me forward. I was going to get my revenge. I felt a hand stretch out and try to grab me, and barely registered Corrigan reaching out, but I sidestepped and sprinted faster. The fire took over, all consuming. His Voice tried to compel me to halt but nothing was going to stop me. Red flickered in my vision and my fingertips began to tingle with heat. I neared the tree runes and slowed, starting to stalk with intent. There was definitely something there. I focused all my senses on the one large, dark shape. There was only one creature, at least, but it looked big, and definitely malevolent. It didn't matter what it was, though. It was going to die.

I came out from under the canopy of the trees and finally saw the whole thing for real in sharp technicolour vision. Whatever it was, it looked to be about twenty five hands high, had horns on top of its furred head and stood on two bowed legs. Steam puffed heavily from its nostrils. The monster took a step towards the trees - towards me - but the instant its foot touched the ground the earth began to shake again in another tremor. This time, however, I was ready. I kept my feet, barely, and pulled out a throwing dagger from my right arm. Zeroing in on its right eye, I aimed and then let the dagger take flight with unerring accuracy. Or it would have been unerring accuracy if the monster hadn't flipped its head to the side with unnatural speed so it caught it in the side of its pointed ear instead, barely scratching its skin. With another heavy crunch, it took a step, this time with murderous intent drawn all over its hideous face. The ground rumbled again, shaking me off my feet again and sending me tumbling to the sand.

I leapt up in an instant, reaching for my other dagger. The monster flicked shimmering black eyes onto me and roared deafeningly. The bloodfire was wholly in control, however, and I didn't flinch. I was about to fling the dagger at the creature with everything I had when a shape flew out of the trees behind me and launched itself at it. It was a were-panther, sleek and gleaming in the moonlight. It slammed into the beast's body, the force of its collision making it stagger backwards slightly, setting off another surge through the ground. The panther's jaws snapped and snatched away at a clump of the beast's flesh but it hung onto its side.

From the left spread of trees, three transformed shifters pounded out and went for its leg. Three others came from the right and attached themselves to its huge tree trunk of an arm. It stamped its feet, roared again and shook them off, sending them into the dunes with a chorus of pained whines. The ground shook again. The panther sprang from the thing's side to its shoulder, claws digging into it to cling on while it roared again and flailed around trying to pull the cat off. I saw my chance and threw again, aiming for its hand. And this time, I didn't miss, as the sharp pointed embedded itself in the creature's palm. It howled in agony and clutched at the dagger, trying to pull it out, momentarily ignoring the panther.

Another wave of shifters attacked in concertina. The monster kicked out at one werefox, catching it on its hind legs, almost immediately snapping the bone with a sickening crunch. Tom, in wolf form, attacked the monster back, his fangs latching onto its ankle. I sidestepped, trying to gain a better point with which to aid the panther, which stayed clinging onto the massive shoulders, occasionally swiping a giant paw at the side of its head.

My blood wasn't happy. Much more of this and the panther would knock it out before I got the chance to do anything. Anton's bear joined Tom and clawed at the tendons on its back leg. The monster picked up its foot and shook them off in one quick sudden movement. Again, as soon as its padded foot returned to the ground, another earthquake hit, sending shifters flying everywhere. The panther took another chance to claw the beast's head, but this time it mistimed and was knocked off in the rolling aftershock. I saw my chance as it bent to grab the panther and took a running leap onto its outstretched back.

I ran up to its neck, legs powering up the slope of its inclined posture, momentum carrying me, with my hands pulling on clumps of fur to reach the top. Hanging on to a horn with one hand and reaching into my trusty backpack with my other hand for my spare knife, I knew what to do.

Goddammit, Mackenzie, shift now!

Knock it off its feet, Corrigan I sent back calmly.

I sensed, rather than saw, the panther pause for a heartbeat then pull back with all the shifters to the dunes. It seemed as if there was a moment of absolute stillness and quiet before, almost immediately, as one group of fur-balled killing machines, they rushed the monster's legs. The force of their attack flipped it off its feet for just a split second, allowing me to drive the point of my blade into its carotid artery and feel warm blood spilling out over my hands. The creature staggered again, this time falling onto its knees as I sprang back out of the way. With a heavy groan it keeled slowly down to the ground, hands flailing towards its neck in vain. Then, finally, it was silent.

Chapter Eleven

I wiped my hands of the creature's blood on the damp grass and surveyed the damage. My bloodfire was gradually subsiding into a pit of devastation as a part of me realised that this was definitely not what had killed John – its tracks were labored in sharp definition across the sand and heavier ground. And yet, it seemed that it was just too much coincidence that it had taken this moment, a scant two days after his death, to appear in the very same spot where he'd drawn his last breath. There had to be some kind of connection.

I stood up and noted a very naked and very annoyed Corrigan right in front of me. He grabbed me by the shoulders and shook.

"What the hell did you think you were doing?" he growled.

I tried to pull away but his grip was too tight. "I thought that it might have been what killed John. I wanted to kill it back." I managed at least to sound calm, even if I didn't feel it.

"That part I understand," he snapped, "but what fool part of you thought that you could take it on by yourself?"

"Is your pride dented, my lord? Who's the kitten now then?" I said, unable to prevent myself from taunting him softly. Hah, who was frightened of the big scary Lord Alpha? Not me, no sirree.

"I compelled you." His liquid green gold eyes bored intensely into mine.

I shrugged complacently. "So in the heat of the moment it didn't take. You're not my alpha, remember."

His grip tightened even more and I winced in pain. "I am the Lord Alpha. I am everyone's alpha."

"Hey, you're new at this game, remember? It's not my fault if you've not fully come into all your lordly power yet."

The answering glare was absolutely terrifying. I rather belatedly considered that I should not be antagonising this shifter in any way at all. In fact, I had the sudden unshakeable belief that he was about to literally tear my head off. My temper would get me killed long before any of the Brethren ever realised the truth about me. And I had to remember that it was more than just my life on the line. There was the rest of my pack to consider too. Bugger.

I cast my eyes down submissively but I didn't tremble. Well, not much, at least anyway. I still wasn't scared of him, I was just pretending to be scared. Honest to goodness. "I'm sorry, my Lord. My disappointment at realising this was not my alpha's murderer along with the adrenaline from the fight has caused me to speak out of turn. I bow to your ultimate authority, in accordance with the Way." Way Directive 73: Any shifter who challenges their alpha's authority is bound to accept whatever punishment is deemed necessary. I could take it.

I hadn't thought it was possible, but his grip tightened even further for just a brief second before he abruptly released me and turned away. "Your punishment shall be meted out in due course, shifter.

Your role in taking down the beast is noted in your favour."

I peeked a glance up. He was stalking off towards the monster's body and I was apparently dismissed - for the time being at least. I raised my head and saw that all of the shifters around me, in various states of nudity, were looking aghast at my foolish bravado. I guiltily noted that Tom's eyes were the most horrorstruck, while Anton's proclaimed that he'd always known I'd do or say something stupid like this before long. Lucy looked like she'd swallowed a small furry creature of her own.

Shit, I was such an idiot sometimes. All I had to do was keep quiet and stay out of the Brethren's way. You wouldn't think it would take all that much effort. My gaze fell on the massive prone body of the beast we'd just killed. I should probably focus and see what I could find out about it rather than trying to engage any more shifters in small talk.

Ignoring the continued stares of the others, I headed up to the beast's head and crouched down. It was definitely an ugly looking thing. Its black eyes were fixed sightlessly to the horizon, as if it was waiting for whatever had summoned it to this plane to come and help. A few of the shifters came over as well and stood over it, looking down. As I tilted my head, something glittering on the side of its cavernous nostril caught my eye. It was a little silver stud pierced into the side. I appreciated its glitter for a moment before I reached over and hooked my fingers inside the nostril itself, finding the butterfly keeping it in place and pulling it out.

One or two of the shifters beside me looked faintly ill. Whatever. I liked shiny things and this would find a place in my little wooden chest with all my other memorabilia.

Alex came up. "Whatcha got there?"

I showed him, wordlessly. I wasn't sure I could trust myself to speak yet without incriminating myself further.

He looked at it and grimaced. "Lovely," then focused on the beast itself. "Sweeet! A terrametus beast! How did you get it in the air?"

Staines appeared in front of us. "We knocked it off its feet for a second at her," he nodded to me, "behest. Then she killed it. It did not fly."

Alex seemed rather impressed. "It didn't need to. That moment away from the ground would have done it. Terrameti get their strength from the ground, as soon as they lose contact with the earth they become as weak as kittens. Nice work, Mack Attack!"

There was a glint of skeptical approval in Staines' eyes. He turned to Alex and raised his eyebrows. "Where were you during the attack, Mr Floride?"

There wasn't a trace of embarrassment anywhere to be seen on Alex's face. "Dude, I told ya on the phone. I don't fight. I'm a…"

"Lover, not a fighter?" It popped out before I could stop myself. I was really going to have to stop doing that.

Fortunately the mage didn't try to kill me or grab me as Corrigan had done, he just laughed instead and licked his lips suggestively, "Something like that."

Corrigan himself had apparently recovered enough from the trauma of having someone speak back to him because he strode arrogantly back over to us.

Alex touched his forelock in mock obeisance at the Lord Alpha and grinned at him easily. "That's not the first time I've seen pack members' rage mean that an alpha's compulsion doesn't work properly. You guys are taking this death pretty seriously."

I blinked in surprise and tried not to appear too pathetically grateful at the mage offering me a get-out clause. Corrigan grunted slighted and ignored me completely, focusing on Alex. "Do your thing, then."

He jerked back slightly. "What now? But I thought…"

"We haven't got all day, or night. The thing that killed the Cornish alpha left no traces." He jerked his head at the terrametus. "That did. So you need to scry and tell us what you can see."

"Alpha dude, I'll do better than that, I'll show you."

I was surprised that Corrigan didn't try to rip Alex's head off his shoulders too for calling him dude. Instead he just folded his arms and rocked back on his heels. Disturbingly he was still naked from his shift back to human. So was everyone else but somehow Corrigan's nudity demanded more attention. At least I'd spent enough time around the pack to avoid moving my eyes to anywhere other than his face. It wasn't easy though.

I decided that looking at Alex was probably a safer option. The mage had closed his eyes and I noticed with fascination that blue sparks were forming at the clenched fists he had down by his sides. There was a faint hum in the air then he opened up his palms.

Blue light sprang forward, snaking through the air. It streamed past the body of the terrametus as if it wasn't even there and instead curved through in stretched coils to the top of the dunes. That was where the seven coals were. The light coalesced there and formed a shape. I screwed up my eyes, trying to work out what it was.

"Can you tell what it is yet?" asked Alex in a mock Aussie accent.

"Try harder, mage," Corrigan ordered in a low rumble of a voice.

Up until that point I had been very impressed with the mage's offerings. Clearly this was just kids' stuff and there was a lot more to come.

The light swirled around some more. It looked oddly human shaped: there were two arms, two legs, and it wasn't that big either. At least not when comparing it to the corpse next to us anyway. The features tightened somewhat and I realised that I was looking at a woman. She had long hair that spread out behind her in the non-existent wind and a smooth unlined face. Her blue lit arms lifted gently and moved almost musically in the air, as if she was conducting an orchestra. She was facing us, and towards the spot where John's body had lain. My eyes drifted down her body, noting a flowing gown, much like the one I'd expected to see Alex in actually. Then I realised that her feet weren't touching the ground.

"Is she meant to be floating? I mean, is that a side-effect of the scrying?" I asked.

Alex's eyes were screwed shut in concentration and it was Corrigan who answered. "No. What you see is what was here. Neither would the dunes have shifted that much in the last forty-eight hours. She is hovering above the ground."

"Fuck me," I breathed.

Corrigan looked at me for a second and seemed about to say something before he clearly thought better of it and switched his attention back to the mage. "Is that it, Mr Floride? Is there a trail?"

The blue light shifted slightly from the woman's shape but did little else. "No trail," Alex said, with some effort.

"Then we're done," said Corrigan. "The money will be transferred to your account within the hour. Can you take care of this?" He asked, motioning towards the earthquake monster. Alex nodded and, with that, Corrigan snapped his fingers and shifted back seamlessly to a panther. The other Brethren, and Anton I noted, also shifted, then twisted back in the direction of the keep and bounded off. Just before the tree line, Corrigan's head turned and his panther eyes, as green gold as his human ones, glanced back towards me for one second, before snapping back to the front and disappearing into the night.

Tom stood there and looked hopelessly at me. The desire in him to join them and be part of the Brethren, even if only just for the brief trip back to the keep, was so overwhelmingly transparent that I waved at him irritably. "Go."

Gratitude flashed in his eyes and he was gone, leaving just Alex and I alone in front of the dunes, with the terrametus and a few fading blue smoky tendrils.

Chapter Twelve

Before too long the only sound left was the gentle to and fro of the waves lapping on the beach behind us. Alex pulled a small round object from the pocket of his jeans and began to murmur something. I watched in fascination. The tiny sphere grew and lifted itself into the air then moved to hover above the corpse of the terrametus. All of a sudden, light exploded from it, showering the body and causing me to shield my eyes. A heartbeat later all that was left was a faint shadow outlined on the sand.

Alex reached out and the sphere flew back, returned to its original size and landed in his opened palm. He stuffed in back into his pocket and looked at me.

"Now the beast dudes are gone, perhaps you can tell me what a human is doing here. And why you smell so – different."

I was still momentarily mesmerised by his display of power but I shook myself out of it and gazed at him assessingly, wondering how far I could trust him. He could reveal my true nature to the Brethren at any point. But there was just something about him that made me feel comfortable and I figured that if he'd been going to tell all my secrets, he'd have already done so by now. And he had managed to explain away why I'd ignored Corrigan's compulsion. I felt the sudden overwhelming desire to unburden myself. I rarely brought the subject up with the pack because it made them uncomfortable to be reminded of what I was. Even Tom tried to change the subject whenever I'd spoken about it. Added to which, I was starting to both like and admire the gangly mage. In for a penny in for a pound, I supposed.

"I don't know who my father was," I said softly. "And my memories of my mother are rather hazy. I have flashes – I know she was petite and dark haired, unlike me, with a kind voice and a good heart. I remember little things, like driving through the snow and wishing I could make a snowman. She stopped the car in a layby and we got out and did just that – built a tiny one by the side of the road, even though we had no gloves and it had to have been below zero. She made things fun."

I paused, remembering. Alex stayed silent. "I know that we were always on the move and we never stayed in one place for very long. She discouraged me from making friends and it was if we were always running from something. At least I certainly never knew where we running to, so I suppose that we were trying to escape from something. Or someone.

And then one day we ended up here. It seemed like she knew where she was going and that she knew who the pack were. But she must have been human because that's what I am so I don't know how she knew of them. She walked straight into the keep without knocking and was stopped by John in the hall. He asked her what was going on and all she did was push me at him. Then she turned and walked out. Before she left the threshold of the keep, she turned and said, 'No-one must ever know. You are all bound to keep her secret.' And she left. She never came back. I'd sit by the window of the library for hours and days, and then weeks, watching for the car to come and for her to jump back out and take me away with her, but she never did.

The words that she'd said must have had power to them because no-one in the pack has ever been able to talk of me to another. They tried – John later told me that he had called up the Brethren for help with what to do with this human child they'd suddenly found themselves lumbered with and found he couldn't speak. He'd said it was like having a weight clawing his tongue to the bottom of his mouth, and that the pain inside his head when he even thought of revealing to an outsider who I was had been excruciating. After trying to break the geas himself, and failing repeatedly, he compelled the others never to attempt it themselves either.

I laughed, sharply. "They weren't happy to have me. John was always kind but sometimes back in those early days he had a look in his eyes as if he'd like to just drown me in the nearest well. There were others who were less kind.

But the longer I stayed, the more they got used to me. The pack here aren't particularly violent or even particularly active. They keep the Way and follow the Brethren's orders from London but they're not monsters. Before they knew it, I was part of the furniture. I made friends. Tom, the wolf who was just here, and Betsy, a werelynx. And others too.

John started to train me and I quickly worked out that even though I couldn't shift, I could be just as strong as they could. I helped hunt. I helped keep them safe."

I swallowed. "And then when it was my eighteenth birthday, John bit me. I wanted it, so badly. I didn't care what my shift was to be, I just wanted to be like them. And it was a pain that I've never experienced before or since. The shifter virus ate through me for days. It felt as if my whole body was crawling and turning itself inside out. And after three days, I was still me. Still human."

I kicked angrily at the sand.

"But you stayed," Alex said, his eyes projecting empathy. At least it wasn't pity: that I didn't think I could deal with.

"This is my home. There are still one or two who wish I was gone – or worse - but for the most part, the pack accept me. And besides, where else would I go?"

Alex nodded, understandingly. "So if the Brethren found out, they'd…"

"Kill me," I answered flatly. "Maybe kill the rest of the pack too, I don't know. Even though it's not their fault. The geas my mother placed on them meant that they couldn't tell anyone. So either they murdered me and disposed of my body, or just accepted me in. And like I said, they're not monsters. Not this pack." My last sentence was heavy with meaning.

Alex frowned at me. "Are you sure the Brethren would do that? I mean, I know they used to hold with all that 'death to anyone who discovers our secret' shit," he sketched imaginary quotation marks in the air, "but I don't think they're still like that."

I snorted. "John seemed pretty sure they'd react violently. So do all the others now. And I've heard proof with my own ears of what Lord fucking Corrigan himself thinks of humans."

"Really? Word on the street is that he's a strong alpha, maybe stronger than they've had for centuries, but that he's not a bad dude."

"I don't care what word says," I answered. "I just need them to do their thing and leave so I can carry on with my life."

"And the alpha? I mean, John, the Cornish alpha?"

"I will find that bitch who slaughtered him and left him here to die and I'll kill her," I said matter-of-factly.

Alex looked at me quietly. "Do you know, I just believe you might."

I faced him head on. "So you understand the consequences if you tell them who I really am?"

"Tell me why they can't smell that you're human first. Shifters have noses like bloodhounds."

"I wear a lotion that Julia, our new alpha, created. It mimics a shifter smell. I think the actual result is a cross between a hamster and a rodent. As long as I keep applying it, they won't be here for long enough to smell a rat. So to speak."

Alex moved a bit closer and sniffed, experimentally, before stepping back and shaking his head. I guessed that mages didn't have superior smell as one of their super powers then. "I still don't think they'd do the whole killing you thing if they found out."

I hardened my gaze.

He sighed. "I won't tell them. I have nothing to gain from getting involved in shifter politics. 'Sides which, I wouldn't want to be responsible for the bloodbath that the Mack Attack would create." He winked suddenly and punched me on the arm.

I smiled at him. I really did feel better now that someone else knew my secret. It also seemed oddly better that he was a virtual stranger. And lightning hadn't struck me or him down yet either. I punched him back lightly and began to search around in the darkness for my throwing daggers. Alex helped me hunt for them in the gloom. One had landed next to the ring of black coals which I pointed out to him. He stared back down at the tree runes from the top of the dune, frowning.

"So it was a woman who was conjured by the scrying?" he asked.

I was puzzled that he didn't know and it must have shown on my face because he continued with, "I don't see who I scry because I need to keep my eyes shut to maintain my power. Which admittedly doesn't make it a very useful tool for a solitary mage to use."

I laughed slightly and described the blue vision to him. He nodded slowly as if considering the matter.

"So tell me what else has happened."

As much as I had decided I liked him, I hadn't exactly gotten the impression of someone who wanted to help beyond what he was being paid for. "Why do you want to know?" I asked warily.

"'Cos I think I like you Mack. And you need help." He looked in the direction of the keep for a second, even though its distant outline was submerged in the trees. "A lot of help. I might be able to draw on my wizardly skills to do something. Not physical something, you understand, but you never know what I might be able to do to get this sorted out."

I was tempted for a second to tell him that I could manage this on my own and that it was my fight and no-one else's, but I realised that no doubt there were things that he might know or could help me puzzle out. I'd be a fool not to take him up on his offer of help.

I sat down on top of the dune, but not too close to the ring of stones. Even though I knew that they were just coals, they gave me the creeps. He sat down beside me and stretched out his legs. I started at the beginning, sketching out everything that had happened, including what I'd found out at Perkins and the shadowy CCTV shape that Nick had shown me.

Alex pursed his lips. "I don't know that I can offer much about who this woman might be. Obviously the fact that she had to break into a local store to get coals means that wherever she's from, or wherever she came from to here at least, doesn't have those sorts of materials ready to hand. She must have some magic training though to be able to create a triangulated grid."

"A what?"

"The runes of seven and the stones here. They form a triangle which would have allowed her to trap your alpha in the middle and hold him. Or summon a terrametus."

"So we need to destroy the grid so she can't do it again then!" I stood up and almost jumped towards the ring of stones, picking one up and throwing it towards the sea.

Alex stayed on the sand and shook his head. "The runes and the stones are needed to form the grid but once that is done they aren't required any longer. The power remains until the creator is killed."

"So she can still use this at any time to do anything she wants?" Even I could hear the rising panic in my voice.

"Yeah, man, she can. But I can put a warning ward around so if there are any signs of magic or transportations then we'll know about it."

I remained deeply unhappy. "But I thought you needed a portal to transport from one plane to another?"

"Portals are more economical with energy, but they're not great if you want to be a circumspect dude."

I tried not to roll my eyes at Alex's ability to use the words 'circumspect' and 'dude' in the same breath and changed tack. "What do you think the electric screwdriver was for?"

"Now that one I have no clue about it." He shrugged and stood up, brushing sand from his jeans. I was pretty sure it was a wasted effort. It doesn't matter what you try to do to keep sand away from you, once it was in your clothes, it was staying. Even if it had been six months since you'd last visited the beach, somehow, somewhere, sand would still linger. Alex continued, "But there is one thing I can definitely help with."

I raised my eyebrows hopefully.

"The wichtlein. Give me the stone and I'll track it for you."

"But won't it have disappeared back down whichever hole it came from?"

"Not if the death and destruction it warned of isn't over yet. And the appearance of the terrametus dude would lead me to believe that it's not."

The hope that I'd felt earlier in the police station began to re-surface. "Then what are we waiting for? There's no time like the present." The pebble was in a pouch in my backpack so I pulled it out and offered it to him.

"Won't the Bros want to be involved?" He made no move to take it from me.

"I think I've made my feelings about them perfectly clear already." I hiked my backpack on my shoulders to make it more comfortable and tightened the straps.

"Yeah but they do have mad skills. And if Corrie finds out you've been off doing more stuff on your own, he'll be even more pissed off with you."

"I'd like to see you try calling him Corrie to his face, Alex. Anyway, he's not the boss of me and they're all leaving tomorrow afternoon because they could only commit to three days. And I won't be alone because you'll be with me."

Alex paled slightly.

"Don't worry," I said calmly, "I'll keep you safe. And no fighting, I promise."

Unfortunately a cloud took that moment to pass over the moon and throw a shadow over us. It didn't exactly boost Alex's look of confidence. I didn't want to wait any longer, however, because if too much time passed then the trail might go cold. I held the stone out to him again and tried my best puppy dog eyes.

He grimaced, and took it from me. "Fine. Just don't look at me like that again – I don't need to be any more scared than I already am."

Chapter Thirteen

Using his index finger, Alex circled the wichtlein pebble that he held in the palm of his hand. A smoky blue snake of light escaped from it, just as before with the shape of the woman. This time it wound its way into the wood, heading away from the beach. Without saying anything further, we followed it.

It took us along the path to the keep for a few hundred metres before curving to the right – and the eastern perimeter where I'd last seen John. We ended up being forced to pitch into the tangled undergrowth.

"Your trailing spell doesn't pick easy routes to follow, does it?" I was suddenly starting to feel very tired. It felt like such a long time since I'd had any proper rest, and I was well aware of the continuing ache in my side. As far as my memory went, the fight with Anton could have been last week for all that had happened since, however the pain in my body reminded me that it had been just that morning.

Behind me, Alex gasped in exertion. "It's not GPS, dude. It doesn't conveniently pick the nearest motorway to drive along."

The blue snake took that moment to decide to dive through a patch of nettles. Great. So far, I'd been cut by briars, beaten up by Anton and Theresa, attacked by a giant horned quake beast, chewed out by Nick, almost killed by Corrigan and now I was trying to commit death by stinging plants in the middle of night. Oh yeah, and John was still dead.

Alex muttered further complaints from behind me. "Get with the programme, surfer boy," I said, trying not to snap. "We're going to follow this if it kills us." Under my breath I cursed that it just might.

The wood around us was alive with the sounds of the night fauna. A midge buzzed by my ear and I slapped at it in irritation as I ploughed behind Alex's blue trail. I wasn't happy about being eaten alive on top of everything else. Then, without warning, I found myself being forced to steady my body briefly against a tree as a light wave of dizziness caught me unawares.

"Feeling tired, human girl?" There was definitely a note of sulky petulance in Alex's voice. I gritted my teeth and pushed myself away from the tree, carrying on into the wood and ignoring him. If we could catch the wichtlein then it would all be worth it. I just prayed that we found it soon or I wasn't sure I'd manage to stay conscious for long enough to do anything.

After what seemed like an age later, we came to a stream. The trail passed directly over it and I felt my heart sink. Oh for fuck's sake. I placed one foot into the icy water and gasped as I felt it seep slowly into my trainer. The stones underneath were slimy and slippery and, even though it was only about calf deep and two metres wide, it took everything I had to get across. I tried desperately to find my bloodfire so I could heat it up and fire it through my body, but even my insides felt dull and damp. By the time I reached the other side of the stream I was panting with exertion. Sweat clung to my forehead as I struggled to stay upright.

And then I heard something. I clutched Alex's arm behind me and pointed, holding my breath. There, just up ahead and not far from the clearing of a few days ago, sat what I was suddenly sure was a wichtlein. It was eating something, gnawing at it with sharp teeth that gleamed in the moonlight. I tried not to look too hard at whatever it had decided to snack on for dinner and instead focused on the fact that I finally felt a flicker of heat in the pit of my stomach and the surge of imminent success.

The wichtlein appeared to be about two feet high and was completely covered in inky dark fur. It had a pointed nose and clawed fingers that were gripping its evening meal while behind it lay a short stubby tail. I was fairly certain that with its underground habits it was bound to be almost, if not completely, blind. That meant that its hearing would overcompensate for this shortcoming. Even the slightest rustle would warn it of our approach. So how to get close enough to catch it without scaring it off? I certainly didn't want to harm it – well, not yet anyway. I needed to find out what it knew and if it had targeted John specifically. As a harbinger, maybe it even knew exactly what was going on and who the blue cloaked bitch was. I was very much aware that I might not get another shot so I had to make this count.

Thoughtfully, I ran through a mental checklist of the tools in my backpack. There was definitely a rope in there somewhere. I wondered if I'd be able to lasso the creature from this distance. My line of sight was clear enough to swing it through and hook round the wichtlein's body but I didn't dare take another step towards it in case it heard me, and I wasn't sure the rope I had would reach it from this distance anyway.

Could I even unzip my backpack to find the rope quietly enough? Damnit. But then, I remembered that Alex was here too and that I was still gripping his arm tightly. I could perhaps use him somehow. If I could send him round to the other side of the wichtlein, where he'd be upwind of it, then it might smell him and run in my direction. Then I could nab it.

I released my grip on his arm and half-turned towards him, motioning with my hands that he should move back out of the stream the way we'd come, and skirt round to the other side of wichtlein. He looked confused and I felt a spark of exasperation. Hadn't he ever watched any war films for goodness' sake? I tried again, making two little feet motions with two fingers and pointing round the surrounding to the back of the little creature. Unfortunately at this point I'd forgotten that he was still stood in the stream. He shifted his weight slightly to see where I was pointing towards and, at that moment, slipped and landed with an almighty splash on his back.

The wichtlein immediately looked up in our direction with a wide-eyed yellow stare and then heaved itself up, discarding the carcass it had been gnawing on and started running in the opposite direction. Fuck fuck fuck. Without pausing further, I sprinted after it, pulling the rope out of my backpack as I did so. At least it didn't move that fast – thanks to the fatigue and pain I was pretty sure that even with the aid of the bloodfire I wouldn't be able to keep up with it for long. I sped up slightly, shaking my head to clear the fuzziness and focusing my vision on the small ball of black fur. I began to swing the rope overhead.

Up ahead was a clump of close-knit trees. I had to reach it before then as I knew I'd never be able to snag it with the rope with all those other obstacles around. I looped the rope faster in the air and then let it go.

The noose sailed through the air and, for a moment, I was sure that I'd missed. Then it arced downwards just in time to catch the wichtlein. As soon as it curved over the small running body, I yanked hard. The creature was suddenly pulled backwards and let out a high-pitched shriek. I wrenched harder on the rope and dragged it towards me for a few more feet, then walked unsteadily towards it, keeping a tight hold of the end of it. When I reached the wichtlein, I paused at looked down at it squirming uncomfortably. Its little clawed paws were scrabbling at the tight lasso, trying in vain to get it off, and it made little huffing sounds that were becoming more and more panicked. I bent down and scooped it up, then held it in front of me at arm's length.

Yep, its eyes were a dull opaque so it was a given that its vision was virtually non-existent. Nonetheless, I hardened both my eyes and my voice.

"You set a stone here, two days ago, for a shifter. Why?"

It wriggled in my hands, still trying to escape and squeaking incessantly. I squeezed its body.

"Answer me!"

"Won't speak. Let Craw go!" The wichtlein spat, shrilly.

Alex appeared at my shoulder, dripping wet. "Craw will speak or wizard will act." He spun his pinky in the air, generating more blue smoke.

The wichtlein cowered and clawed at my arms. "Let Craw go!"

Alex jerked his pinky forward and the blue snake floated steadily towards the little animal.

"No no no no no no no no! I speak! I speak! Stop!"

I briefly wondered what it was about Alex's magic that had the wichtlein so terrified. Perhaps there was more to my rather unfit newfound friend than I had previously thought. I couldn't worry about that now though. The night air around me was starting to feel heavy and oppressive and I was fairly certain that it wouldn't be long before I passed out in a heap. I concentrated on the flicker in my stomach, encouraging it to rise and keep me going long enough for me to get the information I wanted. It gave a feeble answering warmth in return. That would do for now.

I shook the wichtlein and repeated myself. "You placed a doom stone here two days ago for John Arton. Why?"

"He die soon. She kill him," it squeaked, still squirming.

"Who she? I mean, who is she?" I tightened my hands on the wichtlein.

"Iabartu! Iabartu!"

"And who is Iabartu?" growled Alex.

"Sky god human woman." The wichtlein stopped its pointless clawing and fumbling and raised up its head. "She seek wyr blood."

"What? You mean dragon blood?" I was confused. We had a few little dragons occasionally rear their heads in Cornwall, but they popped up all over the country, much like the one I'd bagged for my first kill. This neck of the woods wasn't special in that regard at all, and I couldn't think for the life of me why John's life would have been forfeit for one.

"Not little wyr, fire girl. Draco Wyr."

"What did you call me?" Fire girl? How the hell did it know about my bloodfire? And what on god's earth was a Draco Wyr? I shook the little beast, hard.

The wichtlein cackled unpleasantly. "Craw know many lots. Craw know who Draco Wyr. Man beast know who Draco Wyr. Man beast try stop Iabartu take Draco Wyr. Man beast die." A single claw scratched my arm with intent. "You fault man beast die."

My heart thudded. "My fault? Why my fault? I don't know this Draco Wyr! What do you mean?" It couldn't be my fault he'd died, could it? But why should I believe the wichtlein? I shook it even harder. "You're lying. Tell me the truth." My fingers curled round its whole body and, despite my condition, my bloodfire rose even further. The wichtlein shrieked in answering pain and began struggling again.

"It's telling the truth." Alex's voice was quiet.

"You're wrong!" I snarled, trying desperately to think of what I could to get the wichtlein to stop prevaricating and 'fess up without killing it.

"Mack, I'm not." He touched my arm. I turned and looked at him and saw it in his eyes. I stared at him dully for a second, then back at the little black creature.

The heat was gone. "Why is it my fault? What did I do?"

But there wasn't any answer. I dimly heard Craw cackling again. Blood was thumping in my head and the edges of the world were going blurry. I couldn't keep my head clear this time. I shook myself but the edges blurred further and I heard a roaring in my ears. My grip on the wichtlein loosened. Then everything went completely dark.

Chapter Fourteen

When I came to, I was lying against a tree. Alex's face loomed towards me, concerned. "Mack Attack? You okay?"

I struggled to sit up. I felt very nauseous and the wound in my side screeched at me with sharp pain. I pulled up my t-shirt and looked down at the blood that was seeping through the bandages.

"Shit, Mack! Where the hell did that come from? Have you been bleeding this entire time?"

I tried to focus. "Craw?"

"He's gone. You dropped him when you passed out. To be honest, it was either catch you or catch him. I went for you."

I cursed and tried to sit up again. My head swam. "You need to get Julia." It was a strain just to get the words out.

"I don't even know who Julia is, Mack!" Alex's voice was high-pitched and tense.

"Keep." I gasped. "Older woman. Grey hair. She'll be the new alpha when the Brethren go."

"Okay, okay." Alex nodded and started to move away then abruptly came back. "How the hell do I get back to the keep? And how can I leave you here alone? Shit, shit, shit."

"Go west." My vision turned dark for a second before returning. "I'll be fine." My daggers at least were re-strapped to my arms in case anything nasty came close.

"Okay." He nodded again but remained where he was, looking at me.

"Alex? No Brethren. No matter what." My life wasn't worth the consequences of them finding just how very humanly weak I really was.

"Okay."

"Go!"

"Okay."

He turned and ran out into the dark trees. I leaned my head back and closed my eyes. I tried to think about what Craw had meant about it being my fault. Had I met a Draco Wyr before? Perhaps I'd killed one? I was drifting in and out of consciousness and couldn't work any of it out. There must be a reason why the bitch woman – Iabartu? – needed him. Goddammit, my brain just wasn't cooperating. I gave up and opened my eyes to the stars instead, marveling at how they seemed to be moving around the sky as if they were dancing. Milky Way, Ursa Minor, Cassiopeia…so pretty and shiny….I blinked slowly. I was starting to feel very cold and shivery. I tried to pull my knees up to my body to curl into myself and generate some warmth but a shooting pain ran through me instead and my vision started to cloud over. Closing my eyes, I felt my whole body fall into shut down mode. A stray thought crossed my mind that if Alex didn't get back here with Julia quickly, then I might soon be talking to John himself. A quiet smile curved my lips and everything went quiet again.

"Mackenzie!" *Mackenzie!*

Someone was shaking me.

"Mackenzie! Look at me!" *Now.*

It was Julia, not John. Go figure. I forced my heavy eyelids open and looked away from the sky and at her. "Hey, Jules."

"Hello, dear. I need you to hold on to Mr Florides' hand for me, please. This is going to hurt."

Alex's face swam up. "Hi, Alex. Where's your blue smoke?"

"Hush, dear. Hold his hand and grip it tight."

"'kay."

He placed his hand in mine and I held it. I looked at him and told him how pretty the stars were. He just looked back at me solemnly. I was aware of Julia pulling off my blood-soaked bandages and taking a jar of something from a bag beside her. It smelled awful and had a very green tinge to it. She scooped a dollop out.

"I'm sorry, Mackenzie." Julia's hand smeared the green gloop onto my wound and I screamed. I heard Alex next to me moaning as I squeezed his hand. Julia started rubbing in the ointment and I screamed again. Nothing had ever hurt this much before; nothing had existed before this pain. I fainted again.

*

This time, when I woke up, there was a wolf looking at me with pale yellow eyes. Tom. Julia was still there too.

"What the hell did you do to me?" The pain had gone but the memory of it still remained.

She put her hand on my forehead. "It's an old remedy called trieswater. Particularly dangerous to humans, I might add, Mackenzie. You're lucky that Mr Floride found me when he did. Much longer and I don't think it would have worked." She removed her hand and looked satisfied. "There's no fever at least. You'll live. Although you're a damn fool for staying out after a fight like that considering your injuries."

"John…"

"Is still dead and nothing you do will change that. Can you stand? We need to get you back to the keep. Dawn will be breaking soon."

With Alex's help, and Tom nudging me gently, I managed to get to my feet.

"Tom will carry you back to the keep. You should get some sleep. Mr Floride here has already filled me in on most of your night activities. For your information, the Lord Alpha confirmed my status as the new Cornish alpha after he returned last night and will be returning to the capital. He is, however, leaving behind a delegation to investigate further, thanks to the encounter with the terrametus."

"What? He can't do that!" I burst out.

"He can do whatever he wants," chided Julia, gently. "They have pressing business back in London to attend to but have decided that the situation here needs to be taken care of too. They're going to ask Mr Floride here to do some more work before they decide what to do next."

I swore violently. How many of Julia's lotions and potions was I going to need to depend on to continue hiding from the Brethren? Speaking of which… "Why haven't I heard of this trieswater before? I feel a hell of a lot better."

"It accelerates healing in humans, although it often sends weaker ones into a coma before it can really start to work. You've avoided that part of it, fortunately. It does have some rather unpleasant side effects, however."

"Yeah, I felt those," I commented.

"I didn't mean the pain, dear. Shifters don't use it to heal, they use it as a hallucinogenic drug."

"Uh…what?"

"You'll feel a lot better very quickly but if you start to see things that don't make logical sense then you will be hallucinating. It's why I have never given it to you before."

"Great," I muttered.

"Trippy," grinned Alex, helping me onto Tom's furry back.

I curled my fingers into his fur to prepare myself. "Thank you, Alex." I said quietly, looking at him. "Not just for getting Julia. For…"

He ruffled my hair and shushed me. "You gave me a scare there, dude. Glad you're okay though."

I smiled at him weakly and Tom took off.

*

When we arrived back at the keep, the sun was reaching higher into the sky and the sunny daylight allowed the darkness of the night before to fade away into a bad memory. I was in desperate need of a good night – or day's – sleep, however. I slid off Tom's back.

"I'm going to owe a lot of people a lot of favours by the time all this is over," I murmured, half to him and half to myself.

He whined softly in return. In front of the oak doors, a gleaming limousine sat waiting. The scratched car from the other day seemed to have disappeared. Perhaps it offended his sensibilities to be seen in anything less than perfect. Nothing but the best for the Lord of all Alphas, I thought sardonically. From within the keep itself, I could hear his raised voice barking out indistinct orders. I briefly considered trying to enter through a back door and slipping up to the dorm unnoticed when Lucy wandered outside.

She waved enthusiastically. "Hey! Can you believe how freaky that thing was last night?"

For a stupid moment I thought that she was referring to the wichtlein and wondered how on earth she knew about it, before I realised that she meant the earthquake monster.

"Yeah," I nodded fervently in response. "Freaky."

"You were kind of freaky yourself too," she added. "I've never seen Lord Corrigan so mad at anyone before."

Next to Lucy, a giant four poster bed, draped with satin covers and plumped up pillows, hovered in the sky. I looked down at Tom.

"I don't suppose you can see a bed floating in the air next to her, can you?"

Tom looked about as concerned as a wolf can possibly ever look and shook his head. Okay then, I guess the hallucinations were starting to kick in.

"It must be a gift I have," I said to Lucy, trying to ignore the allure of the bed. I guessed that taking a running leap and diving on top of it would look pretty dumb when what I'd end up doing was a face plant onto the gravel.

She smiled at me. "I'm going to be sticking around and helping you guys out with all this."

I bit back my retort that we didn't need her aid and tried to look gracious. "That's…um…great."

Anton came round the corner at that point, noted Lucy, and smoothly greeted her with a kiss. Mr Charm himself. He completely ignored me and began chatting to her. Little forked devils danced around on his shoulders, poking him in his ears and blowing kisses at me. I really needed to go and sleep this off. Then I could start working out what on earth a Draco Wyr was and why the wichtlein thought all this was my fault. I swallowed hard and bit my lip.

Leaving Tom in the courtyard, I walked past Lucy and Anton and into the keep. Not far to go now. My legs were starting to feel like leaden weights as I dragged myself up the stone stairs, keeping my eyes fixed on the ground lest any other unexpected visions decided to crop up and surprise me. I was fairly certain that a few of the old portraits on the walls were making faces at me, but I refused to look at them directly just in case. I finally reached the dorm room and was about to turn the doorknob when I heard a voice behind me.

"In the doghouse, Miss Mackenzie?"

I supposed it really had been too much to hope that I'd manage to completely avoid Corrigan. "Whatever do you mean, my lord?" I asked, turning but keeping my eyes downcast. Let him think he'd beaten me into meek submission.

"This, if I'm not mistaken, is the girls' dorm. Not the room you share with the wolf."

Oh, yeah. "We're, uh, re-assessing our relationship in light of recent revelations."

He stepped closer. I just hoped that the last remnants of the shifter lotion were going to hold. "I just bet you are," he said smoothly, "especially given that you are clearly only just arriving home. Who was it this time? The human? Or perhaps a new conquest with the mage?"

"I spent all night self-flagellating for my behavior towards you, my lord," I answered sarcastically. Shut up, Mack, just shut up. I raised my eyes to meet his. They were so green, with those little flashes of gold that sparkled. And the way his dark hair hung over his brow in gentle waves - he was actually really very good-looking. I realised that I was still hallucinating all this of course when a little winged baby carrying a golden bow and arrow floated past him.

"That mouth of yours does get you into a lot of trouble, doesn't it?" He looked at my face for what seemed like a very long time. "Just because I'm leaving, doesn't mean that I won't forget that you need to be punished for your infantile behavior."

"Infantile? Why you fu..," Shut UP, Mackenzie, whispered the voice. "Yes, my lord," I finished.

Deep amusement sparked in his eyes. Bastard. He was clearly enjoying himself. "I thought you should know," his deep voice drawled, "that I was impressed with the wolf's fighting skills last night. And yours. You might consider joining the ranks of the Brethren.

Assuming that you can learn some manners, of course."

In your dreams, catboy. "How thoughtful of your lordship to think of us. You would do better to engage your attentions elsewhere however, I fear."

"Indeed," he said. He moved even closer to me until the distance between us was bare inches. It was a definite struggle not to step back. "Well, till next time then, kitten. Perhaps then your hair will be back to its normal colour. I am a fan of Celtic red hair."

I tried not to tense too obviously in annoyance, inclining my head just in time to see a spotted snake with an apple in its mouth slither past me into the dorm. How strange. "My lord." I made my escape and shut the dorm room door firmly behind me. He was leaving and that was all that mattered. The rest of the Brethren at least didn't seem so circumspect in their attentions.

I looked at my bed and almost ran to it, sinking down into the mattress and stretching out my toes to curl off the end. Sleep.

Chapter Fifteen

When I woke up, the dorm room was dark. I was aware of the sounds of others sleeping around me and hoped that I'd only lost a day. I had a lot to do. Swinging my legs over the side of the bed, I glanced at the green glow of the clock on my bedside table. It flashed 3.20am. At least that meant that I'd have some peace as everyone else would be in the land of nod. I was still wearing my clothes from the day before so I lifted up my t-shirt and gingerly prodded my side. It was sore and tender but nothing more. Even better. Pushing myself until I passed out had not been my smartest move ever – at least the green gloop from Julia had put the kibosh on that happening again. And with Lord Shifty himself gone from the keep, I'd have more freedom to arrange my thoughts and continue my investigations properly. The other Brethren members didn't seem capable of jumping without his say so, meaning that it would be a lot easier for me to stay out of the way of those remaining.

I pulled out the shifter lotion from the drawer in the table and padded into the bathroom. I undressed and surveyed the damage. I was covered in scratches and bruises, a mesh of different rainbow colours from angry purple to fading yellow. Lovely. I'd have killed for a long soak in the tub but was mindful of Julia's warning about bathing. Sniffing my skin experimentally, I wrinkled my nose. I was normally a bit of a stickler for good personal hygiene and the stale smell wafting off me was not pleasant. There was nothing I could do about it, however. If the remaining Brethren stayed away from me because of my unwashed reek then it was probably all for the better. I gently rubbed the lotion all over, taking care to cover every inch of my skin. I'd been lucky with it so far, but didn't want to leave any part of me uncovered. Even with Corrigan gone, there was still a danger that the remaining Brethren would work out what I was, and the longer they stayed, the more real that danger became. I could leave nothing to chance.

With that done, I pulled on a clean pair of black leggings and a snug dark button up shirt. I turned up the sleeves and ran a brush through my hair before tying it back into a high ponytail. It was still strange to see myself in the mirror without my usual shiny red. At least I could let the dye grow out quickly now that the truth about that part of me was out. I tried not to think about Corrigan's comment that he wanted to see my natural colour.

I cleaned up after myself then tiptoed out of the dorm. I had several avenues to cover. I now knew who had killed John, but didn't know who or what Iabartu actually was. And then there was the wichtlein's assertion that it had been my fault, along with the Draco Wyr details, and a few loose ends such as the black cloth I'd found next to the clearing and the mystery of the electric screwdriver. I also had no idea what had happened over the last twelve hours I'd been asleep for, although there wasn't much I could do about that until the rest of the keep awoke.

I weighed up my options and decided that I could worry about motives later – Iabartu and her whereabouts had to take priority. With that resolve, I headed for the library and the communal computer. It was high time I saw what the Othernet could offer.

The silence that hung around the keep was a pleasant welcome after the incessant buzz that the Brethren's presence had caused over the last few days. I made a quick detour for the kitchen to make myself some strong coffee and then let myself into the library and stood for a quiet moment, inhaling the musty scent of the books that surrounded the walls. It was possible that I could try researching the old fashioned way, using the library's offerings to find any mentions of Iabartu in the books, but I was pretty sure that the Othernet would allow me to do the same but more quickly.

Moving over to the computer, I turned it on and waited for it to boot up. The Othernet was an electronic gateway to the Otherworld. The human internet was great, but the Othernet was our very own specialised version and covered discussions, forums and websites on every conceivable magical aspect of the world that was kept hidden from most people. When the computer was ready, I clicked onto the search engine and typed in Iabartu. Instantly, several answers appeared.

I clicked on the first one and started reading. It turned out that the bitch was one of seven daughters of Anu, a Messopotanian sky god, and his human consort. I frowned. There was that number again – seven. Not only that but a half breed goddess would be difficult to beat. It did explain the floating above the dunes part, however. If Anu was her father, then she'd possess the ability to control the air currents and appear as if she was flying – or hovering. According to the Othernet page, she lived in an Otherworld realm and didn't bother herself with our earthly plane. Well that information was certainly out of date. I opened up several other sites but couldn't find any details on how to defeat her or disable her. No matter. I'd work it out.

I had still had over an hour until dawn and the keep began to stir awake, so it was time to start on the Draco Wyr. I was nervous about what I might find with this one. I didn't want any confirmation that it had anything to do with me, that my own human blunderings had caused them to take their revenge and kill John in return.

Heart in my mouth, I typed in the words and hit return. Images of different coloured dragons appeared at the top of the page. They were definitely larger than your average wyvern. The first website returned was a gossip column, which I ignored, but the second one was from Otherpedia. That would do it. I opened it up and read.

Draco Wyr were intelligent members of the dragon family. They possessed the ability to shift into human form and were known to regularly visit the human demesnes. They were reported to be an average size of eleven feet tall, with impenetrable scales covering their dragon form. The Draco Wyr also had some magical abilities, mainly from the power inherent in their blood. Legend states that anyone who drinks the blood of a

Draco Wyr will be able to converse with animals and gain the strength of twenty men. Most scholars believe that this is an over-exaggeration, however, as there is little evidence to support such a theory. What is known is that the blood of a Draco Wyr contained enough magical properties to be used as both a deadly poison and a cure-all medicine for a range of ailments. There have been no eye-witness sightings since 1666 and the Great Fire of London, which is believed was caused when two Draco Wyr lost their tempers and attacked each other near the site of Pudding Lane.

I looked back at the artists' renderings. The pictures indicated old-fashioned full-on fairy tale dragons, complete with red scales, pointy tales and sharp, gleaming teeth. They also all appeared to be about the size of a two storey house. Nope, I'd definitely never come across one of them before. So what on earth had the wichtlein meant when he'd said that the Draco Wyr had been involved in John's death but that it was my fault? I didn't feel that I was any closer to finding out anything of any real significance. And it had been three hundred and fifty years since anyone had even seen one anyway. Despite what Alex had said, Craw must have been lying. But then there was also John's computer password to consider – that had been the Basque word for dragon. Was that a coincidence? And how about the fact that John had hidden the increased Otherworld activity from the rest of the pack? And, in particular, me?

I leaned back in the chair and pondered my next move. With my research on the dragons creating more problems and questions than answers, I had to focus my efforts on finding Iabartu. It would be good to know what the Brethren and the rest of the pack had achieved the day before. Maybe Alex had uncovered some evidence of her trail. If not, then my best move would be to do something to draw her out into the open where I could attack her. I had no idea yet what that might be.

Figuring that Betsy would be a good person to deliver all the gossip on what had transpired over the last day while I'd been sleeping, I headed back to the dorm room to see if she was awake yet. I was just about to push open the door to go inside when Anton came out, clutching something white and scrunched up in his hands. What the hell?

I growled at him and his eyes snapped up from what he was holding.

"Human," he hissed.

I answered in like. "Prick." I looked at down at his hands but he stuffed them behind his back. "Sneaking around in the girls' room now, are you? What have you stolen? Let me guess, someone's dirty underwear so you can sniff at it at your leisure."

Instead of the usual smart reply I was expecting, Anton actually blushed. Okay, now I had to know what it was he'd taken. I reached behind him, but he sidestepped and snarled.

"Stay away from me."

Not a chance buster. I eyeballed him with my best steely gaze. "Then give me what you've got there and I'll leave you alone."

His body tensed and I could see dark spots appearing under the skin on his face. His were was trying to get out. I narrowed my eyes further. Something was definitely up.

"C'mon, Anton," I coaxed, trying to reach behind him again.

He backed away against the door frame. "Fuck off."

I rocked back slightly before feinting left and whirling round behind him, pulling the piece of material away from him. It ripped as I yanked it out of his hands. I looked down and saw my bloodied t-shirt from the day before which I'd left stuffed in the dorm's laundry basket. Now I was seriously freaked out.

"You're stealing my clothes? With my blood on them?" Was he going to take the t-shirt to the Brethren to prove to them that I wasn't human? The hackles on my back rose and I felt hot inside. I'd known he hated me but I hadn't thought that he'd really put the whole pack in jeopardy just for a little revenge.

Tufts of dark hair began to spring out on his cheekbones. "Keep it. I don't need it," he bit off and pushed past me down the corridor. Fear and fury rose inside me and I was about to go after him with a vengeance when a door on the floor above slammed shut and I heard a couple of Brethren talking loudly as they came out. Resignedly, I watched him disappear round the corner. This was definitely not good. I considered telling Julia what he'd done. That felt a bit like running off to the teacher but he must have worked out some way of getting round the geas to tell the Brethren who I was - and that put everyone at risk. He was getting far too dangerous for his own good. I looked down at the t-shirt. I was going to have to dispose of it before I did anything else. It hadn't occurred to me that leaving it in the dorm was a bad idea but clearly I was going to have to be a lot more careful from now on.

I went straight into the bathroom and found some bleach in a little cabinet. I poured it liberally over the shirt and stuck it into sink, watching the brown red colour slowly disappear. Betsy wandered in, wearing pink frilly pyjamas and yawning loudly.

"Now you're cleaning, Mack?"

I told her what Anton had done and she looked alarmed. "I know he doesn't like you, babe, but I don't think he'd tell them you're human. Besides anything, the geas would stop him. And with Julia confirmed as alpha, she can stop him from doing anything at all."

I stared down at the sink. "Please don't call me babe, Bets."

She rolled her eyes. "I mean it, *Mack*. We still don't know enough about how the Brethren would act if they worked out what you were. Anton might be a wanker but he's loyal to the pack."

"Then why was he taking my clothes, Betsy?"

"I don't know," she answered softly. "But Lynda likes him and I think he likes her. I'll get her to hang on his coat-tails for the next few days and make sure he doesn't do anything. Maybe he'll confide in her."

My fists clenched. "I do not need him screwing things up at the moment. There's enough to do and enough to worry about as it is."

"Yeah, especially with that spooky portal that the mage uncovered."

I looked at her. "Portal?"

"Oh, yeah, you were asleep all day. He did some kind of uncloaking spell. It turns out that there's a portal on the beach, not far from where John died."

"A portal? As well as the seven stones? And you're only telling me about this now?" My voice was rising to a screech.

"Jesus, Mack, give me a chance. No-one's gone into it because we don't know where it leads to. Even the mage can't work out where it goes. The Brethren are staking it out in case anything else comes out. They reckon that's where both the terrametus and the woman came from."

"Iabartu."

"Huh?"

"The woman is called Iabartu. She's some kind of demi-god."

"How did you....?" She shook her head, "Never mind. Most of what you do is a mystery to me, Mack."

I ran water into the sink to rinse off the bleach. "Does Julia have a plan?"

"I think she's letting the Brethren make the decisions for now."

Fuck that for a game of soldiers. This portal was clearly where the action was going to be. I wrung out the t-shirt and dumped it in the bin. At least now I knew where to go next.

"You've got a scary look on your face, Mack."

"Get Lynda to stick with Anton, as you said. I'm heading to the beach."

I started to walk out of the bathroom when Betsy called after me. "Are you sure that's a good idea? By all accounts you were half dead yesterday. The Brethren have got things under control."

"I feel fine. And I know things they don't. If you see Julia, tell her about Anton and where I've gone," I flung back, then picked up my backpack and made sure I had everything I might need. Time to rock and roll.

Chapter Sixteen

By the time I reached the beach, the sun was high in the sky and glinting off the glittering sea. There were some human shaped figures at the far end, closer to Trevathorn. I figured that Alex would have already set up some kind of warding spell to stop any innocent person on a morning stroll from haphazardly stepping through the portal into another dimension.

There were also a couple of Brethren shifters a few hundred metres away. I briefly debated whether or not to stay hidden but reckoned I wouldn't really manage it for long. Julia's lotion might mask my human stink but it didn't mean that I was scentless, and the eddies of wind swirling around the beach would advertise my presence before long.

As I got closer, I recognised the shifter I'd taken for a werefox on the first day and another Brethren male. They were both standing on the sand, their backs to me. Ahead of them I could just make out the portal. It shimmered with light purple waves. Few pack members had ever stepped into one of the gateways to other planes. Shifters didn't possess the ability to conjure portals, and, unless you were very sure that you knew where one was leading, it was pretty much advisable to leave it well alone. There wasn't a Way Directive about them but there probably should be. There were plenty of nasties that wouldn't take too kindly at all to a stranger, even a shifter stranger, stepping into their living room. By the time you'd worked out where you were and what was going on, you could easily find yourself lying in a puddle of your own entrails. It had happened before.

I had seen a few portals before – not usually out in the open like this – and they were virtually the only way that Otherworld creatures could travel from one demesnes to another. The friendly ones would usually give us warning that they were coming, and would establish their gateways out of the way. The unfriendly ones would materialise anywhere and start attacking anything that came near. There had even been one in Julia's herb garden once when a particularly ugly gnome had decided that it would be far easier to nab some of her plants, than take the time to grow them himself. She had not been impressed and had dispatched him to the underworld before he could pick even one delicate primrose.

Mackenzie? How's the pain?

I started and almost tripped over my own feet. It was Julia, at least, not Corrigan. His Voice wouldn't work from great distances; no-one's did. I relaxed minutely. *It's fine,* I sent back silently. *The green stuff worked a treat and I enjoyed seeing pixies and flying babies. Did Betsy tell you about Anton?*

She did. He is on his way to talk to me.

I didn't fancy being in Anton's shoes right about now. Served him right. *I'm almost at the portal,* I thought at her. *I'm going to stay here and see what happens.*

Be careful dear. Mr Floride updated me with what you had found out. There may be more to all this than meets the eye.

There is. I flashed up an image for her of what I'd uncovered on the Othernet.

She was silent for a second, then spoke in my mind again. *A demi-god will not be easy to defeat. I should inform the Brethren.*

It won't make any difference, I urged. *If nothing happens for a day or two then maybe they'll leave. You know that I'm strong. I can deal with her myself.*

I don't like this. I had a sudden vision of Julia pacing around the office.

Julia, trust me. I wasn't trying to inflate my own skills. I had as much physical power as any of the pack shifters, and I had no doubt that I could match most of the Brethren too. If all this did have something to do with me – if it was my fault that John had died – then it was probably related somehow to my humanity. And that meant that the less the Brethren knew, the better.

She sighed mentally, then agreed. *Fine. But be careful. Remember that we need you, Mackenzie. I don't have any more trieswater to bring you back from the brink again.*

I will.

I sensed her pulling back and moving away. I walked up behind the two Brethren.

"Hi!" I said with forced cheeriness.

Neither one turned. Corrigan had them well trained. I moved round so I could see their faces although they kept their stony eyes trained on the portal. At least they took their sentinel posts seriously. There was one time that Tom had been sent out to guard a newly opened portal that opened up near Penzance. He'd fallen asleep and missed several faeries emerging. They'd caused particular havoc that night, and the local police were kept extraordinarily busy stepping in between several faerie induced street brawls. Nick had even been called in from the sticks to provide support. He'd later told me that he'd never seen anything like it before and that the superintendent suspected that some city based drug dealers had infiltrated the town and spiked drinks in pubs and clubs from one end of Penzance to the other. John had put Tom on kitchen duty for a month as punishment, which ended up being punishment for everyone. The food had tasted even worse than it usually did and we were all glad when his penance was up.

"I thought I'd keep you company out here," I said, again with the cheeriness in my voice.

One of them flicked their eyes at me for just a second then focused back on the purple portal. "Whatever."

Friendly talkative pair. Deciding that there was no point trying to engage them further, and as they obviously weren't going to make me leave, I moved a few feet away from them and sat cross-legged on the sand. I stared at the gateway. If I strained my ears, I could just make out a low humming sound emanating from it, like the buzz of electricity. That probably meant that it was still very active. Good. Hopefully I wouldn't have to wait too long until Iabartu or more of her minions decided to appear again. I planned out defensive and attacking strategies in my mind. I had my throwing daggers attached to my arms, as always, and my curved knife in my backpack. It was a shame that again I'd been forced to leave the silver back at the keep, but wielding it would raise far too many awkward questions. It was still annoying though.

With no information from the Othernet to go on as to how I could kill Iabartu, I'd just have to settle for good old-fashioned brute strength. The 'daughter of a sky god' part might prove tricky, given that if she could fly it would be difficult to catch her. The only way would be to catch her unaware when she stepped through the portal.

I looked around. The Brethren guards were in a good position to see the portal opening but it did mean that she herself would be able to see them as soon as she materialized as well. It would make more sense to cut around so I could flank her. When her attention was taken by the Brethren, I'd be able to sneak up behind and slit her throat. And that would mean that I would get my revenge personally. Sweet.

Standing back up, I started to move for the rear of the portal. Although it was transparent from the front, despite the purple shimmers, it was obvious which was front and which was back, because from the rear there was nothing to be seen at all. In fact it was as if there was nothing there at all. Before I'd taken more than three steps, however, I heard voices coming from the direction of the trees, the words becoming more distinct as they drew closer.

"What you have to understand, Lucy, is that humans don't think like us or act like us. Effectively they're cattle who get in the way and mess things up."

I immediately stiffened.

"Yeah but the mage is human, isn't he? And we're half human."

"The mage has skills. He's part of the Otherworld. And we might have a human side but we'll never be that stupid or that vulnerable. You know that joke, right? What do you call a human with a half brain?"

"Errr…"

"Gifted." The Brethren arsehole began to snort with laughter.

Heat swirled around me. I turned in their direction and assessed them carefully. Lucy's petite frame was dwarfed by the fuckwit who'd decided that he was superior to the whole of humanity. He looked strong, with ripped biceps and a chunky neck - no doubt I'd discover it was red if I had the wherewithal to check under his collar. I could take him easily. I took a step towards him and dug my fingernails into my palms.

Lucy shouted down to the two stoic sentinels who hadn't budged a millimeter. "Hey guys, we're here to relieve you of your duties. Any activity yet?"

I took another step.

One of the waiting guards said something back to her, but I didn't hear what his actual words were. I could already visualise myself breaking the idiot's nose with a satisfying crunch. I didn't even care that he'd shift and immediately regenerate. It would still be worth it.

At that moment, Alex stepped onto the beach from the trees. He took one look at me and his eyes widened, although I barely registered the movement; I was already shifting into an attack stance. I was vaguely aware that he had quickened his step but my focus was on the Brethren shifter. Then he stepped into my direct line of sight, blocking my attack route.

"Hey Mack Attack!" he called over, with emphasis on the Attack part of my latest irritating nickname.

Lucy craned her neck to peer round his body. "Mackenzie! I didn't see you there. Are you joining us for the stake-out?"

"This'll be good," said the arsehole, stepping out from behind Alex's protective shield. "This girl is what I meant. Smart, strong and a million times more useful than a human."

Hah! The irony of his statement wasn't lost on me. I forced myself to breathe and tried to calm my boiling blood. Alex came closer and wrapped his arms around me.

"What the feck are you doing, dude?" he whispered in my ear.

"You heard what he said," I growled.

"I'm starting to see why the wolf calls you Red. That temper of yours is seriously scary. If you attack him because he's an ignorant idiot, all that will happen is the other Brethren will be forced to take his side. Which will make you mincemeat. Now, given all the trouble I went to save your sorry hide last night, I will be very pissed off if that happens."

I pulled free and looked away. "Fine," I muttered.

The arsehole came up and stuck out his hand. "Pleasure to finally make your acquaintance. There's been a lot of discussion about you since we arrived. I do hope that you decide to leave this rural hell-hole when all this is done and come with us to London."

I reluctantly took his greasy palm, and shook it. I will admit that I tried to crush the bones in his fingers at the same time. He pulled his hand away and shook it in mock, or (as I hoped) real, pain.

"Wow, that's a strong grip you've got there, tiger." What was with all of the cat nicknames I seemed to be garnering recently? My lips tightened and he eyed me curiously. "What's your were, anyway? You smell kind of funny."

"Hamster." It took some force of will to get the word out.

He looked surprised. "Uh, really?"

I shrugged, not trusting myself to say anything else, and walked back to the other side of the portal. He remained there for a second or two, still looking puzzled, until the other two Brethren moved impatiently, and he shook himself, and turned round to switch places with them. Lucy did the same. As the first two guards walked towards the trees and back to the keep, he continued to stare at me through the portal. I felt my ire rising again, but Alex put a hand on my arm and made a face. I rolled my eyes at him. Whatever. I sat back down on the sand and started to wait.

Chapter Seventeen

Lucy and the human hater took up the same positions as the previous two Brethren had, and maintained the same stoicism. I was faintly surprised that Lucy was as strict about her vigil as the others had been but guessed that Corrigan's stranglehold on the Brethren was viciously strong. I, meanwhile, was going to preserve my strength and energy for when something – hopefully Iabartu – finally appeared. I was confident that I'd hear the change in tone as the portal prepared to eject someone long before they actually arrived. Keeping an upright, straight backed, military style stance was a waste of time.

I pulled out a couple of cans of Coke from my backpack and offered one to Alex. He sat down beside me and we pulled the ringtops. I hoped that the Brethren idiot on the other side could hear the satisfying hiss as the carbon dioxide was released although I did feel slightly guilty about Lucy. Then again, given what I'd already discovered about her tastebuds, she probably wasn't too bothered. Alex sat down next to me and stretched his legs out in front of him.

"What gives, Alex? I thought you weren't the fighting type?" I asked him, archly.

He took a swig of Coke and regarded me seriously. "Oddly I find myself suddenly invested in what happens in this quiet little corner of England.

Not that I'll be squaring up to any heebie jeebies any time soon, you understand," he added hastily, "just that I find myself wanting to stick around. You never know when there might be a damsel in distress who needs me to run away in the opposite direction for her."

I laughed and clinked my Coke can against his then became serious. "What Craw said – about it being my fault that John died. You really think that was true?"

He sighed heavily. "All I know is that the wichtlein definitely thought it was true. And, no, before you ask, I don't know anything about what a Draco Wyr is, other than it must be some kind of dragon."

"So where do we go from here?"

"We do what we're doing right now and wait to see what comes out that." He nodded towards the portal and I was rather taken aback at the confidence in his voice. For someone who was a self-professed non-combatant, he actually displayed a lot of guts.

We sat in companionable silence for a few moments before it occurred to me that I really didn't know very much about him at all. I could do small talk – at least it might make the time pass by a bit faster. I cast a look over at him. "So what would you be doing if you weren't here?"

"Nothing much of anything. I spend a vast amount of time in London tracking down lost objects and trailing unfaithful spouses. You'd be surprised at what a fickle bunch the Otherworld pop can be."

"I don't doubt it," I said drily. "But you don't always work for shifters?"

"God, no!" he said. "My services are for hire to the highest bidder. I have to work within the dictates of the Ministry but for the most part I can be employed by virtually anyone. Fae, vamps, trolls, even a unicorn once. I've worked for them all."

"Have you ever worked for a human?" I asked softly. "I mean, an out and out human who's not a mage or a wicca or anything?"

Alex was silent for a second. "No," he answered heavily. "I'm afraid I've not."

So there was no-one like me then. I changed the subject. "You look rather, um, young to be doing all this."

"I might make the same comment about you, dude."

I acknowledged his point. A plane rumbled softly overhead and we both leaned back and tracked its jetstream through the sky.

"It really is very lovely here," he commented after it was long gone. "I can see why you are so keen to stay."

"Yeah," I sighed. "It is lovely. But that's not why I stay. These guys are my family. Since my mum split, I've never had anyone else I could depend upon. But the pack, they're always there for me. Even though..." my voice trailed off and I looked at the Brethren.

"You don't get bored?" he asked, changing the subject.

"Of beautiful weather, pristine beaches, lots of friends? Yeah, I get bored. But no-one's life is ever perfect, Alex. And these last few days have reminded me that living in interesting times isn't always what it's cracked up to be. I'd give anything to be bored right now, instead of trying to hunt down the vicious murderer who killed my alpha."

"You think of him – John – like that? As your alpha?"

"Yeah, I do." I finished off the Coke and scrunched up the can in one hand. "I might not be able to shift, but I feel like a shifter."

He nodded with a serious expression on his face and lay back in the sand. I traced little figure of eights in the sand and watched the portal with half an eye. The sun was getting hot, but at least there was a cool breeze wafting in from the sea.

Mackenzie? Are you still at the beach?

I sat up a bit straighter. *What's up, Julia? Did you talk to Anton?*

Yes. He's not trying to expose you, dear.

What? I got up to my feet, drawing the Brethren's attention. I ignored them completely and started pacing. *Julia, he had my t-shirt. With my blood.*

Hmmm, yes. Well that's rather interesting, dear.

I scoffed aloud.

It appears that since your fight, Anton now has developed something of a …taste for your blood.

Say what?

Julia continued. *He's convinced that it's good for him. And it seems that he will go to lengths to get more of it.*

I was absolutely stupefied. *Is that normal? He is turning into some kind of shifter vamp?*

That's not physically possible, dear. I don't know why he's decided that you're suddenly so tasty but he's certainly still being kept to the geas.

I didn't know what to say. Could this be some kind of weird ruse that he'd cooked up? *Jules, are you sure he's not lying?*

I compelled him. Even though he wishes you were gone from the pack, he was telling the truth.

He's not sworn to you yet, none of the shifters are. Technically, they all still had the change of alpha get out clause to use as an escape if they wanted to leave.

Actually, he is. He swore on the Way while you were out for the count yesterday. Almost everyone did.

Oh. I was surprised. I'd been sure that he'd want to hold out and see if he could get a place with the Brethren. Then I realised what Julia had said. Hold on, 'almost' everyone?

Julia, who didn't swear?

Tom and Betsy.

"FUCK!"

Everyone on the beach was looking at me now. I knew in my heart of hearts that neither of them would ever betray me, geas or no geas, unless compelled to by whoever their new alpha became. But I had a pretty good idea about who they wanted that new alpha to be. Tom had made no secret that he had the burning desire to join the Brethren's ranks. And with Betsy apparently besotted by him, she'd probably follow him wherever he wanted to go.

How could they be so naïve?

Mackenzie, dear, they have to make their own choices.

Well, what if Corrigan compels them to talk about me?

207

Unless he specifically asks if you're human or not, or to tell him every single detail they've ever known about you, which I imagine would take several days of telling, then they won't have to reveal anything they know. And Corrigan has no reason to suspect that you're human. Are you sure that your anger is less to do with your worry about what they might say and more to do with your friends leaving you?

No. I paused. Sodding know-it-all. *Okay, maybe.*

They will always be your friends, no matter what they do or where they go. And the Brethren might not want them. I don't think either of them has made their intentions known yet.

But Corrigan had already told me that he did want Tom. And Betsy had acquitted herself well in her evaluation so I couldn't see why they'd turn her down either. I sat back down on the sand.

I have to go, projected Julia. *Anton seems to be getting rather worked up because Lynda won't leave him alone. Stay safe, Mackenzie.*

Yeah, I sent back, and Julia severed the link.

Alex was sitting up and looking at me rather alarmed. "What the hell is going on with you?"

"That was Julia. It's just…it's nothing." I didn't want to get into it. Tom and Betsy's potential defection was simply too complicated to explain and I wasn't sure that Alex would understand my feelings about it. And the information about Anton was just too disturbing.

"Mack? What do you mean, that was Julia?"

"Huh? Oh, she can project to me the way that she can to the rest of the pack." I said absently, my mind on other things.

"And could John do this too?"

I didn't answer.

"Mackenzie, this is important. Could you hear John's Voice too?"

"Sure. And Corrigan's as well."

"That doesn't make sense, Mackenzie." He pulled me by the shoulders and looked into my eyes. "Only alphas can use the Voice and only then with their own shifters. Corrigan of course can use it with everyone, but then he's mega powerful. But even he wouldn't be able to use it on a human."

I looked at him stupidly. "Alex, he can because I'm human and I can hear him. No alpha has ever had cause to use the Voice on a human so they'd never know if it works or not. And besides, John always said I could hear him because I spent so much of my formative years with the pack. It's not a big deal."

"Dude, it is so a big deal. Do you really think that alphas haven't tried to compel humans before now? They've spent centuries trying to do that. Imagine the power they'd have if they could. They can't, believe me."

I became aware that my mouth was gaping open at him. I snapped it shut. "He can't compel me though. And even you knew I was human straight away, Alex. "

"Well, yeah, and you still seem human. But you can't be. Even without the compulsion side of things, there is no alpha, no matter how strong, who could use the Voice on an out and out human."

I wasn't quite sure how to handle this new piece of information on top of everything else. I'd spent so long wishing desperately that I wasn't human, and I'd come to accept that I couldn't change who I was no matter how much I wanted to. And now that I was resigned to being human, I wasn't sure I wanted to be anything else. I'd heard John's Voice for so long that I hadn't ever thought to really question why I could. I struggled to find a reason why. "Can you hear an alpha's Voice?"

"No, only shifters can, I told you." Alex's voice was emphatic.

I felt more doubt creeping in. "And I'm definitely not a shifter."

He sank back down. "No, you're not. There's nothing shifter-like about you. But I'm still telling you that it doesn't make sense that you're human either."

Great. I was just a freak. Now I wasn't a shifter or a human. Could my week possibly get any worse?

I noticed that Lucy was looking concerned but trying very hard to keep her gaze focused on the portal. At least the distance between us and the hum of the gate, meant that she wouldn't have heard any of my conversation with Alex. I tried to look nonchalant and unconcerned by crossing my legs and leaning back. Unfortunately I was feeling anything but that. Alex stood up and walked towards the water's edge. I had to admit that part of me wondered if he was trying to stay away from me now that I was clearly something very strange indeed. Perhaps I was contagious. The pit of my stomach felt warm with hurt and confusion. And then I wondered if the fire I felt in my blood when I got worked up, wasn't just a side-effect of a red-head's fiery temper. Maybe it was something else. Maybe I was a monster. Maybe that's why it was my fault that John was dead.

I lost myself in my thoughts. At some point Alex came and sat back down next to me but I barely registered him. At least he left me in peace to sort through what I was thinking. After a while I roused myself slightly and looked at him. I thought I'd ask him what he thought about my bloodfire, and whether it might be connected somehow to everything else. In fact, I'd even drawn a breath to speak when, all of a sudden, the ripples in the portal began to fluctuate wildly and the humming increased dramatically in volume. Something was coming through.

I immediately leapt to my feet and pulled out my left dagger, poised for action. Across the sand, I could see both Lucy and the racist prick tensing. Being shifters, they didn't particularly need to carry weapons – their shift did more damage more quickly than virtually anything else even remotely legal would. Alex was backing away slowly from the portal itself. I gripped the dagger's hilt tightly.

"Come on Iabartu, you bitch," I whispered. "Let's finish this."

There was a terrible rumbling and a figure started to emerge slowly. Initially it was difficult to make out what it was. Unfortunately, however, it was also immediately very clear that whatever it was, it wasn't Iabartu. She'd been about five feet tall in Alex's scrying and this figure looked to be about twice that. It was definitely humanoid, however. I squinted, trying to make it out. One muscled leg that looked the size of a tree trunk came into sharp focus. Its foot was bare but very hairy with long sharp looking toenails. Ick. I shifted my stance deciding to aim for its Achilles' heel.

Helen Harper

I wasn't sure exactly what would happen if I attacked it in mid transport - it would usually be considered extraordinarily rude to do so – but circumstances dictated that this was not someone here to pay a friendly visit. I could end this in a second if I managed to hit the right spot though.

I snapped back my wrist and let the dagger fly, when, at the same moment, a furry shape barreled into the thing's knee, knocking the entire vulnerable spot that I'd been aiming for out of the dagger's trajectory. My weapon thudded uselessly into the sand. Fucking idiot shifter. Who had half a brain now? Before I could react further, the rest of the creature materialized completely, reaching down with one fell swoop and picking the offending were-cougar up, before shaking it violently and flinging its body away. The human hater's were shape lay broken and still.

Lucy had shifted as well, into her sleek honey badger. She at least had more sense than her buddy, however, and held back, eyes watchful and assessing. I called on my fire and let it seep throughout my veins from my heart to the tips of my fingers. It thudded and flickered in intensity. Bring it on. The thing was completely focused on Lucy and roared at her so loudly that I felt the vibrations through the sand under my feet. It remained stupidly unaware of me at its back, however. She bared her sharp teeth and prepared to attack, giving me a chance to perfect my aim, hopefully without any interruptions this time.

I threw, and knew straight away that I was close to the mark. My shot wasn't quite swift and true enough however. The dagger embedded itself in the beast's ankle, just missing the vital Achilles' heel. Shit. It shuddered in pain though, head whipping around. Involuntarily I took a step back. It only had one huge eye, smack bang in the middle of its face. Christ, a Cyclops. I took in its long dark hair, tied back with a piece of rope and its skin that was swarthy and weathered. A loincloth covered its genitals but other than it was completely naked. I supposed I should be thankful for small mercies. A naked ten foot tall one eyed beast was not at the top of my 'Otherworld neighbours I'd like to meet' list. Something dangled off the string at its waist but, at this distance, I couldn't quite make out what it was. It didn't look large enough to be a scary weapon at least. The Cyclops roared at me and, even from metres away, I felt globules of warm spit on my face combined with the hot rank air of its breath. No, I was not a fan.

It turned back to the front, seemingly dismissing me as unthreatening, so all I was presented with was its lean back. I prepared to attack again while Lucy made her own move, rushing the Cyclops, and snapping and biting at the same ankle I'd already injured, but it dodged her teeth and ran past her. And towards Trevathorn.

Chapter Eighteen

I stood for one brief moment, then reacted and took off after it. Lucy joined me, scampering along the beach and yet easily keeping up. I pelted down the shore, feet scuffing the sand as I sprinted in hot pursuit. Alex yelled something behind me but it was indistinct and his words were whipped away in the sea wind.

It was imperative that we stopped it before it reached the village. I dreaded to think what damage it might incur if it got there. Imagining busloads of eager tourists being swept aside by the Cyclops' long arms, I ran even faster. This was probably not going to turn out well if I didn't stop its parade fucking fast. Way Directive Twenty-two: Wherever possible, the human world must be shielded from the Otherworld.

The Cyclops was an ungainly, clumsy thing, but its long legs enabled it to keep just ahead of the pair of us. It gouged out huge prints in the soft sand as it skewed its way along the edge of the dunes. At one point it leapt over a salt crusted log, stumbling ever so slightly as it landed on the other side. This was our chance. I jumped at it, feet first, and struck it in the back before I fell back onto the sand. It collapsed onto its knees and roared again, and Lucy sprang onto its back and held on with her sharp teeth, ripping into its flesh.

I jumped back up and pulled out my knife, taking advantage of its position to move in front of it and block its path to Trevathorn. I swiped at it a few times but couldn't quite connect, so I lifted a booted heel and kicked its lowered face with every ounce of power and strength that I had. It groaned and pulled itself up, scrabbling at Lucy on its back, connecting with her body and throwing her off before taking off in the direction that it had just come from. I ran after it again, starting to pant with the exertion.

Other shifters were starting to run onto the beach from the forest. I noted a bear – great, Anton again – a grey haired tiger which I took to be Staines, and a couple of wolves. The Cyclops spooked and turned again, this time heading right for me. I slashed out with my knife, connecting with its skin and cutting it deeply, and jumped out of the way, landing on my feet, but it only paused momentarily, then headed back in the direction of the village. Goddamn Brethren. I'd have finished this thing off well before now if it wasn't for them.

One of the wolves caught up and overtook me. As it passed by Lucy curled up by the water's edge, it leapt at the Cyclops and gained purchase on its arm. The monster tried to shake it off as it loped even closer to the settlement, eventually managing to fling it down onto its back. The wolf rolled back over onto its feet, not seriously harmed, but looking slightly dazed. It shook its fur and ran after the Cyclops again.

This time it was the tiger that launched at it from a few feet away, fanged mouth chopping at the Cyclops' skin. The monster howled and wheeled yet again, running zigzagged back in the direction of the portal. Staines' tiger snapped at its heels. Blood was dripping from it in all directions, spraying onto the surface of the sand. Its great head turned to me, the one great eye blinking. I noted idly that it had impossibly long lashes that any large cosmetics company would be thrilled to use in a campaign. I kicked out at it again, and heard the satisfying crunch of a rib snapping from within its great cage of a torso. It moaned yet again but continued running. I was starting to wonder just how many times I'd have to chase it up and down the beach before this ended.

Anton started lumbering towards it, shiny fur shaking with the exertion. The Cyclops leapfrogged over him, however, and carried on. Its injuries were definitely starting to slow it down considerably however, and I could see I was gaining on it. The shifters behind me were catching up too. I reached a hand out to snag its ankle and bring it down once and for all but hadn't realised how close we were to the portal. Just as my hand started to curve around its leg, it escaped into the purple shimmer and vanished. I was left grasping at air and only barely managed to stop myself from falling headlong into the gateway after it by skidding into the sand and digging in my heels.

Shit.

I took a few steps backwards and watched the portal carefully in case the Cyclops re-emerged. Staines, Anton and the two wolves joined me, and we all stood there, waiting. But there was nothing.

I cursed again and plonked myself down on the sand, thoroughly pissed off now. Alex reappeared from behind a dune.

"Oh my God, dude. Did you see that thing?"

"I could hardly miss it, Alex," I answered, barely disguised irritation evident in my voice.

He put his hands up in the air. "Jeez, way to attack the innocent party. I tried to help but you didn't listen."

I looked up at him and waited for him to elaborate. Staines, beside me, still in tiger form, did the same, feline eyes narrowed.

"I told you. It's an ispolin. A Bulgarian giant."

"It's a fucking Cyclops," I hissed.

"No," he answered patiently. "It's an ispolin."

"Wandering around a beach in Cornwall? Why the hell can't these things stay where they belong? Between earthquake monsters, Basque dragons and one eyed ispo…"

"Ispolin," offered Alex helpfully.

"Whatever."

"What Basque dragons?" It was Anton. He'd shifted back to a human and stood there naked as the day he was born. I looked down. Yeah, still unimpressed. Then I remembered that the Basque dragon part had come from me breaking into John's computer. Oops.

"Uhhh…last week, when you were in Penzance there was one," I lied, badly, and then changed the subject quickly by directing it back to Alex. "Anyway, what do you mean, you tried to help? I didn't hear what you said."

"Blackberry bushes."

"Excuse me?"

"Blackberry bushes," he repeated slowly, as if I was hard of hearing. "Ispolin are terrified of them. They get caught in them, or something, and can't move. I'm a bit hazy on all the details to be honest, dude, but just get some blackberries and you'll have it screaming like a girl for its mummy."

"Wow, that's so helpful, Alex, thanks. This beach is clearly teeming with blackberry bushes all over the place. If only I had thought of attacking it with one."

"Alright, dude, alright, no need to get snarky. Anyway, it's interesting that you mention dragons cos I'm sure that ispolins' nemeses are dragons."

Why did it keep coming back to dragons? "Well, next time then I'll look for a fucking dragon hiding in a fucking blackberry bush."

There was a feline growl next to me and I turned to watch Staines painfully shifting into human form. He clicked his jaws a few times to aid his transformation back into human form before speaking. "This is not helping. We have our people to aid."

I suddenly remembered Lucy and her bird-brained colleague. I turned round and scanned the beach. The guy was still lying crumpled where the Cyclops – sorry, ispolin – had thrown him. I didn't think he'd moved an inch since then, which wasn't a good sign. One of the wolves was now beside him, just sitting there, ears flat. Lucy, meanwhile, was limping up the now semi-destroyed beach, which looked as if someone had dug potholes all around it. At least the tide would take care of that side of things in a few hours' time. Checking that the other wolf, Anton and Staines remained beside the portal, I jogged down to meet her.

She was holding her arm awkwardly and it was clearly broken. A gash on the side of her head trickled blood and she was half bent over, clearly in a lot of pain. When I reached her, she all but collapsed into my arms, deathly pale. My fingers twitched again with heat. How the hell did we let this happen? I tried to push aside thoughts of rage at the monster's very painful destruction and picked her up in a fireman's lift, slinging her over my shoulder. It might not be very dignified, but at that moment it was the best I could offer.

Back at the side of the portal, but far away enough away from it to react should anything else decide to come flying through, I laid her gently down on the sand. Alex came over from the other shifter's body and shook his head at me slightly, then bent to check over Lucy. My body shivered with ire. I might not have liked the were-cougar, I might even have wanted to punch his lights out, but he didn't deserve to die. I turned to look at the portal. Staines, however, reading my thoughts, gave me a warning glance and for now I acquiesced and crouched down to join Alex. Staines pulled out a mobile phone from his pocket and began tapping furiously at the keypad.

"I think she's ruptured her appendix," Alex said, gently poking at her stomach.

She moaned softly, and I winced in phantom pain for her.

"We need to get her back to the keep and call in a proper doctor. Even with her regeneration ability, she needs serious medical attention."

We had Julia, who was good for herbal treatments, and a few other pack members such as Larch who were fairly skilled in first aid and basic medicine, but I doubted that they had enough experience to help her properly. One of the drawbacks of being in a pack where serious injuries were so few and far between.

"There's a guy in Somerset," I said. "We can call their alpha and get him here within a couple of hours."

Staines snapped his phone shut. "There's no need. The Lord Alpha is on his way as we speak, with our doctor in tow. We look after our own."

Despite the seriousness of the situation, I was tempted to stick my tongue out at him. Whoopdedoo. Their own special doctor, because normal pack ones couldn't be trusted, and their stupid lord were coming. We were all saved, after all, I thought sarcastically.

"I'll take her back then," I said instead, reaching over to pick her body back up again. The wolf beside the Brethren corpse had shifted and was already scooping him up for the sad walk back.

"No," ordered Staines. "Anton, take her to the keep. Be very careful with her."

Anton shot me a smug glance that was blocked from Staines' view by Alex. My teeth clenched. "I am perfectly capable of helping carry her."

"But not perfectly capable of shifting to help us even out the fight," bit out Staines. "You take this mourning thing too far. Anton, go now and don't delay."

Anton nodded and took Lucy from the sand, surprisingly gently. He immediately began a brisk walk back, although I could see that he was being careful not to bump or jolt her. Sometimes, when I wasn't involved, he really could be a nice guy.

Alex had tensed beside me, no doubt waiting for the explosion. I couldn't even get angry at this one though. Staines was right. I might have been able to stop the ispolin from hurting the others if I'd been on my own, and I might have been fairly certain that I could have brought it down before its other foot touched the sand if the were-cougar hadn't gotten in my way, but I was also fairly certain that if I could have shifted, even into a sodding werehamster, then I could have done more too. Perhaps enough to stop their friend from dying. I just stared at Staines, mutely.

He turned to Alex. "Can you bind the portal for now so that nothing else gets out?"

I stepped forward to protest. How would we catch Iabartu if the gateway was blocked? However, Staines silenced me with one look. Given their grief and state of mind, now probably wasn't the best time to go around flexing my muscles. If only I could rein in my temper like this all the time then my world would probably be a better place.

Alex nodded solemnly. "It's only a temporary measure though. It won't last for more than twenty-four hours."

"That's fine." Staines looked towards the trees where other shifters, including Tom, were starting to emerge. When they had all appeared, and were quietly assembled in front of us, gazing down with drawn faces at the cougar's body in the wolf's now human arms, Staines spoke again. I had to strain to make out exactly what he was saying, however, because he was so very quiet. "Where were you?"

Someone coughed awkwardly. The remaining Brethren looked guilty.

I was proud of Tom when he chose to speak up. "We were playing football in a field away from the keep. We didn't realise what was going on until Boran," he jerked his head at a large upset looking guy, "finally managed to find us. There are no words to express how we have failed you."

"It's not me you've failed. It's Thomson and Lucy who you've failed," Staines said. It occurred to me that I hadn't even known the werecougar's name until this point. I felt vaguely ashamed of myself.

The shifters' bodies sank even lower.

Julia joined them from behind. Her back, in contrast to the others' however, was straight, and her voice was clear. "And if Lord Corrigan had been here, he could have used his Voice and everyone would have been here in force. But he wasn't. And that's not their fault. It's not yours either, or probably even Corrigan's. But that's the way it is and we can't change it now."

I applauded her silently. Staines looked furious for a moment and then nodded slowly, as if it cost him a great effort. "I need five of you to stay here at the portal. The mage will need time to set up a temporary binding and you still need to guard it just in case it doesn't hold." All the shifters immediately put up their hands and he pointed at five of them in turn. "The rest of you, go back to the keep. We need to prepare the rites in accordance with the Way so we can transport Thomson's body back to London for a decent burial." He looked at me. "You are local. Go to the village and make sure that no damage has been done and no suspicions have been raised."

I raised my eyebrows at Julia, questioning, and she nodded. Fine by me. Hanging around the keep at the moment was going to be about as much fun as sucking on one of the ispolin's yellowing toes would be. I walked off, without rushing. Following a sensible order didn't mean that I needed to look like I was one of Staines' eager soldiers. I heard the others behind me begin to move, but I continued on to Trevathorn without looking back.

Chapter Nineteen

As I walked towards the village, dodging the huge ispolin footprints as I went, I pondered whether Iabartu had deliberately sent both the terrametus and the ispolin through the portal. If that was indeed what had happened, then why hadn't she bothered coming herself? She'd taken the time to come through on her own to deal with John. And, if it was the case that she was responsible for both monsters, then I was still unclear about the reasons why she was hell-bent on causing such havoc.

Obviously, she felt that her business was as yet unfinished. Had John had something that she wanted? Information or maybe some kind of object to do with the Draco Wyr? If so, then he'd died rather than give it up, meaning it must be important. But then perhaps she'd achieved what she'd wanted when she killed him and now had just left the portal hanging open, in that careless and disdainful manner Otherworlders sometimes displayed. I discarded that idea almost as quickly as I'd thought of it, however. I might not know that much about portals, and might never have entered one myself or know the mechanics of how to create one, but I was aware that it took power to maintain one, which is why it was so unusual that the portal on the beach was still there. Even as a so-called demi-god, Iabartu would find it a strain to leave it usable.

There were so many things that just didn't add up. I tried to avoid thinking about Craw's assertion that it was my fault that John had died because it just hurt too much. I was already uncomfortably aware of the sick feeling of guilt in the pit of my stomach that, if I could have shifted, I might have saved Thomson from dying and Lucy from getting hurt. Which led me on, of course, to Alex's revelations. I wasn't a shifter, but was I actually a human at all? It seemed that whichever direction my thoughts took, I was confronted by horrible implications and terrible scenarios.

My eyes stung with the threat of tears and I swallowed hard. If I was going to get to the bottom of all this, then crying like a little girl was not going to help. Being strong and calm would. I rubbed at my eyes with my cuff and squared my shoulders, focusing instead on how to allay any suspicions that might be forming in Trevathorn. An elephant had escaped from the local zoo, perhaps? Except the nearest zoo was about 120 miles away so that was probably rather unrealistic. Ummm…

Why didn't you shift?

Corrigan's growl in my head startled me so much that I almost tripped over the log that caught the ispolin earlier. He couldn't have gotten that close to use his Voice that quickly, surely? Staines had only called him twenty minutes ago. God, just how powerful was he? As well as being stunned into silence by the revelation that his Voice could carry hundreds of miles, I didn't have any answers for him that made sense so I just kept quiet.

Answer me.

I sighed inwardly. Everyone wanted answers and there were just none to be had. Or at least none that could be shared without more violence. Instead of feeling angry, I just felt tired. I should probably think of a way to reply to him before he used compulsion though.

Are you trying to suggest that it was my fault that this happened, my Lord? If I hadn't been there it would have been even worse. It wasn't me who decided that only two guards were going to be a good idea.

Silence. I didn't feel proud of myself for trying to shift the blame onto someone else, but at least I'd managed to deflect him for the time being.

Eventually he answered. *That was a mistake. It won't happen again.* There was unmistakable regret in his Voice that gave me a twinge of guilt.

So I guess none of us are completely infallible then, I sent back quietly.

I don't suppose we are. He sighed mentally. *I'll be at the keep in a few hours, so let me know if you need any help with damage control in the village.*

I wondered just how in the hell I was supposed to manage that when I couldn't contact him by Voice and he wasn't exactly on speed dial. He seemed to realize that, however, and rattled off a phone number that I could call him on. Fine. There was one more thing that I did need to know as well though.

How is Lucy?

Corrigan might not be at the keep yet, but I had no doubt that Staines was keeping him updated. Who else would have told him that I was going to Trevathorn to make sure that everything there was alright?

Not good.

Pain was reflected in his Voice and, for a moment, he seemed more human than shifter. He was silent for a moment longer and then broke off the contact. I kicked the log, hard, and cried out, feeling the sharp pain in my foot briefly overtake me. Then it faded and I was more alone on the beach than I'd ever been before.

*

I eventually entered Trevathorn via a small cobbled side street that led from the beach. There was a small crowd of people standing beside the square at the Hanging Bull. This didn't look good.

I strode up with purpose, figuring that if someone had seen or heard something, they'd be broadcasting it to the entire village. Secrets didn't stay quiet for long in any small village, and Trevathorn was a shining example of how to put a rumour mill to perfect use. In fact, I'd heard the barman in the Bull quip once that if you were caught unaware in the woods and had to answer a call of nature, then everyone would know about it before you barely managed to get home. Even though, as the local 'cult', the pack wasn't exactly a real member of the community, there was still a part of me that appreciated that feeling of living somewhere where the neighbours cared enough to gossip about you. The only thing worse than being talked about was not being talked about.

As I got closer to the clump of humans, I realised that they seemed to have formed some kind of semi-circle around whoever was doing the talking. So perhaps there was just one witness then. That would make any reports of giant one eyed beasts with ugly toenails easier to discount at least. My money was on Mrs Arkbuckle, the local postmistress. If there was a story to be told, then she would be the person most likely to know it. She was the human version of Betsy. I'd heard a scandalous rumour last year that she'd been steaming open any interesting looking envelopes that came her way, in order to know as much as possible about what everyone was doing. I think most people had forgotten that in this day and age of email, most letters were confined to boring and official business matters. Smoke doesn't always equal fire. And that was what I'd have to make sure that everyone thought now.

Unfortunately my heart dropped to the bottom of my stomach when I saw that it wasn't Mrs Arbuckle at all. In the centre of the circle was a cameraman, pointing a black video camera at a trim woman with perfect skin. She was holding a microphone and flashing a curved row of even white teeth. Shit, shit, shit. I stepped closer to hear what she was saying.

"Are we ready?" She tapped her earpiece, and cocked her head quizzically.

The cameraman began counting down from five, pointing at the woman dramatically as he said each number. I briefly considered rushing them both, tackling her like a rugby player, and taking her down before she could say anything to the world at large. I doubted that would help matters, however. Holding my breath, I pushed closer into the watching crowd, earning myself a few scowls in return.

"Good afternoon, Martin." Her voice modulated itself into an almost perfect version of received pronunciation and she gazed into the camera lens with a happy concentration. I figured that the invisible Martin must be the anchor 'back in the studio'. "I am here in Trevathorn in Cornwall, reporting on the recent wave of seismic activity that has sent the local villagers running for cover. There were several small earthquakes here on Tuesday evening, each measuring around 2 on the Richter scale, and large enough to send roof tiles crashing into the quiet cobbled streets and vases tumbling to the floor from the top of mantelpieces."

I immediately relaxed. Oh, the drama of a little quake. It was hardly on a par with the San Andreas fault, but I supposed the tremors caused by the terrametus had been strong enough to warrant a mention in the remarkably unturbulent British Isles. And no doubt, the appearance of this minor celebrity in town, coupled with the vague promise that they might catch themselves on television, meant that both the locals and the tourists had stayed glued to the action here, instead of realising that the real drama had been unfolding just half a mile away. Every cloud had a silver lining, I supposed, and at least there was one less thing to worry about.

The journalist turned to a woman at her side. So the ubiquitous Mrs Arbuckle was there after all, I noted. I turned away rather than listen to her take on what would no doubt be transformed even further into terrifying earthquakes of biblical proportions. That was when I noticed Nick across the street, watching the action with his arms crossed. He glared at me for a moment and then pointedly ignored my presence. It probably wasn't worth the effort to try and appease him, and I was pretty certain that he would have no further details on the robbery at Perkins. Demi-gods were no doubt rather accomplished at staying hidden from any human investigations into their undertakings. And Cornwall's finest weren't exactly CSI. I felt bad about hurting his feelings but it was better for him in the long run.

There was an old red telephone box on the other side of the little square. I was pretty sure I had some change in my pocket - should I call Corrigan and tell him everything was okay? Then I thought of Julia. This was her home and she'd be more concerned about the village than Lord Shifty. I was annoyed with myself for not thinking of her first. She was my alpha – sort of - she should always come first. I thrust my hands into my pockets and stalked over to the phone. Julia wasn't the kind of technologically advanced person who possessed a mobile, although admittedly while I had one I was always forgetting to bring it with me which meant I might as well not own one at all. I called the keep itself. No-one picked up so I left a message.

I put the phone down and gazed unseeingly at the years old graffiti etched into the paint, trying to decide what to do next. It was ridiculously dangerous, but maybe I should try entering the portal. If all Iabartu was going to do was to send minions through who would wear us down bit by bit, then surely it was high time to go on the offensive instead. The problem was that I'd have no way of finding her, or my way around once I entered her demsenes. It could very well be a vast plane of existence, which I'd spend the next sixty years or so wandering around in a clueless fog before eventually dying of old age. I drummed my fingers against the glass and absently traced a small tag written in black that proclaimed that 'Blake woz ere'. Inspired words. Truly.

Then I paused and remembered the black piece of cloth that I'd found in the clearing and which had been shot through with silver. It was just possible that it had belonged to Iabartu. It seemed strange that she'd just have left it hanging there, and there hadn't been any evidence of her presence anywhere other than at the seven stones and tree runes at the beach. But who else could it have belonged to? Alex would be able to tell me if it was hers or not by scrying it. If it wasn't hers, then at least it was likely that it belonged to another of her servants who might be able to lead me to her. And if it was…

I was confident that Alex would be able to put a locator spell on the material to find its true owner. He had already said that one of his regular jobs was to help owners find lost objects. It must be an easy process to reverse and help lost objects find their owners. I felt instantly invigorated. Let the Brethren and the pack take care of matters here. I'd get Alex to help, grab some of the silvered weapons, and sort the bitch out.

Awesome.

Chapter Twenty

I ran through the woods towards the keep with a renewed sense of purpose. Now that I finally had a proper plan, both adrenaline and warmth trickled through me. I ducked under a couple of branches and leaped over a bush, avoiding the usual path so that I could take a shortcut and get back quicker. It was my sense of impending achievement, however, that made me so blinkered, and so dumb.

Traces of the Otherworld are evident everywhere, if you know where to look. I did know where to look but today I wasn't seeing them. As I hopped over some roots without breaking my stride, I blundered straight into an invisible wall and was immediately thrown backwards. Slightly stunned, I staggered to my feet, daggers already pulled. But there was no physical enemy – I'd become trapped inside a sodding faerie ring.

"Fuck!" I slammed my shoulder against the edge of it, even though I knew it was a useless gesture.

Faerie rings are perfect circles of woodland mushrooms, left in random areas of countryside by the more irritating members of the Fae. Many older rings were now defunct; they didn't tend to hold their power for long. However the ones with enough juice in them to still work were not only annoying, but also dangerous. Time, for the Fae, moves differently to what it does for almost everyone else. They survive for millennia in Earth terms; and once in the Fae demesne itself, you could spend one day and then return to find that decades in the 'real' world had passed. They'd set faerie rings to capture foolish humans, and would then force their hapless prisoners to dance themselves to death. It was said that just one beat of faerie bells was enough to set your toes tapping and your hands clapping, and that once you started you'd never be able to stop. Even worse is that with time lacking any importance for the Fae, often years would go by before they'd check on their faerie traps. It would be impossible to force my way out of here on my own, and of course my mobile phone was back at the keep. After leaving the message on the answer machine that all was well, no-one, not Julia nor Corrigan, would be using their Voices to get in touch and see where I was. If I had some iron on me, then perhaps I'd manage to break through it, but even more stupidly I was pretty sure that my usual iron knife was currently sitting happily on my bedside cabinet waiting to be cleaned and sharpened after I'd used it to slit the throat of the terrametus.

I emptied out the contents of my bag, anyway, just to be sure. I'd put the empty Coke cans that I'd shared with Alex on the beach back inside but they were made of aluminium, which was next to useless against anything other than a recycling plant. There was the half empty canister of hydrogen peroxide that reminded me painfully of John for a second, but which offered no help in terms of usable iron. There was a small first aid kit, a couple of energy bars, a tatty book that I'd been reading when routing out the rabbits had become just too unspeakably dull for words, but absolutely nothing that would help me get out of the ring. Even my daggers were made of an alloy that wouldn't contain enough iron to work. Sometimes modern technology was a curse. I tried anyway, stabbing randomly at the invisible wall. Of course nothing happened.

I flung the contents of my bag to the ground and moved around the entire circle, checking it for any vulnerable points. Nothing. I felt rage and frustration shivering all over me. It wasn't fair! I knew that someone would find me long before I'd ever have to persuade any of the Fae to let me go, but I needed to get out now and get into the portal.

I thumped myself down, cross-legged, in the centre and slammed my palms against the mossy ground, stirring up a fine dust as I did so. I kicked out uselessly at the edges of the ring. It was no good; I'd just have to wait till someone came and rescued me.

*

Several hours later, dusk was beginning to settle. I was curled up, dozing, and waiting.

Where the fuck are you?

Corrigan! I sat up with a snap. Finally. I didn't think I'd ever be pleased to have his Voice inside my head. I was about to answer when Julia spoke to me, with a high note of panic.

Mackenzie! We need you!

Oh shit. *What's going on? What's the matter?* I had no idea whether both Julia and Corrigan could hear me at the same time, but it didn't matter. Something thing was clearly very wrong.

It was Julia who answered, and her words made the bottom drop out of my world. *The keep is under attack. We need you. Now.*

I…Julia…I'm stuck. I'm in a faerie ring and I can't get out.

There was silence on the other end. *Julia? JULIA? CORRIGAN?*

They'd gone. What did that mean? Who was attacking them? If it was Iabartu and I was stuck here, if the pack got hurt, or worse… I stood up and began flinging my clenched fists against the edge of the ring, over and over again, screaming at it to let me out. I pummelled the invisible wall with fury and felt my whole body on fire with an intense heat. I kicked and punched and threw myself at it with every iota of strength I had. Hot tears of frustration pricked at my eyes as images of the pack and the Brethren's bodies lying broken inside the keep while faceless monsters prowled through the rooms attacked me.

I hit the wall harder, and cried out in pain as my knuckles slammed against it. But I didn't stop. My fists were red raw from the repeated impact. I kicked again and punched again. What was I going to do? My vision was blurry with tears as I continued to attack the ring's outer edges. Come on, come on! I kept a furious battery of assault with my fists while my bloodfire screamed at me to continue.

And then, all of a sudden, I was falling through the circle into the outside world and onto the hard ground. The momentum carried me through till I banged into a tree and looked up, dazed. I'd actually punched my way through a faerie ring. Feeling a moment of utter befuddlement, I looked down at my hands. My knuckles were smeared with blood. I stared back at the ring in confusion then shook myself and got up, running in the direction of the keep. I was free, that was all that mattered. And now I had to go help my people.

I flew through the woods, feeling branches whip at my face and thorns catch my trousers. This time I made sure I looked at where I was going so I didn't foolishly fall into any other traps. I ran and ran, heart pounding in my ears praying to whatever was out there that my friends were okay. I couldn't handle more bloodshed and death, not now. Not when I could have prevented it by looking where I was going and avoiding getting trapped by a stupid faerie ring.

When I emerged from the woods and saw the keep, I was horrified. I couldn't see anyone outside, friend or foe, but one of the great oak doors was hanging off its hinges. I stumbled for a second and then ran faster, clutching my daggers. No no no no no no no. Not my home and the rest of my family as well as John. I couldn't let that happen.

My feet crunched into the gravel as I reached the driveway, and I started to slow. I still couldn't see any signs of life. I felt very hot, and very sick. Gripping the hilt of both daggers I stepped into the keep. The lighting was dim, and there were signs of utter devastation everywhere. The corpse of some kind of hideous creature lay face down on the shabby red carpet. Lamps had been overturned and, as I walked further into the hall, I could feel shards of glass snapping under my feet.

I resisted the urge to call out, not knowing what might decide to answer. The door to the office was open, and I glanced in, seeing paper strewn all over the place as if a miniature hurricane had swept in, caused utter havoc, and then immediately faded away. I continued forward, holding my breath. Where the fuck were they all?

I jogged to the gym and checked inside. Nothing. My chest felt tight and I was getting more and more panicked. Those fucking faeries! If I'd been here then I could have helped. A sound came from deeper in the bowels of the keep. I froze. It had sounded as if it was coming from the kitchen. A quick clatter of something falling to the ground. I tightened my jaw and tiptoed in that direction.

Pressing my back against the wall, I pushed open the door with one hand then peered around. The table was on its side, but I couldn't make out anything else. I was about to move into the doorway when something launched itself at me, biting into my arm with sharp teeth and growling viciously. Despite the pain, I felt a wave of relief.

"Tom! It's me!" The growling continued and his fangs sank deeper into my flesh. It was as if he'd not heard me. "Tom! It's Mack. Look at me!"

The rumble in his throat died and a pair of pale yellow eyes gazed up at me balefully. He immediately released my arm. Blood was streaming down it, and I could see a smear of red on his teeth. His huge tongue lapped at his lips for a second and he looked briefly puzzled. Then, he turned back into the kitchen and I followed, grabbing a dish towel hanging on a hook and wrapping it around the wounds.

"Tom, what the fuck is going on? Where is everyone?"

He whined, but didn't turn back to look at me. Instead he padded out of the kitchen and through the small door that led into Julia's herb garden. I had no choice but to follow. What met my eyes when we emerged back into the cool night air was a scene of controlled chaos. Limp bodies lay around the space, with shifters in various stages of transformation tending to them. Part of me noted the squashed herbs underfoot and thought of how angry Julia would be when she saw what had happened to her precious plants. But then I saw Julia.

She was lying in a corner, face turned away from me. Her arm was broken, and spread at an awkward angle. A man I'd never seen before was crouched down beside her. It looked like her right leg had been ripped off at the knee. Corrigan was stood, naked from the waist up but wearing jogging bottoms below, with his arms folded. He was staring down at her with a look of intense worry and concentration. Several members of the pack were doing the same. I spotted Lynda, with tears running down her face, clinging onto Anton for support. Betsy was there too, and Johannes, both covered in blood.

I was rooted to the spot with fear and felt my tongue cleave its way to the roof of my mouth. Was she…?

"She's not dead," a soft voice said beside me. It was Lucy. I ripped my eyes away from Julia, though the image of her broken body was now seared into my eyeballs, and looked at her blankly. She was pale and clearly still in a lot of pain after the ispolin's attack. No doubt the Brethren doctor had helped her already impressive regenerative powers, but she would need a considerable amount of time to heal. I wondered if she'd been involved in the fighting despite that fact and felt frustration that even a shockingly wounded shifter had been there to help when I hadn't. She continued, "She's not far off though. The Doc will do what he can for her, make her comfortable, but..." her voice trailed off.

I found my voice. "What happened?"

"We were attacked. I don't know by what. The mage is trying to work out what they are. They came completely without warning, from the front and the back. A few got in through the doors," she nodded towards the other side of the keep, "and others came in here. Your alpha was in the garden. I don't think she had time to even shift. We've lost three other shifters altogether."

I wanted to ask if they were Brethren or pack but I didn't dare. Lucy understood though and her gaze hardened slightly. "They were ours, not yours."

She limped away inside, back ramrod straight. I couldn't worry about her hurt feelings right now though so I turned back to Julia but caught Corrigan's eyes blazing angry gold at me instead.

"I called you. Why weren't you here?" he snarled.

The other shifters looked at me. I could the weight of their accusing glares and my whole body tensed. I'd failed them, and Julia. Again.

"I...was trapped. There was a faerie ring," I stuttered.

He took a step closer, and his eyes seared into me. "Then how did you escape?"

"I don't know. After I heard your Voice – and Julia's – I hit the edge of the ring. A lot. And then it gave way. I don't know why." I was aware that my voice was high-pitched with stress, trying to justify to everyone listening that my reasons for not being present to protect the keep were genuine.

"That's not possible. Did you have iron?"

I shook my head, mutely.

He towered over me. "Seems awfully convenient, that this is the time you chose to suddenly get yourself trapped by the Fae. And then miraculously escape."

Now I felt angry. Was he insinuating that I'd deliberately excused myself so that the keep could be attacked? "If I'd had a choice, I would have been here, my *lord*." I placed heavy sarcastic emphasis on the word. "I would not have abandoned my pack. And I think that between the terrametus and the ispolin, I've proven my loyalty. I was stupid and I didn't look where I was going but if you're trying to suggest that I'm some kind of traitor..."

"And yet, even with the ispolin, you still didn't shift, when you could have."

"And you know my reasons for that." At least my pack knew my reasons for that, anyway.

He glowered at me with the threat of violence contained within the stance of his body. "I'd compel you to tell me everything, Miss Mackenzie, and yet I wonder if it would work after, as you say, what happened with the terrametus."

Oh what a tangled web we weave. I opened my palms to him, in a marked display of submission. He seemed to be getting closer and closer to the truth. But once I got inside the portal, it wouldn't matter. Because either I'd kill Iabartu or she'd kill me. And in killing her, her portal would close and I wouldn't be able to return. Fucking Corrigan and his clever eyes, and the fucking Brethren with their all too obvious air of superiority, would never find out I was human. Despite Alex's clever assertions to the contrary, I knew I felt human. I couldn't for the life of me really contemplate being anything else. There was the bloodfire, sure, but I didn't really have any special skills that I'd not gained through hard work and years of training. Wanting to be a shifter wouldn't make me one. And, anyway, being human would not stop me from redeeming myself and getting revenge for John, Julia, and everyone else.

The shifter, probably the doctor, who'd been crouching down by Julia interrupted us. "My Lord Corrigan, we need to move her inside. I will try my best to heal her but she may be too far gone."

I felt ill and briefly shut my eyes before forcing them open again. Corrigan nodded briskly and looked at me. "The keep's perimeter needs to be repaired. You will make sure that it is. And then you had better get that taken care of." He looked pointedly at the bite marks from Tom. Although blood still dripped from them, soaking into the dishtowel, I didn't feel any pain. Not physical pain, anyway.

I motioned acquiescence and fixed my attention on Julia. "Anything she needs," I said to the doctor, "anything at all, tell me."

Corrigan growled at me, but the doctor nodded in sympathy. I hitched my backpack on my shoulder and went inside.

Chapter Twenty One

I couldn't shake the image of Julia's broken body from my mind. I wasn't sure I could cope if she died as well as John. Oily nausea rolled through the pit of my belly; I only just made it to the bathroom in the time to retch up the meager contents of my stomach.

Splashing cold water on my face, I stared miserably at my pale reflection in the little mirror. I was supposed to help protect my pack. Instead, as long as the Brethren were around, my presence endangered them. Not only that, but when they really needed me I hadn't been here. No wonder Corrigan had looked ready to murder me. If I could stick to my plan, and get inside the portal, then I'd just have to hope that I could make things right.

I walked back out into the hall and made my way to the front door. Pragmatically speaking, fixing the entrance seemed to be the best way to secure the keep. Not least because, if we didn't, then anyone who came knocking, such as the local postman first thing tomorrow morning, would immediately think that some kind of massacre had taken place. Which it actually had. Iabartu was kicking our butts.

Johannes joined me, shaking his head sadly. "Sad days these, lass, sad days." He was carrying a toolbox which I took from him.

"What's happening, J? I don't understand why we keep being targeted."

"Aye," he said heavily. "We have summat that someone wants. Trouble is, we dinna know what."

I thought about that, and what I'd uncovered so far. Was this related somehow to the Draco Wyr that Craw had mentioned? I could pretty much lay my hand on my heart and attest to the fact that we were not hiding any dragons anywhere. We weren't concealing anything, other than that we were a bunch of shapeshifters. Perhaps Iabartu had something against the were. But then that didn't make any sense because why would she target us in isolation? Why not go straight to the heart of the shifters and aim for the Brethren in London? Strategically it was a stupid move.

Johannes moved the door back into position and held it, while I clambered up on a ladder and started to connect the hinges back into place. It was awkward getting this done with a dishtowel wrapped round my arm, but not impossible. I pulled out a heavy iron nail. If only I'd had this in my pocket a few hours ago. I pushed it into the hinge bracket and began hammering, imagining that it was Iabartu's face that I was hitting. I just couldn't think of anything we had that a demi-god would so desperately want. Up until now, I hadn't examined in much detail what her motives might be, but perhaps if I could understand why she was doing this, I'd have more chance of understanding her. Know thy enemy.

"J, can you think of anything we have that someone would go to this trouble to get?"

He sighed. "Nah. There's nothing that I ken of. We dinna have onything locked away because it's too valuable to be seen by others."

I paused. Actually we did. In John's office there was the magically sealed drawer I'd been unable to open. It was just possible that there was something inside that Iabartu was after. I couldn't think of any reason why John would have wanted to keep anything hidden away from the rest of the pack, so whatever was in there must be important.

I knocked the nail into place. I needed to get into that drawer. Unfortunately I'd not seen Alex since I returned and he would surely be my best bet for breaking through a ward. Remembering the melted pen, I figured that attacking it myself might not be best the idea. But silver could work. I needed to get some anyway for when I went through the portal so I reckoned that there was no time like the present. Quickly finishing up the door, I shouted down to Johannes to try closing it. The heavy oak slammed shut into place. Perfect. At least if Corrigan caught up with me again I could prove that I'd been busy.

"I need to take care of a few things, J," I said to him as I climbed back down the ladder.

"Aye, lass," he nodded, "you do tha'. 'n' make sure ye catch that fecker 'n' all."

No prizes for guessing who that 'fecker' was. At least someone still had faith in me.

*

I had to make sure that none of the Brethren saw me returning to the keep. I was pretty sure that if I was caught shirking the orders that Corrigan had given me, they'd throw my sorry ass down the disused well at the back of the keep and wipe their hands of me. Before I did anything, however, I had to find Julia.

As I was confident that she'd been taken to her own room, where she could be made the most comfortable, I headed back inside the keep but avoided the main stairwell. Off the great hall was a small door that led to a staircase that had been used by servants in times gone past. I reckoned that the Brethren wouldn't know about it yet – and even if they did, they'd have no cause to use it. Despite my gut feeling that I wouldn't bump into any of them along the way, I moved cautiously up the steps, trying to be as silent as I possible could. When I reached the third floor, where Julia's room was located, I carefully pushed open the door just a chink and peered through.

I could just make out her room at the other end of the corridor and voices coming from inside it. I watched for a few moments and then Corrigan and the doctor emerged. The looks on both their faces were grave. Swallowing hard, I waited till they had headed to the main stairwell and begun to descend before I made a move. There was one heart-stopping moment where Corrigan seemed to pause and sniff the air, and I pushed myself back against the wall and held my breath, praying that it wasn't me he could smell, but then he continued onward murmuring something inaudible.

Tiptoeing forward, feeling like a thief in my own house, I made my way to her room and inside, gently closing the door behind me. Her pale broken body lay on the bed, unconscious. I didn't have much time before someone returned to check on her, but I had to do this. I knelt down beside her prone form and placed my hand on her arm. Her skin felt clammy to the touch and a wave of despondency ran through me.

"It's all my fault, Julia," I whispered. "The wichtlein said so. I don't know why or how, but it is. And if," my voice broke slightly, "if I could have been here when you called then I could have saved you." I gulped in air and tried to swallow down the tears. "I'll make it right though. I promise I'll make it right. Just stay strong until I return." I smoothed a strand of hair away from her brow and slowly stood up. This was my battle now. I was going to do what I should have done from the beginning. I turned and left, without looking back.

*

After leaving the third floor, I snuck up to the south garret where the silver weapons were kept, managing to avoid any Brethren along the way. The door was kept locked, simply because of how dangerous silver was to shifters, but everyone knew where the key was. I reached up onto the dusty sill of the door frame and felt around. My fingers found it before too long and I managed to unlock it quickly.

Inside, the little room was spartan but clean. I pulled a bow off the wall and tested its string. It twanged with a pleasing tautness so I slung it round my shoulder, then opened up a battered chest and pulled out the silver tipped arrows. There would be a limit to how many I could realistically carry – and I still had to get out of the keep without any of the Brethren spotting me – so I only took eight and stuffed them into my backpack. The length of the arrows were such that it looked like it contained weapons. As long as no-one asked me to open the bag though, I'd probably be okay. Next I unhooked a small dirk from the other wall and hefted it in my palms, feeling its weight. It was perfectly balanced and would suit me well. It was light and easy to carry so even if I found myself wandering around the portal's other plane for some length of time trying to find the bitch, then at least it wouldn't weigh me down. I tested the blade gently against my skin and made a small nick. It would cut through even the toughest hide. Excellent.

My next stop was the dorm. I'd have to bandage up my arm to stop it from bleeding any further. Some Otherworld creatures, shifters included, could smell blood at fifty paces. There was no point in giving myself away too easily. And I was pretty sure that I still had some of Julia's yarrow ointment to slather on too.

I headed back down the narrow stairs and almost banged straight into Staines as I rounded the corridor. Shit. He scowled at me and then wrinkled his nose. Damnit, when was the last time I'd put on the scented lotion? I couldn't remember, but it had definitely been more than eight hours ago. His eyes narrowed suspiciously at me, so I headed him off at the cross.

"I stink of human after being in that town. And blood too. Makes me feel unclean. The trouble is that we only have a limited supply of hot water and I have a horrible feeling that the girls will have already used it all up." I was vaguely aware that I was babbling. "I don't suppose you have that problem in London though, do you?"

He looked at me like I was slightly demented. Which was fine. Then he strode off without saying a word and I made a face at his back. Manners cost nothing. Another one of Julia's favourite sayings. I winced at the thought of her and quickly picked up my pace.

Fortunately no-one was in the dorm. I was hoping to avoid any of the pack, because I didn't want to blurt out my plan to them, in case they tried to stop me or, worse, tried to join me. This was a one way mission and I was going solo. I changed my clothes, slapped on some lotion and then carefully cleaned and bound the bite marks on my arm. Tom's reaction times must be improving to have latched on so quickly, I thought idly. He'd make a strong pack warrior one day, assuming of course that the Brethren didn't vanish him away first. I supposed I'd never know now which way he'd decide to jump.

Once I was safely dehumanized, I went out in search of Alex. I didn't know which room Julia would have put him into, especially with the Brethren already occupying all the guest rooms on the floor above. However there were a few spare rooms on my dorm's floor, such as the one that Tom and I 'shared', so I wandered along in the dim corridor light, swinging open a few doors as I went. All the rooms were bare and unslept in apart from one on the far side, facing north. As the door squeaked open and I peered around, I noticed there were a few bags dumped on the floor by the window and some odd chalk marks on the floor. Probably some kind of paranoid mage runes, the equivalent of a teenager's Stay The Hell Out sign. I reached into my bag and pulled out a scrap of paper and a pencil and scribbled him a note, sticking it to the inside of the door, and telling him to come and find me, either in the office or outside the keep, as a matter of urgency. Hopefully he'd come back soon and read it. In the meantime, I'd have to keep my fingers crossed that the silver dirk would be able to break through John's magic.

Vaguely remembering an old war film I'd watched years ago, where the British spy in enemy territory had commented that you had to look as if you belonged and knew where you were going and what you were doing to evade capture, I strode out of the dorm and down into the office, trying to make it appear as if I definitely wasn't skulking and was still working on Corrigan's 'repair the keep' orders. I needn't have worried. I passed a few pack members, and a few Brethren too, but they were all lost in their own thoughts and own grief and paid me little attention. Ally gave me a ghost of a smile as I tripped again on the hole in the carpet going down the stairs, but didn't say anything. It had seemed that everyone had forced themselves to bounce back quickly after John, but with the threat of more imminent attacks, and the shocking events of just a couple of hours ago, it felt as if the will and the spirit of the keep had been stripped away. The feeling was almost as depressing as thinking of Julia upstairs fighting for her life. And it also gave me reason enough to keep going with my plan.

I had a couple of ready made excuses prepared in my head, in case anyone, especially Corrigan, was inside the office, but I was in luck and it was empty. Someone had already started to tidy up some of the devastation that the invaders had caused, but whoever it was had left a few tidy piles of papers and then disappeared. It suited me perfectly. I carefully twisted the knob on the door to John's study and stepped inside, flicking on the light switch.

It was exactly the same as it had been when I'd last been in, breaking into his computer. I ignored the machine this time around, however and bent down to the bottom drawer of the old desk. There was a tiny brass keyhole fashioned into the wood, where I guessed the source of the magic ward would be. I could feel it pulsating even from where I stood, broadcasting to keep out and stay away. Sorry, not this time. I pushed my index finger towards it, experimentally, and felt the cold burn of the barrier. I drew back quickly and tried the sides, knocking the lower edges of the wood that encased all the drawers. The buzz of the ward was there too, although a bit fainter. I tried reaching underneath, to the bottom of the drawer, but jolted back with a hiss as again I met painful resistance. Then I pulled out the drawer above, completely taking it out of its place and peering down. It was a pitch black well of nothingness.

Despite the situation, I was rather impressed at John's attention to detail. I wondered if he'd conjured it up himself, dabbling a little in the black arts as a hobby as he'd occasionally been wont to do, or if he'd hired a mage like Alex to do it for him. He didn't like strangers, no matter who they were, but this was a complex ward that demanded a pretty high level of appreciation. I just hoped that it wasn't impervious to silver. The little dirk was secreted away in my bag, so I pulled it off my shoulders and unzipped it, hand curling round the hilt. I tugged on it to take it out, but it seemed to be caught on something, one of the seams of fabric perhaps. I tugged harder and was about to yank it free when a shadow suddenly fell across the desk and I heard Corrigan's furious voice.

"Just what the fuck are you doing now?"

Chapter Twenty Two

I sent an internal prayer of gratitude to myself that I'd not yet pulled the dirk free. Holding silver would be something that even the ridiculous lies I'd so far managed to fashion for His Great Lord Shiftiness couldn't cover. I straightened and blinked at him, a picture of innocence. If all else fails, then try the truth, I mentally shrugged.

"What does it look like I'm doing, my lord? I am trying to find a way to open this drawer."

I couldn't fathom what the expression on his face was saying. His green gold eyes bored into my soul and I felt a small shiver run through me. "And why exactly would you be doing that?"

"Well, it's obvious isn't?" I answered brusquely. "The fact that we keep being targeted for attack must mean that we have something that the blue woman wants." I certainly wasn't prepared to give up Iabartu's name to him just yet. "This is the only place that I can think of that is locked and where there might be something that John would have hidden away. If we can find it, then we might have a better chance of understanding what is happening and stopping it."

"An interesting conclusion, kitten," he murmured. Oh, great. We were back to endearments again. I just barely managed to keep from rolling my eyes before he continued. "And why," he said silkily, "didn't you think to mention this drawer to me before?"

"First of all," I ticked off my fingers, "I couldn't find you. And I was pretty sure that you'd have your hands full dealing with the death rites. Second of all, if I'm wrong and there's nothing in here apart from a couple of shifter girlie mags, then I'd look pretty stupid. And thirdly, you've already made it pretty clear that you don't trust me. For all I know, you'd try to suggest that I planted whatever was in there myself."

"I see," he drawled slowly. "I must beg to differ on one point, however."

I waited. Amusement glinted in his eyes but I was damned if I was going to ask him what that point was. He still didn't elaborate further. Oh for fuck's sake, fine then. "And what would that be?" I finally asked.

He smiled. Was that a flicker of triumph? Bastard. "I think you'll find, kitten, that I do trust you. And despite the fact that you're the most annoying, unpredictable and difficult to control shifter I've ever come across, you do appear to have useful skills. I'm not sure I trust you enough to stay here in the countryside on your own before you manage to cause complete devastation. But I think that you've proven yourself enough for me to tell you that my offer to join me in London still stands."

Join *me*. Not the Brethren. Oh God. Was that a deliberate choice of words on his part or did he just think of the Brethren as an extension of himself anyway? I swallowed and looked up at him. "Even though I might have deliberately engineered falling into a faerie ring so that I could be absent when the keep was attacked?"

"Mmmmm," he answered non-committedly, "you're going to have to tell me one day how you really did escape from that."

I didn't even know myself how I'd managed to get free, so I didn't think I'd ever be able to tell him. "I honestly have no idea, my lord," I answered truthfully. "Perhaps it was just an old ring and didn't have much power left."

"Yes, perhaps, kitten, perhaps." He stretched out his arms and linked his hands behind his head. I was suddenly very aware of the stretch of the dark fabric of his t-shirt against his tanned muscular biceps.

Irritation exploded out of me. "Will you stop fucking calling me that?"

"What?" he taunted, softly, eyes glinting.

"I am not a cat," I said through gritted teeth. "I am a hamster. And my name is Mack, not kitten."

"Well then, maybe I should just call you Hammy, instead," he purred.

My stomach squirmed into knots. He was flirting with me. After everything that had happened, and all he'd already said and threatened me with, he was flirting. Why me? This could not happen. I'd rather face an army of ispolin than this.

"Well then, maybe I'll call you Pants," I snapped at him.

He laughed, and opened his mouth to say something else. Oh no, it was high time to put an end to this. "My lord, perhaps you could help to open the drawer." And get your fingers frozen off instead of mine, I thought silently.

He cocked his head at me, with another glance that I couldn't quite interpret, before replying with a cocky business-like air, "As my lady wishes."

I resisted the urge to slap him around the head and stepped out from the desk. He brushed past me, and I had to try very hard not to flinch at the warm hard heat of his body against mine. I quickly moved away and nearer the door so I had a quick exit if I needed it. Humour flashed across his face again, as if he knew exactly what I was thinking. Fuck. Off. If he knew who I really was then he'd snap my neck like a twig and forget all about me in an instant. I just had to keep remembering that.

He bent down to look at the drawer and frowned. "Huh, this a pretty powerful ward."

He stood up and gazed at me, all serious now. "Did John have magic skills?"

"A few parlour tricks," I shrugged, glad that we were off the topic of pet names for each other, "nothing like this. Not that I knew of anyway."

He jerked his head in brief acknowledgement and then crouched down again. His very large hands reached out to the drawer, then he drew back suddenly, as if scorched. Hah! That would teach him.

"Stand back," he ordered.

I bristled at the command but did as he asked. With a look of intense concentration on his face he pulled back his hand and formed a fist. I wondered if he was seriously going to try to punch his way through it. That would be completely idiotic. He'd rip his hand off for sure. I took another step back, just in case.

His whole body tensed and then, quick as lightning, he slammed his fist forward. There was the sound of breaking, splintering wood, and a flash of blue light. He shook his hand a few times, and I could see that it was red and beginning to swell, but he grinned at me like the cat that got the cream and stepped aside with a flourish. You have got to be kidding me. I walked gingerly round and stared down at the mess of the desk. He'd actually snapped through the ward, and the fabric of the wood itself, leaving a hand sized hole. I gaped at him.

He laughed. "Impressed much, *kitten*?"

I became aware that my mouth was hanging open so I snapped it shut and glared at him, trying vainly not to appear over-awed. Shit, clearly there was a good reason why he'd been voted in as the new head Alpha.

"Big deal," I said, with far more nonchalance than I was feeling. I stuck my hand into the destroyed drawer and felt around, noting the remaining bristle of magic tremble against my touch. There was nothing there apart from what felt like a paper folder. I tugged at it, trying to yank it out, and cursed when it wouldn't fit through the gap.

Impatient, I knelt down and pulled out the drawer, lifting out the folder. It was unmarked. I raised my eyebrows at Corrigan and showed him it, then lifted the flap. At that point, the study door was flung open and Staines and Alex came through.

"What in god's name was that?" Staines shouted.

Wow. Talk about being annoyed at missing the party, I thought.

Alex chipped in. "Jeez, I think the whole keep felt that tremor. What did you do? Break through a…" He stopped and stared at the desk. "You destroyed a level five ward?" He looked at me for a second but I shook my head and pointed over at Corrigan. I supposed that at least I wasn't the only one who was seriously impressed at his power.

Concern flitted over Staines' face. "My Lord Alpha, your hand."

I realised that Corrigan was still clutching his hand and felt a sort of grim satisfaction that at the very least he'd slightly hurt himself.

He, however, just growled, "It's fine."

Staines pulled out a sleek looking phone and began to jab at the numbers. "I'll call the doctor."

"No." Steel laced Corrigan's voice. "He has better things to be doing right now. Besides, I confess to a sudden curiosity at what the Cornish alpha was so keen to hide." He jerked at the folder in my hands.

I looked down and went instantly rigid when I saw what the visible half of the front sheet displayed. It was my name. Oh fuck. Blood drained from my face. I snapped it shut and just stared at Corrigan. "Er….." He could NOT read this.

Alex suddenly flinched dramatically. "Something's approaching the front."

Corrigan's whole body stilled. "Shifter?"

"I…uh…can't tell."

Staines growled and turned smartly out of the study. Corrigan looked at me, eyes narrowed. "You will wait here." The bastard was trying to compel me. So much for trusting me.

I tried to smile graciously and inclined my head. "My Lord."

He stalked out the door. I turned to Alex and breathed again. "Oh my God. We need to hide this, Alex, now. They'll be back as soon as they realise no-one is there."

"Someone is there," Alex said, surprising me. I thought he'd just noticed the look on my face and cleverly created a diversion. "Human though. Male, I think." He glanced down at the folder that was now burning in my hands. "What's in it?"

"It's about me," I gasped. "It must say that I'm human. Corrigan can't read this, Alex, he just can't."

"Okay," he said. "Damage control." He took the folder and pulled out the contents then spun me around and unzipped my backpack, stuffing the papers inside. He raised his eyebrows at me as he saw the other contents of the bag. "Silver?"

"I'll explain later," I muttered.

Alex pulled a book off the shelf. "Spells for the Uninitiated," he read. "This'll do. Page 107, if I remember rightly."

"What's on page 107?" I asked, as I watched him rip it out and place it inside the folder.

"Love Spell," he said, with a great deal more calm than I felt. "With any luck, Lord Corrigan will believe that your alpha was just trying to get a bit of sneaky bed action."

"That's ridiculous," I said flatly. "No-one would ever believe John would stoop that low."

He looked at me, quietly. "Do you have a better idea? They're on their way back."

"Fuck. No. Give me that," I snatched it back out of his hands and shoved it into the folder, just in time to see Corrigan return.

"Your policeman boyfriend is here," he sneered.

"Nick? But…"

"Go and get rid of him." He pulled the folder out of my hands.

I tried to protest weakly but he pushed me out the door. The weight of the backpack on my shoulders now felt constricting. Between the silver weapons and the proof of my true identity, if anyone opened it, it would seal my doom. And perhaps the rest of the pack's too. That might work out well for Corrigan, I thought bleakly. With no Cornish pack, then there'd probably be no more attacks to worry about and he could scuttle back to London in his showy limo and forget we'd ever existed. Oh, this was all so very very bad.

Nick was already in the hall when I entered through the study. It was difficult to concentrate on why he was here with everything else that had just happened. I tried to put on my game face.

"Nick. What brings you here?"

He looked around the hall. "There were some reports of loud noises from this vicinity," he said slowly. "Had some trouble have you?"

Most of the devastation from before had been tidied up, but one of the paintings had a great rip right through it and there were still some shards of glass from one of the lamps in the corner. At least the dead monster had gone.

"Yes, we...er...were having a party," I gabbled. "It got a bit out of hand. Most people are away sleeping it off." I tried to smile disarmingly at him.

He frowned at me. "Apparently it sounded more like a riot, than a party."

"Crazy times, Nick, crazy times. Thanks for coming over to check it all out though."

"Would you tell me if something was wrong?" he asked softly.

"Yes," I lied, looking him straight in the eyes. I was becoming too good at this.

"Okay, then." He paused for a moment. "Do you mind if I have a look around?"

Yes. "Ummm..."

At that moment, Tom, bless him, appeared. I waved at him frantically. He looked oddly wary of me but came over anyway. "Actually, it's kind of late and we were going to go to bed." I flung an arm round Tom's waist and smiled at Nick apologetically. "How about tomorrow morning instead?"

His face went cold. "That won't be necessary," he said stiffly. "Call me if you need anything."

He walked back outside. I watched him go, feeling sorry for him. In another world, we might have worked as a couple, but... The oak door slammed behind him and Corrigan's voice drifted towards me with a deceptively laidback tone. "That was fast work."

I realised my arm was still round Tom and snatched it away, whirling round. Corrigan's eyes were entirely expressionless - and he was still holding the folder.

"I was just doing what you asked, my Lord."

His gaze flicked to Tom and then back to me. "Whatever you say. Better get some rest. It's late and we need everyone rested in case there's another attack tomorrow."

"And what if there's one tonight?"

Corrigan sighed and looked at me tiredly. "I have watchers all over the keep. Do not presume to tell me my job, Miss Mackenzie."

He walked up the stairs, with Staines behind him like a faithful dog.

"Do not presume to tell me my job, Miss Mackenzie, kitten, servant of my own bidding," I mimicked once he'd gone. "Tosser." I didn't think I'd ever seen someone flick between hot and cold so quickly.

Tom looked across at me. "What the hell is going on, Red?"

"It's…complicated." I pulled him in the direction of the kitchen. "Come on, let's get Alex and get a coffee and I'll tell you."

Chapter Twenty Three

The three of us congregated around the now upright kitchen table. I set the large copper kettle on the stove to boil and began preparing some coffee, setting out three mugs. Tom kept sending sidelong glances to Alex until exasperatedly I hissed that he could be more than trusted and knew everything that was going on.

"Including…?" The question in Tom's voice was obvious.

"That she's human? I'm a mage, dude, I knew within about 0.5 seconds."

"Alright, *dude*," Tom sarcastically snapped back.

"Hey boys, let's chill, shall we?" I commented, try to aim for a light tone. It was an unusual day when I was the one trying to keep the peace. I guessed that the stress and fear was getting to everyone.

Both of them slumped slightly and looked guiltily at each other. I continued on, all business-like. "So what's with the funny looks, Tom?" I really wanted to ask him if he was planning on joining the Brethren but, given the circumstances, decided that I'd have to leave that topic alone.

He started. 'Eh?"

"After you attacked me this afternoon,…"

"I thought you were another monster!" he protested.

I shot him a look and said drily, 'Thanks. Like I was saying, after you attacked me this afternoon, *mistakenly*, you kept looking at me like I'd sprouted horns or something. What was that all about?"

He coloured and coughed slightly. "Your blood."

I looked at him blankly.

"It tasted funny," he said. "As if it was hot…and," he fiddled with his cuffs, "tasty."

Both Alex and I stared at him.

"It's not my fault! It tasted nice, okay? And strange. But not like anything I've ever had before."

I opened my mouth to speak but Alex beat me to it. "Have you tasted human blood before?"

This again. Alex was clearly still convinced that I wasn't actually human.

"Of course not!" Tom replied defensively.

"So you've got nothing to compare it to then," Alex said slowly.

"What do you think I am? I might be a shifter, but I don't go around eating people." He had a disgusted look on his face.

"Anton," I said suddenly.

"What?"

"Anton sneaked into the dorm and stole my t-shirt." I was starting to feel a bit sick.

"Uh, what's your point? Are you trying to tell me that he's secretly had the hots for you all these years and wanted to steal your clothes? Or that he's a closet cross dresser?"

I held Tom's eyes. "It had my blood on it. He told Julia that he," I paused and swallowed, "had developed a taste for it."

"The bloodfire!" Tom exclaimed suddenly.

Alex looked confused so I explained. "When I get angry or upset, I feel hot inside. Sometimes very hot. Like fire. It helps me to think and seems to make me... stronger. And sometimes I can call on it if I need some help to focus."

"I told you!" Alex almost shouted so that I had to hush him in case we woke anyone up. "You're not actually human. And you're just telling me about this fire stuff now. Honestly, dude, for a bright girl sometimes you are duuuumb."

"Of course she's human," Tom said, puzzled. "She's always been human. She smells human. I mean, not right now with Julia's lotion on, but usually. " He looked directly at me. "You're strong, Mack, but you're not Otherworld strong."

I took offense at that. "I can beat Anton. And I can beat you."

"In skill, sure, but not strength. Not really."

I scoffed slightly but couldn't really argue. Alex took up the thread again though. "Why can you hear Corrigan's Voice? Why could you hear John's and Julia's?"

"They can't compel me," I pointed out. "And I can touch silver."

Alex shrugged. "Minor points probably related to the fact that you're not a shifter. Does your blood do anything else?"

I was about to say no, when I suddenly thought of how I'd managed to escape from the faerie ring. There had been blood on my hands by the time I punched through it. "Er..."

At that moment the kettle on the stove began to whistle. I sprang up, glad to have the excuse of tending to it and pouring the coffee. Could it be true? Could I really not be human? I felt both elated and deflated at the same time. Both Alex and Tom remained silent until I'd placed the cafetiere on the table, along with the mugs.

"It's time you open that file," Alex said softly.

"What file?" asked Tom.

I filled him in on what had happened in the study, trying to stall having to actually open the damned thing. I wasn't sure that I wanted to know any more. But there had to be a reason why John had papers about me kept in a magically locked drawer. It'd be pointless having something that secure which just said I was human, wouldn't it? Everyone in the keep already knew that.

"Mack Attack…"

Tom raised his eyebrows slightly at my newly acquired nickname. Wait until he heard the kitten one.

"I should go and visit Julia first, and make sure she's alright." I neglected to mention that I already had. Perhaps I didn't need to know what was in the file after all.

"There's nothing you can do," Alex replied calmly. "She's sedated and being looked after by the doc. She won't even know you're there."

"I'll know that," I growled.

"Quit trying to put it off," he said, firmly. "I can vouch that Julia's not going anywhere, not yet at least. Look at the file first, then go."

I took a deep breath. I wasn't going to be able to get out of this. "Fine." My backpack was in the corner of the kitchen beside the door, where I'd dumped it when I came in. I carefully kept my back to Tom, blocking his view. I still didn't want him to see the flash of silver because there was no way I was going to give him the chance of trying to be a hero and volunteering to come with me through the portal. All this file and human/not human stuff was just a speed bump. Once Tom was safely out of the way, I still planned to get Alex to do his stuff and put a tracer on the cloth.

I pulled out the clump of papers and sat back down at the table, nervously smoothing them over.

"We can give you some space," Alex said kindly.

"No," I replied quickly. "I'd like you to stay here. Both of you." I didn't want to do this alone.

Each of them nodded. I felt a shiver in my stomach and turned over the first sheet.

It was a photo of me, aged seven, clipped to a letter. I scanned down to the bottom to see the signatory and the world suddenly stopped. It was from my mother.

I lifted my eyes to Tom and Alex and gulped out the words. "It's from my mum."

"Your…. But, how, can that be?" Tom burst out.

I shook my head in confusion. Alex told me to read it out.

Dear John,

I know it has been a long time since I've contacted you, and, believe me, I wouldn't be doing it now if I thought I had another choice.

I'm in trouble. They're getting closer and Mackenzie is in danger. If they catch her, you know what they will do. I need to know that she'll be safe. It's a lot to ask, especially because of pack rules, but I need you to look after her for me. I know that she'll be safe with you. I'll be in Cornwall in a few days' time and be able to leave her at the keep. She doesn't understand what is happening, and it's probably better that she never does. If she stays with you, then she never needs to know the truth. She's strong, and she can look after herself, but sometimes when she gets angry I feel afraid. I can see the power inside her. Maybe you can turn her when she's older and then it won't matter. I have no idea if it will work. But they can't find her, John, no matter what.

Please believe me that if there was another way then that's what I'd do. You're my last hope, and my daughter's.

Martha

My mother had already known John before she left me here? And what did she mean that she was afraid of me? "What am I?" I whispered, aghast.

Tom was tense and motionless, but Alex reached out and gently touched me on the arm.

"It's okay," he said. "Whatever it is, it'll be okay."

I flipped to the next page, heart in my mouth, terrified at what I might read next. It was a medical form with my name at the top. I had a faint memory from not long after I arrived, of John taking me into his study and pulling out a needle. I'd been so frightened and had tried to back away, but he'd soothed me and said it wouldn't hurt for long. That it was just in case there was an accident and they needed to do a blood transfusion. I hadn't even understood what that was at the time but something about the look in his eyes made me trust him so I'd offered him my arm and let him draw my blood. I wondered why I'd not remembered that until now. John had certainly never mentioned it again after that day.

I stared down at the smudged piece of paper.

"Red?" prompted Tom, softly.

I passed it over him and he read over it, drawing in a sharp breath and then turning it over to Alex.

"Oh my God," Alex breathed. "Now it all makes sense. This is why you are so strong, and feel fire in your blood. This is why you can hear Voices. And this must be why Iabartu…" His voice trailed off and he looked at me sadly.

"Uh, who's Iabartu?" Tom asked, brow furrowed.

Tears filled my eyes. It was my fault after all. Craw had been right. John had died protecting me, hiding me. Julia was lying upstairs fighting for her life because of me. Four Brethren shifters were dead because of me. I fought the tears back and felt rage and fire fill me. Without thinking, I stood up, violently kicking back my chair and flung my mug against the tiled kitchen wall, spattering it with dark coffee stains and shattering the porcelain. An inhuman cry fell from my lips and I picked up the chair and began hitting it against the wall.

"No! It can't be me, it can't be my fault," I gasped, slamming the wooden frame against the wall, again and again and again, until a small wooden leg was all that was left in my hands. I threw it to the side and doubled over in pain, hugging myself. It was my blood that the bitch wanted. I howled in grief, anguish and anger.

I was part dragon.

Chapter Twenty Four

Once my sobs subsided, and I was hiccupping in a ball on the floor, Alex came over and picked me up, hugging my body to his.

"It's not your fault," he said gently. "You didn't know and you couldn't help it." He pulled out another chair from the table and sat me down. I gazed dully down at the grains of wood, and traced a whorl with my finger.

"I don't understand." Tom came round the other side of the chair. "What does this mean?" He waved the piece of paper at me. "What's not your fault? And, I say again, who the hell is Iabartu?"

I took a deep breath and answered. "She's a demi-god. She's the blue bitch who Alex scryed and who killed John. She's the…thing that sent through the terrametus and the ispolin. She's looking for me because she wants my blood."

"But why your blood?" He looked frustrated and his fist tightened on the paper. 'What does this mean?"

Alex took it from him and glanced at him with a serious, warning look. "Mackenzie is one eighth Draco Wyr. She has dragon blood in her veins. It's what makes her stronger and what fuels the bloodfire. It's also why she can do things that most humans can't. It's diluted enough by her human side so no-one can detect it unless they go looking specifically for it." He waved the paper in the air. "Which your alpha obviously did." Alex looked back at me. "You're still human, Mack Attack. It's only a fraction of you, and it's not your fault. It's not as if you could control it."

"I should have known," I said dully. "You worked out within just a couple of days that I couldn't be fully human. I've lived with this for my whole life. Even though I realised that the bloodfire was strange, I didn't try to work out why I had it. I just pretended that it was normal. And it got John killed."

"But he knew, Mack." Alex's voice was soft and insistent. "He knew and he didn't tell you."

My eyes blazed and I growled. "Are you trying to suggest that it's his fault that he was killed?"

He sighed and ran a hand through his dirty blond hair. "No. What I'm saying is that he was trying to protect you. He was your alpha and your guardian, and keeping you safe was his job. If he'd thought it was something you'd needed to know, he would have brought it up. But he didn't. Remember what you told me about him trying to break the geas when you originally arrived? If he'd had this letter and he knew your mother then he must have made that part up to keep your identity secret even from yourself. Everything you've told me suggests that he loved you like a daughter; that it didn't matter to him that you have the fire of the Draco Wyr in your veins, but it did matter that you were safe. He knew what he was doing."

I sank back down in my chair. "If he knew what he was doing, then why is he dead?"

Nobody answered. After a moment, Tom cleared his throat. "So, this Iabartu half god woman. Why does she want your blood?"

Alex answered for me. "Draco Wyr haven't been seen for centuries." I looked at him, startled. He shrugged at me. "You're not the only one who can do research, Mack Attack. Anyway, as I was saying there's not been sight nor sound of them for longer than even the Fae could remember. Not just on this plane but on any plane. Most people think they didn't ever really exist in the first place. The stories say, though, that their blood is strong enough to bring down an army. Or to cure the most terrible afflictions imaginable. It depends on how it's used. Even though Mack is only an eighth Wyr, there is still power there."

"And Iabartu must need it to kill and destroy or because she wants to open up a pharmacy." My fire was still flickering but I knew with cold certainty what I needed to do. "Tom, I need you to hide these papers. It's still enough to hurt the pack if the Brethren find them."

"But it means you're not human!" He exclaimed with sudden realization. "They won't do anything because now we're not breaking the Way."

He could be really naïve sometimes. "And until now we all thought I was completely human so whether we did break the Way or not, we had the intention of doing so."

Alex frowned. "And the dragon blood is only a fraction of you. In essence, Mack Attack, you are still human."

Whatever. The point was moot as far as the Brethren were concerned. But I looked steadily at Tom and gestured expansively. "You see? Corrigan still can't find this out. Please, Tom. Find somewhere to hide this stuff." I gently touched the letter quietly saying, "This is the first time I've ever seen my mother's handwriting. It's proof that she might still be alive, still exist somewhere. I don't want to lose it."

"Okay, okay, Red. Whatever you need." He picked up the papers and moved towards the door, then suddenly turned, holding up a finger. "Just one thing though – how does a dragon mate with a human in the first place? I mean how did your great-grandfather or grand-mother have sex with a fire breathing lizard?"

I was the spawn of a lizard. Oh my God.

Alex pushed Tom gently towards the exit. "Let's not think about that part for now," he said briskly.

Tom nodded slightly and finally left. Alex looked at me silently for a second before speaking. "So, what do you have in mind?"

"Whatever do you mean, Alex?"

"You know what I mean. You couldn't wait to get rid of your wolf friend. And I'm getting to know you, Mack Attack." He placed emphasis on the 'Attack'. "You have a plan."

I nodded briefly. "I have to get into that portal."

Alex gave a sharp intake of breath. "I'm not sure that's wise…"

"It's what I was planning to do all along anyway, Alex. And now it makes even more sense. It's me she must be after. If I go to her, then all this will stop." I gestured around the kitchen and at the still present signs of the invasion. "You know it makes sense."

"I know Lord Corrigan is planning something."

I interrupted. "Lord Corrigan can go fuck himself." I felt a brief twinge of something as I said his name. Regret? Fear? I wasn't sure but I pushed it way and focused on the here and now instead. "Only I can do this. And I need your help to do it." I held his eyes. Please, Alex.

He was silent for a long moment before speaking. "Okay, then, Mack Attack. What do you need?"

*

We walked outside into the cool night, heading for the little outhouse where the bolt of cloth was situated. Even after the Brethren had examined it, they'd left it where I'd placed it, unwilling to bring the death streaked material inside. It also meant that Tom wouldn't know where we were should he manage to quickly hide the papers and then return looking for us. This was my fight.

Only the porch light leading from the keep was on, so we had to carefully pick our way along the path. I was alert for signs of the watchers that Corrigan had so arrogantly spoken of, but everything seemed quiet. Perhaps the Brethren weren't as good at their jobs as he thought they were. So much the better. Neither of us spoke until we entered the small hut. I winced slightly as the old hinges creaked when the door opened, but there were fortunately no sounds of alarm from the keep behind us.

Inside it was pitch black. I sensed Alex make a movement beside me, and the interior was suddenly glowing with a soft light.

"That's a handy trick," I grunted.

He shrugged and walked over to the cloth, recoiling slightly as he got closer.

"This reeks of power and death. Are you sure about this?"

I didn't even deign to answer. He lifted up his palms slightly in acknowledgement and got to work. I watched him, still fascinated at the display of magic. His eyes closed, much as they had the previous time, and he began to chant softly. After a moment, the now almost familiar swirl of blue smoke curled around the cloth then began rising into the air and filling the small space. I felt my bloodfire warm in anticipation and I knew I was ready for this. It would kill me, but it would be worth it. And the rest of the pack would be safe.

Tendrils started sneaking away from the cloth and curling around my ankles. I felt tingles of cold on my skin and shivered slightly. Alex chanted louder and then fell silent. The smoke bled away into the atmosphere.

"It won't activate again until you're inside the portal," he said softly.

"Good. That means nothing else will see it between here and there," I commented. I deliberately kept the tone of my voice light. "And the portal itself?"

"Let's synchronise our watches," he said, with a ghost of a smile at the spy like phrase. "At exactly 2.15am, I'll open it for ten seconds. I can't give you longer than that though."

"It'll be enough."

"You don't have to do this, Mack. The Brethren…"

"Don't, Alex. I do have to do this and you're not going to change my mind." I picked up the cloth, trying not shudder, and stuffed it inside a plastic bag to avoid the smell escaping. Then I shoved it into one of my backpack's side pockets.

"I can come with you," he offered tentatively.

I laughed sharply and without mirth. "You don't do fighting, remember?" I touched him gently on his arm and tried to put conviction into my voice. "I will be fine and back here in no time."

He smiled slightly at the lie. "I'll wait right here for you then."

I tried to smile in return. "Don't wait up." He looked at me with a mixture of sympathy, hope and understanding. "Thank you, Alex," I said quietly, "for everything."

"Anytime, Mack Attack." He gave me a mock salute, which I acknowledged with a forced grin. Then I turned and left for the beach.

Chapter Twenty Five

As I left Alex and the wooden hut behind, I noticed that there was a light on in one of the third floor rooms, where Julia – and thc Brethren – were housed. A shadow moved across the window from behind the drawn curtains but I couldn't make out who it was. It didn't matter though. I knew this area like the back of my hand and could easily skip in and out of the shadows, staying out of sight, until I could get away into the woods.

Despite my bluster in front of Alex, I was feeling a bit scared. Okay, more than a bit scared, in fact I was bloody terrified. But I knew beyond a shadow of a doubt that this was the right move to make. I skirted behind a tree and then ducked to the fringes of the keep's front garden, hopping over the low-lying fence. I was about to edge into the cover of the woods when I noticed a dark shape moving towards me. It looked vaguely lupine so I figured it was probably one of the Brethren out patrolling. Luckily, the wind was down so my scent wouldn't carry far. I still froze, however, and waited, holding my breath and hoping the figure would turn into the garden rather than continue on towards me.

I counted my heartbeats. One one thousand, two one thousand, three one...excellent. The wolf turned back once it reached the gate and began to head down the way from which it had just come. I breathed a silent sigh of relief and entered the little forest. I paused just before the path, turning back to take one final glance back at the keep. My eyes travelled the length of its dark shape, over the familiar breeze blocks and slightly crooked outline. I prayed desperately that Julia would pull through. It didn't bear thinking about what might happen if she didn't. Hot anger flickered again inside me at what she, and the rest of my adopted family, were being forced to go through on my behalf. If I could stop Iabartu, it wouldn't make amends for the danger I'd put them in or for the consequences my presence had caused them, but it would prevent any further problems. They could return to their quiet little lives, unbothered by the arrogantly superior Brethren or nasties that threatened their very existence. I tried not to wonder if any of them would really be sorry that I was gone. Tom would, probably. Betsy perhaps. I hoped that they realised what a good thing they had going here in our little corner of the world and didn't take the decision to move to London with the Brethren. It was out of my hands now though.

I drank in the whole scene with my eyes and then turned back to the trees. It was time to go.

As soon as I reached the path, I picked up the pace and began jogging. I had about twenty five minutes before Alex opened the portal. I could have tried taking a shortcut and leaving the path, but I was still wary after my spell in the faerie ring earlier on and knew that the path would be quick enough. Part of me regretted throwing the majority of my coffee onto the kitchen wall. Some caffeine would have given me a much needed boost right now. Instead, I focused on the path and the satisfaction I would feel when I drove my silver dirk into Iabartu's black heart.

Before too long I reached the beach. I slowed, knowing that there would still be some Brethren guards out keeping a watchful eye on the portal. Fortunately I'd come prepared for just such an eventuality. I walked slowly over the top of the dunes, arms outstretched just in case any trigger happy shifters decided to attack first and then ask questions later.

As before, there were two guards, standing watchful over the frozen gateway. Both heads whipped immediately in my direction but relaxed slightly when they realised that I wasn't a threat. They still looked stiff and uncomfortable though, and, for just a brief moment, I felt slightly sorry for them. It couldn't be easy being made to stand here all night, in rural Cornwall, and know that their lives and the lives of their friends were being risked for a bunch of not very powerful, yokel pack shifters. My sympathy didn't last long, fortunately.

The one closest to me, the werefox, kept his gaze trained warily on my approach. I figured that they didn't entirely trust me after Corrigan's implication that I had deliberately abandoned them to be attacked. The other had switched her focus back onto the portal itself.

"Hiya!" I forced my voice to be bright and cheery.

Neither of them replied but I continued up towards them. "I couldn't sleep so I thought I'd come out for a walk and see if either of you needed a break."

"We are fine," the fox grunted, as expected.

"Well, how about a drink, then? You must need something by now to keep your energy levels up." I pulled a couple of cans of Coke from my backpack – from a separate compartment to the silver weapons, of course – and offered them out to the both of them, keeping the smile fixed on my face.

The werefox looked like he might tell me to piss off for a second, but clearly his thirst won over and he grudgingly accepted both of them, handing one to his colleague. I checked my watch. Still five minutes to go before Alex would release the portal. I figured it'd give me a chance to brush up on my small talk skills at least.

"So, I'm really sorry about your friends." And I actually was.

Both of them grimaced. "They were all strong brothers," the other Brethren said, still not looking away from the portal but at least swigging the Coke and relaxing ever so slightly. I maneuvered myself slightly so that I was angled towards the gateway. As soon my watch hit 2.15am, I'd make a run for it.

"Let the Way light their paths through the long night," I quoted, and each of the Brethren inclined their heads slightly.

Ummm…what now? I cast around, trying to think of an appropriate topic. The werefox rescued me, however. "So, I hear our Lord Alpha has offered you a place," he said, in a tone of voice that suggested that he thought it was patently a ridiculous idea.

"Uh, yes, he has. The Brethren's not really for me, I think though," I replied.

"It's a great honour," he said stiffly, somehow offended that, even though he believed I wasn't worthy of such an honour, I should be on my knees thanking them for it.

I kept my tone light. "Well, I prefer a quiet life."

"And yet you're such a skilled fighter," said a third deep voice, smoothly.

I turned, heart thudding. I knew that voice. The two Brethren guards immediately bowed, deeply. So they'd take their eyes off their jobs to genuflect at least.

"My Lord." Shit shit shit. "What brings you out tonight?"

His green eyes held mine appraisingly. "You were spotted leaving the keep. I was concerned," he paused slightly before continuing, "for your safety."

"Well, I appreciate your concern, my Lord. However, my skills at fighting, which you so gratifyingly highlight, mean that I am more than capable of looking after myself."

"You wouldn't be thinking of doing anything stupid, now would you, Miss Mackenzie?"

I noticed that he didn't call me kitten when others were around. I filed that tidbit away and smiled at him, returning his gaze without fear. He couldn't intimidate me, not when I was about to enter an Otherworld demesne to kill a god. Besides which, I was part dragon. That beat a were-panther any day. "I have absolutely no idea what you could mean, My Lord."

He stepped closer. I stepped back. I didn't want him to be within grabbing reach when the portal opened.

"From what little I have managed to glean of your nature, Miss Mackenzie, you have about as much sense of self-preservation as a kitten would." His eyes gleamed in the darkness at slipping in the kitten reference. Bastard. "I wouldn't put it past you to try to run into the portal stupidly thinking that you could save the world single-handedly."

I took another small shuffle backwards, hoping he wouldn't notice. "But as you know, my Lord, the portal is closed. Even if I wished to make such a foolish move, I would be unable to do so."

He didn't say anything in return, just folded his arms and gazed at me implacably.

"I couldn't sleep, alright? I thought I'd just come out for a walk and maybe bring your servants, sorry — guards , something to drink to keep their spirits up."

The werefox appeared vaguely alarmed. "I apologise, my Lord. We didn't think there would be any harm in accepting her offer of a drink."

I felt vaguely sickened at the Brethren member's bowing and scraping. So apparently did Corrigan because he bared his teeth slightly and snapped, "You are permitted to fucking drink if you need to."

Both of the sentinels cowered slightly. I wondered at the sort of regime Corrigan was running, that his own shifters were immured in fearful obeisance. Before I could comment on it, and really piss Corrigan off, my watch beeped. Almost immediately, the portal shimmered purple and began to hum. I twisted round in one swift motion and ran. I felt rather than saw Corrigan lunge at me, grabbing a hank of hair, but I managed to pull free, leaving what felt like half my scalp behind in his large hands. Sand kicked up as I sprinted at the portal, just a few metres away. I had to make it before he stopped me. I heard him roar in uncontained rage but the distance was too short for him to pull me back in time. The magic of the portal rippled painfully against my skin, tightening around my entire body as I battled through.

And then I landed in an ungraceful heap in broad daylight on the other side. I was through.

Chapter Twenty Six

I picked myself up, blinking in the unexpected sunshine. Corrigan's roar of rage was still echoing in my ears. I turned back to the portal, half expecting an enraged were-panther to come leaping through, but the purple shimmers were frozen. Clearly Alex had managed to immediately reseal the barrier as soon as I had entered. I felt grimly satisfied. At least the failure or success of my mission would be down solely to me and I wouldn't have to worry about anyone else coming through and getting in my way. Corrigan would realize Alex's complicity straight away but I knew that the mage would be aware of that and would make himself suitably scarce. Let's face it, no-one would want to hang around to see the full wrath of the Brethren's Lord Alpha. I dismissed my thoughts of him.

Surveying my surroundings, I was very much aware of both the vast differences and surprising similarities between this plane and my own. The sky here was so very blue, in fact such a deep rich shade that I'd never before seen anything like it in my life. The air felt cleaner and purer than even Cornwall's fresh salted scents, and the grass too was greener, with an earthy base. And yet something felt completely wrong about it all. It took me a moment to work out that it was because there was a total absence of sound. No insects, no birds, no gentle whistle of wind. The whole place was completely devoid of life.

I was stood on top of a small grassy knoll. There were undulating hills off in the distance, and what looked to be a deep valley cutting into the landscape some miles away on my right. But there were no trees, no plants, nothing apart from the grass, the ground and the sky. It was just as well Alex had cast the locator spell on the black bolt of fabric or I had the feeling that I'd end up trudging through this blue green desert forever.

Pulling it out of its side pocket in my backpack, I held it out in front of me, trying to ignore the smell. Almost immediately a thin blue smoky tendril rose into the still air and then snaked its way towards the valley I'd spotted before. To the right it was then. I slung the cloth over my shoulder and began to walk.

The uncomfortably unfamiliar sensation of fear had disappeared from the pit of my stomach. I was glad that it had gone. It could sharpen my focus and keep me alert, but feeling frightened meant that I was also more than likely to fumble and fail once I finally found Iabartu. It also proved to me that I had made the right decision. It might be lonely out here in this barren land but I felt confident that I was doing what was best for everyone. I began to whistle as I walked. The slightly off tune sound seemed to carry away from me leeching through the quiet atmosphere much in the same way as the blue trail. Let Iabartu hear it, I thought grimly. With the total absence of cover anywhere there was no doubt that I had no chance of the element of surprise. The least I could do was make her feel nervous at my apparent nonchalance.

As I continued to walk, part of me felt irritated that the best my Draco Wyr blood could do was make me feel hot and fiery inside. It would definitely be handy right about now to be able to sprout wings and fly. Especially when I was going up against a demi-goddess of the sky. I wondered about what Tom had said, about how on earth a dragon mated with a human in the first place. Perhaps they could shift into human form? And had it been my great-grandfather or great-grandmother who was a lizard? I considered the fact that John had known the truth all along, dismissing me when he'd heard about my bloodfire, trying to turn me into a real pack shifter when I was eighteen, training me to fight. I fervently wished that he'd told me what I was. Then I could have asked him more about my mother. He'd known her; she hadn't just been some strange human who'd turned up out of the blue one day. Somehow they'd had a history and she thought she could trust him with my life. Instead, my presence had taken his.

I frowned, trying to push the thoughts away. I'd get my revenge when I found Iabartu, one way or another. Even if the effort killed me, the least I could do would be to hurt her as much as I possibly could first. The familiar coil of heat asserted itself inside me at the thought and I concentrated on keeping it there. It would help when I finally uncovered whichever hole she was hiding in. My temper would at last do me some good.

I walked for what felt like hours. My senses were completely alert the entire time but I could feel myself becoming dangerously bored with the green and blue monotony. I tried to amuse myself by playing I-spy in my head for a short while, but there were only so many words I could come up with for grass, sky and valley. Although it wasn't particularly hot on this plane, I could feel the trickle of sweat soaking into my t-shirt and backpack. The straps were starting to rub against the skin of my shoulders and I realised that the stench of my humanity was becoming vastly obvious. I supposed it was just as well that I wouldn't be returning to Cornwall. The Brethren would never know the truth and the pack would be safe, not just from Iabartu but from me. I hoped that Tom wouldn't be too hurt that I'd not told him my plans but I was sure he'd understand. And with any luck Julia would pull through too.

Shifting the damp straps on my shoulders slightly, I continued on. My watch had stopped at the moment I'd come through the portal, which wasn't particularly a surprise given what I already knew about how time on other planes worked. I wondered how many Earth hours I'd already spent here. Or maybe it was days, or even mere seconds. As long as I could find John's bitch of a murderess before she sent anything else through to attack my pack then it didn't matter.

I was so intently wrapped up in my thoughts about how I'd go about ripping the head off her shoulders, I didn't notice for a while that there was something up ahead. The valley had been getting steadily closer but, due to the curve of the steep slopes, I hadn't until now spotted now something standing there in the middle of the grassy floor. From where I was it looked like a dark hole of pure blackness, incongruent against the rest of the landscape. The blue smoke seemed to disappear into the middle of it. At last I was getting somewhere. I began walking a bit faster, feeling the lick of flames inside me rise ever so slightly.

As I got closer, I realised that the patch of black had very straight edges. This was definitely not a natural occurrence. It had to be either man or monster made. In fact it looked suspiciously like a door. When I was a scant hundred or so yards away, I realised that that was exactly what it was. There even appeared to be a doorknob, just as black as the rest of it. I checked it for signs of a letterbox – perhaps I could drop Iabartu a little note, I thought sardonically, but there was only the door shape and the doorknob itself. I couldn't work out what material it was made out of. It didn't look like it was anything solid and, as I could actually circle the whole of it, I noticed that it was paper thin along the edges. As the trail leading from the cloth went straight into it, and didn't appear on the other side, this had to be the way I was supposed to go.

I shrugged to myself and used the corner of my t-shirt as a barrier between my skin and the doorknob to twist it open. There was a prickle across the length of my arm as I did so and then the door swung open. There was nothing on the other side, other than the rest of the valley, but the blue smoke went through it one way and didn't reappear on the other side, so it had to lead somewhere. I tugged out the silver dirk and clutched it in my sweaty palms and took a deep breath then stepped through.

And went nowhere. The smoke might have disappeared through the doorway but I certainly didn't. I was in exactly the same valley and in exactly the same place, just on the other side of the stupid door. That wasn't meant to happen. I frowned and tried stepping through in the opposite direction. Again, nothing. I hopped back and forth through the frame, irritated. What kind of stupid magic door was this? I had the horrible feeling that somewhere Iabartu was watching me on some Otherworld version of CCTV and absolutely pissing herself laughing.

I wondered if it was just me. I knelt down and pulled on a tuft of grass, crying out in surprised pain as it cut deep into the edges of my palm. A few drops of blood welled up, jewel-like. Cursing, I wiped the blood onto my jeans and used the dirk instead, gingerly holding the tips of the grass blades tight. Even though the dirk's blade was razor sharp, I still had to saw through to free them from the ground. That was…different. I definitely wasn't in Kansas any more. I stood up, still pinching the tips of the blades of grass and taking care not to cut myself further then flung them through the open doorway.

Like the blue smoke, they disappeared in midair. Huh. Rooting around in my bag, I found a bottle of water and unscrewed the lid, taking a long swig. Then I threw the bottle cap. It vanished as soon as it passed through the black edges of the frame. So it wasn't a case of just being something substantially from another plane that couldn't pass through. It was just me that couldn't pass through. Perhaps it was to do with carrying silver. I was extraordinarily reluctant to leave my best weapons behind, but they'd do me no good stuck here in the middle of nowhere with no-one to fight anyway. I took the backpack off my shoulders and removed the arrows, placing them carefully on the ground next to the dirk, then experimented first by waving a hand and a leg through the doorway. They didn't seem to go anywhere. There was only one way to know for sure. Casting a forlorn look at the grounded weapons, I tightly closed my eyes and jumped.

I opened one eyelid carefully, peeking first. Fuck. I still hadn't gone anywhere. Opening the other eye, I kicked the doorway in frustration and felt the same prickle as before run up my leg. Yeah, yeah, so it was definitely a fantastic magic gateway in the middle of a fantastic magical Otherworld plane filled with killer grass. It still didn't help me in the slightest.

I kicked the door again, this time shouting at the top of my lungs. "You wanted me, you bitch! Now I'm here! Come on then!"

The door gently swung shut as if in answer. I paused for a second, hopeful, but nothing else happened. It must have just been the vibrations from my kick. Well this was just great. Here I was, striding into Iabartu's home turf, ready to take her on and be the conquering hero and I'd end up having to go back to the portal with my tail between my legs. Except then I realised that the portal was sealed shut again so I couldn't even do that. I imagined Corrigan, shaking his head at me like I was some sort of naughty petulant child. Shaking the image away, I tried to focus my thoughts. Maybe if I destroyed the door instead, then she would come along to investigate.

Picking up one of the silver arrows, I took out my bow and strung it, aiming directly at the centre of the door. I held my breath but the arrow just thudded uselessly into it, then bounced back onto the grass. I kicked the door again, pissed off. Then I scooped up the dirk and stabbed viciously at the black shape with all my strength. It didn't even make a mark, in fact it was as if the door seemed completely impervious to the weapon. That did not bode well. I tried again. Nope. My fingertips bristled with angry heat and I dropped and punched the door, scraping my knuckles against the smooth impenetrable surface. The resulting pain reminded me that they were already tender from my battle to escape the faerie ring – and gave me an idea. If my blood was strong enough to break through a Fae's conjured barrier, then surely it could manage this. And even if it didn't work, I knew at least that Iabartu wanted me, or rather my blood, for whatever nefarious reasons she had cooked up. It could be that she'd sense it once it was spilled on her land.

I knelt down again and grabbed another tuft of glass sharp grass, wincing again as the blades cut through my skin. Instead of wiping the blood away this time, however, I smeared it onto the door frame and shook a couple of drops onto the ground for further effect. Then I stood back, and watched and waited.

I wasn't quite sure what I'd been expecting, but I'd been hoping for something rather dramatic. Wyr blood should surely bubble and hiss against nasty Otherworld materials. Instead, however, there was the faint smell of burning, that reminded me of the times when Johannes accidentally set his own hair alight when trying to light the ancient gas stove with a match. Nothing else happened. After a few tense moments, I reached out for the doorknob again and twisted. This time, the whole thing disintegrated in my bloody hands until I was left staring at nothing but the empty valley again. The blue trail still vanished in mid air, at the spot where the door had been.

Well, great, I thought sarcastically. Now there wasn't even a door to try to enter; it was just a blank space of air. Some fucking saviour I'd turned out to be. Mack Attack wasn't going to be very successful if there was nothing around to actually attack in the first place.

I was so angry with myself that I didn't notice it at first, but once it got stronger and began tugging at my ponytail I began to realize that something was happening. Where there had only been still air that lay as flat as that inside a sealed Egyptian mummy's tomb, now there was wind. And wind that was getting stronger and stronger. It started to whistle around my ears and ripple the cloth of my t-shirt. The black material that I'd been carefully carrying on my shoulder whipped off and danced away, carried on an invisible current. I felt my backpack being lifted up from behind, pulling at my shoulders as if it was being grabbed by an unseen force, a ghostly mugger who wanted all of my worldly possessions. I tried desperately to keep my balance and steady myself, but there was nothing to grab onto and I felt myself falling backwards, landing on the sharp grass and feeling its points pierce into my skin through my clothes.

At that point a shadow passed over my face. I shielded my eyes from the bright sun and looked up, trying to make it what it was. It was moving at an unbelievable speed, getting larger by the second, cartwheeling and spinning through the sky. I tried in vain to scramble to my feet, but the gale around was too strong. It felt as if I was being pinned to the earth. All I could do was watch. There was a roaring thunder in my ears and, oddly, I thought again of Corrigan's loud animalistic ire as I'd escaped into the portal. He didn't matter now though, nothing mattered now. My time was up.

Chapter Twenty Seven

The swooping shape drew nearer and nearer. Despite the situation, I vaguely admired the elegance of the flight. She landed a few feet away from me, causing ripples of tremors to shake beneath me. At least the wind died down though, and the atmosphere returned to the heavy oppressive stillness from before.

As soon as I was able, I sprang to my feet. Belatedly it occurred to me that I'd dropped the bow after I'd tried to shoot the door, and that no doubt it had been carried away in the hurricane. Fortunately I'd had enough sense left in me to hook the dirk through one of the belt holes at the top of my jeans, where it was still secure. I pulled it out and held it in front of me, prepared to take action.

Iabartu stood relaxed in front of me, examining her fingernails, as if she needed to make an emergency appointment with her manicurist. She was the same height as Alex's scrying had intimated and she was indeed floating just a few inches off the ground, as she had been when she had brutally attacked John. A sudden image of his corpse flashed through my mind and I felt the returning flash of fire. I shifted my weight and took a step forward. I was going to everything I could to destroy her.

"Bitch," I muttered, without even realising it.

Her white eyes lifted up to mine. And they actually were white - she had dark pinpricks of pupils, but absolutely no irises. The effect was extraordinarily unsettling. Despite the shudder of revulsion her gaze caused in me, it occurred to me that she looked rather bored of me already.

"What's your point?" Her voice was quiet and yet icily hard.

I swallowed and then steeled myself. She might be ice but I was all fire. I ignored her question. "I believe that you have been looking for me." I impressed myself by keeping my voice steady.

Iabartu arched a thin eyebrow at me. "Why, yes, little dragon, I have."

"You may be rather disappointed," I countered, "I am more human than Wyr."

She hissed, unexpectedly. "That is…unfortunate. But not disastrous or unexpected. It is your human nature that I knew would mean you would come looking for me if I pushed hard enough. Why do you think I left the portal open? Or the cloth for you to track? Your kind are so very sentimental and weak."

"You murdered my alpha," I spat.

A glimmer of a smile flickered over her bow-shaped lips. "Yes, I did, didn't I?" She laughed musically, and the sound grated through every inch of my soul, fanning my flames further. "Just think how much anguish he could have spared you if he'd only given you up at the beginning. Because, like I told him, the end result is still the same. I will drain you dry of every drop of fiery blood until all that is left is an empty husk." She laughed again, but this time the sound was colder.

"Why?" I bit out. "What makes my blood so special to you?"

"Oh little human Wyr, I could use it in ways that you can only dream of. You see, like you, I'm just a half-breed. Half a goddess." Her eyes gleamed. "A fantastically powerful one, but still there are those who seek to bring me down because I am not as pure as they would wish. Your blood will help me destroy them. Just a few carefully placed drops mixed into their mead and they'll be mine to control." She laughed coldly, but I noticed that her fists were clenched.

"If you'd just asked," I commented, "I'd give you a few drops."

The expression on her face was scornful. "And let you loose for someone else to use? I don't think so. Besides," she flipped her hair self-consciously, "I need a constant supply. Your blood has certain…addictive qualities that makes it so useful. There's no point in establishing the need, the desire for it, in one of my foes, and then not being able to control that supply." Licking her lips in a way that made me shudder, she added, "I need it all."

I felt a cold shiver run through me at her words, despite the churning bloodfire that was champing to be let loose. Part of me had hoped that I'd been wrong, that it hadn't been me that she'd been after – and that it hadn't been me who John had died protecting. I didn't really care what she did to her enemies on this plane but I was damned if I was going to let her use part of me to help her continue her terror campaign. And I would have my revenge for John, Julia and all the others.

"Over my dead body," I growled.

She raised a shoulder, shrugging lightly. "Suits me. There are plenty of ways to kill your mind but keep your physical body alive." And with that she lunged forward, trying to grab hold of me.

I dodged, only just managing to escape her grasping hands, and turned on my heel, facing her again. I watched her stance carefully, taking note of the shifts in her muscles, trying to gauge where she would move next. I wasn't going to try to strike her with the dirk until I could be sure of making contact.

She looked amused. "Oh, little dragon, this is going to be more fun than I thought." She shot up into the sky and disappeared.

I whirled, squinting up above me, trying desperately to work out where she had gone. A faint whistling came sneaking into my left ear and my grip on the dirk tightened. Suddenly, I felt a huge force cuff me on the side of my head. I went flying into the sharp grass feeling its blades rip into the skin on my face and arm.

She stood over me again, laughter pealing out. "Don't bleed too much, remember I need all that."

From the ground I kicked out at her leg, connecting with her flesh. She howled in surprise and somersaulted backwards. I sprang up and leapt forward, lashing out with the blade. I felt the satisfying moment when the dirk scratched into her clothing.

"So," she hissed, "the little human can use silver. I'm not one of your shifters, however. I am a god. It won't hurt me."

"Oh, but you're just a demi-god, Iabartu, otherwise you wouldn't need me. And when I stick this into your heart, it will hurt you. A lot."

I was more confident now. She wasn't entirely invulnerable and now I knew that I could reach her. This was not going to be impossible. I ran at her, dirk in front of me, ready to slice her and make her bleed. This time, however, she skirted right into the air before clawing her taloned fingernails at me. They connected with my cheek and drew blood. Iabartu paused, hovering in midair, and examined the little red drops on the tips of her fingers, a fascinated expression on her face.

"I can feel the fire from here," she murmured.

"Then feel this," I spat and attacked again, stabbing at her as the flames inside me roared in approval. The silver sank into her arm before she could pull away, and a dark liquid welled up around it. I managed to keep a firm grip on the hilt and held onto my now only workable weapon while Iabartu pulled back sharply. My slice didn't quite have the devastating effect that I'd been hoping for but at least I got a reaction as her face twisted briefly in pain.

"Enough!" She snapped her fingers and, almost immediately, I heard a quiet rumble in the distance, getting gradually louder as whatever it belonged to drew nearer.

"Afraid you can't beat me on your own, bitch? I might have figured that you'd call someone else in to do your dirty work. Clearly, a half breed like you doesn't have much power of your own." I hoped that I could taunt her into making a mistake but Iabartu had too much ice running through her veins for that just yet.

"You're a half-breed too, human. I notice you don't have anyone rushing to your aid." She swung backwards and out of my reach.

"Because I don't need help to kill you," I retorted loudly. Just as I'd tried to encourage her temper to get the better of her, now she was obviously trying it with me. Of course, my temper was often my best weapon – Iabartu didn't need to know that though.

The sound of whatever she'd summoned was getting almost unbearably loud. With half an eye on Iabartu, who was now floating at the edge of the valley, I turned slightly to meet whatever was coming. Whatever it was, it was huge. And it looked disturbingly familiar.

Iabartu let out a silvery giggle that made shivers run down my spine. "You have already met, I believe? I think that my little friend is anxious for a re-match. After all, you attacked him entirely without provocation the last time."

The ispolin's shape drew closer. "He invaded our territory," I growled.

"For all you know he was popping round to borrow a cup of sugar before you so mercilessly and viciously pounced on him."

I felt an irritating twinge of guilt. She did actually have a point – not about the sugar of course, but about fighting first and asking questions later. But he'd killed that Brethren guy and maimed Lucy. And if he'd reached Trevathorn, god only knows what might have happened. It was the pack's job to keep Cornwall safe from the big bad. The ispolin was certainly both of those.

Iabartu laughed at me again. "That, my dear, is why you'll never be as powerful as me. Why that blood is wasted on you. You'd actually feel bad for giving him a booboo."

I scowled, annoyed that I was so transparent, and struggling to keep my fire in check at least for the time being. "On the contrary, it's what makes me better than you. But if that thing gets in my way, then I'll mow him down. It's you I'm here for."

I'd barely finished my sentence when the ispolin howled in rage and began to charge. Iabartu leapt up into the sky. "Lucky me, I get a ringside seat," she called down. "Don't kill her just yet though, I need her heart pumping when I drain her blood."

I ignored her pointed order to the beast and tensed. It was clearly still bearing the scars and wounds from our encounter on the beach and was looking for a little payback. I understood that, but there was no way I was going to let it prevent me from doing all I could to get my own payback from Iabartu. An image of Lucy's limping form flashed into my head, along with Thomson's broken body. I might not have liked the guy but he was a shifter which made him part of me and mine. This wouldn't be so hard on my conscience after all. I released some of the heat I'd been keeping such a tight hold onto and looked straight into its one great eye. Bring it on.

The ispolin came close enough for me to see that I could see its hairy nostrils flaring. A trickle of dark green snot made its way down its face, making me wonder if the slime that Nick had found at Perkins had just been the remnants of a giant monster sneeze. The heaving nostrils did remind me of a Spanish bull, however, which gave me an idea. I watched it carefully, waiting for it to make the first move. Its muscles rippled and its whole body shifted almost imperceptibly to the left. I sprang right, just in time to miss its barreling shape, and turned to face it again. Without pausing, it rammed its way towards me again, head down and lethal horns leading. For the second time, I managed to jump out of the way. I could sense Iabartu watching impatiently from the air and I took a moment to sketch a bow in the air, almost imagining myself as a bullfighter on a sandy ring. The ispolin pawed the ground and blinked furiously then rushed me again. I skipped out of the way but this time it was expecting it and threw out a fist to cuff me. It connected – barely – but the force was enough to send me spinning to the ground. I jumped up quickly, not before I felt a thousand blades of glass sharp grass cut into my skin all over again, while trying to ignore the sudden sensation of vertigo that the ispolin's blow had created in my skull.

My gaze fell on the black cloth that was lying on the ground behind it. Well, in the absence of red, I supposed that black would be just as good. This time, when it lunged at me again, I ran at it too, then dove headfirst between its legs, noting that its foot hygiene hadn't improved since the last time, and whipped up the piece of material. As I rolled beneath its groin, I also noticed that dangling from its waist was an oddly mechanical looking object. Huh. So that was where the electric screwdriver had ended up. Part of my brain tried to work through what on earth a one-eyed Otherworldly monster would want with home DIY but before I could come up with a reasonable answer I was back on my feet facing the ispolin and holding the black cloth in front of me.

I dangled it to my side, daring the monster to come at me again. I hadn't counted on the blue trail that still snaked its way from it – this time up to the sky to where Iabartu hovered. As I'd picked the cloth up, the smoke had moved with it. The ispolin's huge eye was caught by it, almost entirely mesmerised. I hadn't expected it, but it'd work. I threw myself at the monster in a blur, aiming my dirk for one of the gashes on its side from earlier. The silver blade entered the its tough flesh with surprising ease and began to smoke. The sickening smell of burnt flesh rose in the air. It fell to the ground, clutching the wound as I sprang back and watched warily. The same cutting grass that had bothered me earlier, now bothered the ispolin more, and it howled again, deafeningly. This time it was in pain and not rage however. It rolled over and only succeeded in cutting its hide even more. This would be a handy time to have some blackberry bushes around for it to roll into, assuming that Alex's theory had been accurate.

Its huge arms flailed around in the air and it kept rolling on the ground. I gripped the dirk and was about to attack again when Iabartu materialized at it its head and sank one long taloned nail straight into its one eye, piercing it like a balloon. The ispolin shuddered and went still.

Iabartu looked at me and shrugged implacably. "If you want a job done, then you have to do it yourself," she murmured softly.

Without thinking, I threw the dirk straight at her throat. She was too quick, however, and blocked it, sending the whole blade spinning uselessly behind me and far out of my reach. "Now what are you going to do little human?"

Good question. I reached inside myself and unleashed the full force of my bloodfire. This time there would be no holding back. It felt like my insides were boiling but I relished the feeling and allowed it to take over in a way I never had before. My shoulders straightened and I met her gaze full on. She opened her mouth to speak but my flames wouldn't let her even start her sentence. The time for talking was over. Now I needed my revenge and to do what I could to let John rest in true peace. I attacked.

I had no weapon left, and had to avoid falling on the ground, so I stayed light on my feet and clenched my fists. Smacking into the side of her face, I managed to send her reeling but she recovered quickly and answered with a blow of her own. I felt unsteady on my feet, both from her swipes, the continued blood loss and the ispolin's attack, but the heat inside me wouldn't allow my brain to register it properly. I kicked her stomach, thanking the heavens that I was wearing my boots instead of my soft soled trainers, and was rewarded with a pained gasp from her. She shot up into the air, body circling upwards like an arrow. I span around, trying to spot where she was and where she'd land next. Unfortunately, I wasn't versed enough in the fighting tactics of flying demi-goddesses, and, before I knew what was happening, she was behind me, her slender fingers wrapping themselves round my throat and her nails curving into my skin.

Iabartu's fingers tightened and she leaned over to my ear. I could almost taste the smell of death from her, it was so strong. This made the unpleasant odour of the cloth pale into weak comparison. "I could use my nails to end this now," she breathed. "Rip into your windpipe and have you bleed out in half a pathetic human heartbeat." One fingernail scraped across my skin and I felt it draw blood. Shit. "But that wouldn't achieve what I really want." Her hands squeezed my neck further until I started to gulp for air. Black dots appeared in front of my eyes and my lungs burned. The flames inside me shrieked and raged and I tried to kick back and knock her away, but it was a feeble effort. "Instead all I need to do is to take away your breath for a mere minute. I'll starve your mind of oxygen. You'll be technically brain dead, but I won't let your body die." She laughed coldly in my ear. "I'll keep you alive for as long as I need. You'll be a little dragon vegetable, growing all the blood I'll ever need, just for me." My head was exploding with pain and I could barely hear her words. I needed to breathe but it wasn't going to happen. Even through the haze of oncoming oblivion, all I could think was that I'd failed. Failed John, failed Julia, failed the pack. Even as a supposedly all powerful Draco Wyr with fiery blood, I had still failed. I closed my eyes and tried to accept the inevitable. A tiny rational corner of me hoped that whatever Iabartu was planning to do with my blood wouldn't cause any more harm to anyone, shifter or human, while my hands clawed desperately at her fingers, trying uselessly to pry them away from my throat.

Dimly, I heard a roar and a thunder of steps. Before I could pinpoint what the noise was, I was on the ground, gulping and gasping for air and trying to fill my burning lungs. I didn't even notice the grass this time. My head felt ridiculously heavy, and it took a vast amount of effort, but I lifted my eyes to see a huge bear on its haunches extend a clawed paw out to Iabartu's shape, preventing her from taking off into the air and slamming her into the ground. Seemingly from out of nowhere a sleek black panther pounced on top of her, massive paws digging into her shoulders. It snarled venomously and raised its head for just a brief second to look directly at me. And then it ripped out her throat.

Chapter Twenty Eight

I staggered to my feet, hot angry tears burning my eyes, lungs still screaming in agony, blood leaking from a thousand cuts all over my body, and blood at near boiling. The panther sat atop Iabartu's still body, looking incredibly self- satisfied. I staggered over and slapped it. In theory, I'd flung all my power behind that one blow, but there was little left inside me to offer. The panther reeled back ever so slightly and growled, rising up.

The Lord Alpha began to change. His fangs retracted first, although the traces of Iabartu's blood remained on his white teeth. His muzzle and whiskers twisted into human features, and skin and muscles ripped through the fur. His bare feet straddled her body and he glared at me. "You fucking idiot."

I gasped, trying to get the words out, but my voice felt lost. "She..." I croaked, "She was mine to kill."

Corrigan placed his hands on his tanned bare hips and suddenly looked amused. "And you were doing such a great job of that, kitten, weren't you?"

The sound of more ripping fur and shifting came from my left and Anton sauntered over, lip curling. "My Lord, she attacked you. The Way…"

"Under the circumstances, I'll overlook it," Corrigan said calmly, not looking at Anton.

"I needed to kill her," I whispered hoarsely again.

Corrigan's eyes flashed. "And you presumed to think that you would do it single-handedly? That I didn't have a plan to sort all this out in the first place?" Anger shimmered across the taut muscles of his face.

Okay, so he was pissed off, but it had still been my fight not the fucking Brethren's. I opened my mouth again to say so but the pain of drawing breath was too much and I found I couldn't speak.

"At last, silence reigns. With any luck your vocal chords will be permanently damaged and then you'll be forced to keep that sweet mouth shut for good."

I snarled at him and took a step forward.

You forget yourself, human. Anton's Voice slammed into my mind. I stared at him aghast, with a horrible sense of deja vu. Anton's Voice meant that Julia…

An articulate noise sprang from my throat, grating against my already wounded windpipe. I gasped for breath and pitched forward, caught by Corrigan's hard arms just in time. He looked down at me expressionlessly and cleared his throat.

"She's not dead," he said softly. "But her wounds are such that she no longer has the physical ability to manage your pack. Anton's Voice emerged several hours ago and Mother Nature is doing its job." He paused for a second, appearing to consider his next words. "Funny, I thought it would be you." He said this last quietly, so quiet that I doubted that Anton heard him. Probably just as well; I doubted the bear would take too kindly to hearing the insinuation that a human would make a better alpha than he would. I supposed that on the bright side, it meant that Corrigan still wasn't aware of my true nature. This thought was then suddenly followed by the slamming realization that it had been far too long since I'd used the lotion to mask my human smell. Unconsciously I took a step backward. Shit.

Corrigan's face closed off. "We need to leave. The other portal will not remain open for much longer."

I swallowed, trying to edge closer to Iabartu's body, praying that the stench of death emanating from her would mask me. "Uh….other portal?"

Anton looked at me as if I was stupid. "How do you think they got through to attack the keep? The beach portal was already sealed by your friend," he spat the last out. "There was *obviously* another gateway."

Oh yeah. I'd been so caught up in my grief and horror, not to mention absorbed by the revelations of my ancestry, that I hadn't even considered where the nasties had come from that had maimed Julia. Duh. I was clearly off my game. My lack of sensible brain activity then wasn't stopping me now from picturing just how much danger I was putting the whole pack in right now. I stared at Anton, willing him to initiate another conversation so I could remind him about what would happen if Corrigan decided to inhale past Iabartu's covering scent.

It was Corrigan, however, who looked at me impatiently. "There'll be time to analyse later. You need to shift so all those cuts will start healing and we need to return. I don't want to spend more time around this plane than necessary."

I squeaked and continued to try to implore Anton with my eyes.

"For fuck's sake," exclaimed Corrigan. "She's dead, your alpha's death is avenged, you can shift. We don't have time for this."

"Right," I said, swallowing hard. "Okay, time to shift. Yes, can't wait to finally shift again, if I go too long I get that itch, you know? So it's good, that I can now actually shift." I was clearly babbling.

Corrigan raised his eyebrows. Anton, damn him, looked amused – and slightly hungry. I wondered whether he still wanted to taste my blood and whether I could use that to make him let me stay with the pack. Well, I was fucked if I'd let him get even slightly close after this. He continually seemed to forget that my lack of shape-shifterness put the whole pack at risk, not just me. Without his help I went down the only avenue left to avoid trying to meet Corrigan's obviously impossible expectations. I rolled my eyes back into my head and fainted.

I tried not open my eyes immediately in surprise when Corrigan caught my body before it landed back onto the sharp grass. He cursed and picked me up, holding me against his chest. I fought very hard not to tense up as he did so.

Anton laughed sardonically in my head. *Nicely played, human.*

God, finally. *You idiot,* I hissed back at him. *I've not used the lotion for over a day now. Once we get away from the rotting stench of the bitch, he'll know I'm human.*

And I should care about that why?

Welcome to the new Cornish alpha, ladies and gentlemen. *Because, you wanker, once the Brethren know what*

I am, you will all be in danger. You are the alpha, it's your job to protect everyone.

I could almost feel the cogs whirling in his head. Corrigan muttered something to him and took off smoothly towards what I supposed was the other end of the valley. If Anton didn't get with the programme soon, this was not going to turn out well. I couldn't pretend to be unconscious indefinitely. Not only that but Corrigan had a fast gait and it wouldn't be too long before the only thing he'd be able to smell would be me.

Yes, it IS my job to protect everyone he finally answered. *So I'll do this and help you. And you will leave Cornwall forever.*

WHAT?

I am the alpha, his Voice stated simply. *Your presence puts the pack in danger. Therefore I want you gone from Cornwall as soon as we return.*

As much as I knew that Anton was relishing this moment with every fibre of his being, he was right. I did put the pack in danger by staying with them. Especially now. All this had happened because of me, and although I could acknowledge that I hadn't asked for any of it and couldn't have changed the molecular biology of my blood even if I'd known about it, I knew that I was still guilty. Leaving was the safest option. It was almost a relief to finally have someone demand my absence – perhaps it would help assuage my guilt.

Done.

Give me your word.

I almost growled aloud. *You just had it. Now fucking deal with this.*

"My Lord, I will take her," said Anton somewhere to the left of Corrigan.

Corrigan was silent for a heart-stopping moment. Oh come on. He finally replied, "It's fine. She weighs nothing."

"I am her alpha. It is my responsibility – she is my responsibility. We have not always been on the best of terms but perhaps this way I can demonstrate to her that she can trust me."

Nicely played, I thought. Now when I ran off, I'd be the ungrateful bint who couldn't acknowledge that 'Lord' Anton had rescued me. Bastard. Corrigan halted and passed me over to Anton's arms. Instead of cradling me against his chest as the Lord Alpha had done however, he slung me over his shoulder in an incredibly undignified fireman's lift. I was painfully aware of my bottom waving around in the air from above his shoulder.

"The others will be anxious for news, my Lord," Anton continued. "I do not wish to move too quickly as clearly Mackenzie has many small wounds from which there is a considerable amount of blood. I have no objection if you wish to move ahead and let everyone know what has happened."

I wondered if Corrigan would let himself be manipulated quite so easily. I sincerely hoped so.

Anton continued. "Perhaps then you can alert the doctor to move to the portal to help her as quickly as possible. Mackenzie is usually more hard-headed than this. I am concerned that she has fainted and not yet re-awakened."

I tried very hard not to slap his back for his so-called 'concern'. Nonetheless it seemed to work as, without a word, I sensed Corrigan begin to move away. After he appeared to go a few feet however, he called back, "You are very demanding when you want to be, Anton. I hope that the Way has chosen a true alpha for Cornwall. I would hate to spend more time down here babysitting you."

Hah! Take that bear-man!

Take care, kitten, sounded Corrigan's Voice in my head. I was startled by the unexpected gentleness of the sentiment. At least with my face stuck in Anton's naked back, my surprise didn't show. And with that he was gone.

Anton jostled me forward for a few more uncomfortable moments. I guessed that he was waiting until the Lord Alpha was definitely out of sight. Eventually, however, he put me down, feet first, and gazed at me stonily.

"You will not renege on this, human," his eyes spat malevolent sparks.

I felt the familiar spark of heated irritation inside me and sighed tiredly, "I gave you my word, tosser. I'll do this." Truth be told, although my fainting had be feigned, I was starting to feel rather woozy anyway. I hoped I'd be strong enough to get out of Cornwall first. Talking also hurt an incredible amount. "I just need to get cleaned up and talk to Julia and the others, and then I'll be gone."

He laughed shortly. "I don't think so. As soon as we get back through the portal, you are gone."

I began to protest but he interrupted me. "I don't need to give the Brethren any more opportunity than necessary to find out what you are. I'll inform the others what has happened once they have gone. Your friends," he injected disdain into the last word, "are leaving for London anyway."

Tom and Betsy. I cursed inwardly. I'd been hoping that they would change their minds but considering the alternative, being stuck here with Anton as alpha for the next several decades, I couldn't exactly blame them anymore. Joining the Brethren, though? My body shook with distaste.

Anton eyed me. "How bad are your injuries?"

I didn't kid myself that he was asking out of concern. He just wanted to make sure that I'd get out of his demesne before I caused any more trouble. "I'll live," I answered shortly, squaring my shoulders. I was bleeding from a thousand different cuts and it was still painful to breathe, but there was no way I was going to give him the satisfaction of knowing how much I hurt. "What about my things?" I asked him. The thought of leaving my little treasure chest behind was almost as much of a wrench as leaving behind the pack. Almost.

"I'll arrange for them to be sent to you once you are settled somewhere else," he said dismissively, then moved away wrinkling his nose. "We need to hurry. The Lord Alpha will be sending the doctor to the portal as we speak. We need to get through before he manages to return. And for god's sake stay at least a few feet away from me. Your stench is getting unbearable."

I scowled at him, angrily. Even though he was getting everything he'd ever wanted, he still couldn't resist sticking the knife in. "What? Don't fancy licking my blood any more?" I hissed at him.

"Oh, believe me, I still want it. And I'd have it if I was so inclined." I looked at him, warily before he continued. "But now I'm alpha I need to rise above such base desires. Keep your funny blood, ape. It's about all you have left after all." And with that he turned and started striding away.

My eyes shot daggers after him, but I followed regardless. I wondered if Anton's attitude would change if he knew the truth about my blood. I shrugged. It didn't matter now. I put my head down and concentrated on putting one foot in front of the other, ignoring the dots of bleeding pain from around my body.

It seemed to take an age to get anywhere. The landscape remained entirely uniform throughout – emerald green blades of cutting grass, brilliant blue sky and the walls of the valley. There was absolutely nothing else to be seen anywhere. It was a blessed relief when the purple shimmers of the second portal finally came into sight. Anton turned back towards me briefly, raising his eyebrows with an extraordinarily annoying look of anticipation. Screw him. I wasn't leaving for him or because of his demands – it was for the good of the pack. My friends and my family. I felt unbidden tears rise up and blinked them furiously away. I had to stop thinking of myself though, and start thinking of the others. It occurred to me that I now possessed absolutely nothing. All my weapons were lost, and my 'fainting fit' had meant that I couldn't even retrieve my trusty backpack. I had no money and nowhere to go. And with Iabartu's death, not even at my hands, I now had absolutely no purpose. I felt utterly bereft. I watched Anton disappear through the gateway, taking a moment to compose myself. I was damned if I'd let him see how upset I was.

Digging deep inside myself, I searched for the flare of bloodfire. Once I had it, I let it swirl around me, and I let its waves of heat curl around me my body. I pictured John, and Julia, and everything I was leaving behind. I even reflected on Iabartu's corpse and how I hadn't even managed to kill her myself. At least as long as I was angry, I wasn't going to weep in front of Anton; I wouldn't give him that satisfaction.

I rubbed my eyes with the back of my hand and stepped through the portal.

Chapter Twenty Nine

The sensation of passing through the gateway made me feel oddly nauseous. I pushed it away, however, blinking, and realised that this second gateway was close to the clearing where John had shown me the wichtlein's stone. It made sense now, after all we were some distance from the beach and it had never quite tallied that Iabartu had travelled from so far away instead of going straight to the keep. It seemed a lifetime ago now since I'd been here last. I closed my eyes for a brief second, imagining John in front of me, before composing myself, opening my eyes and looking coldly at Anton. "What will happen to the portal?"

"It's none of your concern," he muttered.

Fuckwit, I thought, enjoying the feeling of my bloodfire rise further. "You can't keep the pack safe with this open, Anton."

"You are pushing your luck," he hissed at me, his breath warm and unpleasant in my face. "The mage will close it now that we have returned. The pack will only be safe once you have gone." His eyes narrowed to slits. "And it's time you did so now."

I took a step closer to him and was rewarded to see that he took a step backwards, away from me. "Oh, I'll go, Anton. But you'd better be the best fucking alpha in the country. Because if I ever hear that you've done anything to endanger the pack, or if you abuse your power in any way, I'll be back." I licked my lips. "And we both know who would win the fight." I dared him to remember the fact that I'd bested him the gym in the Brethren's test. He snarled at me, but I'd already had the last word and meant every part of it. And he knew it. Spinning on my heel, I stalked away, towards the road and away from the keep.

*

Walking through the forest, I knew I'd have to be fast. Corrigan could easily catch me, probably in his human form as much as in his shifter form and there was nothing left that would hide my so-called humanity from him. I scoffed at myself. Humanity? That was a laugh. I wasn't human, I was some weird kind of weak dragon by-blow with stupid hot blood that was apparently addictive.

I picked up the pace. Before too long the road leading to Truro and beyond came into view. I pulled a few large leaves off a nearby tree, using them to rub off the worst of the blood. The last thing I'd need was to be picked up by some well meaning passerby who'd be so horrified by my appearance I'd be taken straight to hospital, no matter what I said. The leaves did a fairly poor job, but they were better than nothing. I started to jog. I had to put as much distance between myself and the keep as possible – not only because Corrigan might find me but because despite my vow to Anton I knew I was in danger of changing my mind and going back to the only home I'd ever known, whatever the consequences. I spared a thought for Tom, Julia, Betsy, Johannes, even Nick. I hoped they'd understand why I'd left.

Suddenly a Voice slammed into my head.

You're running away. It was Corrigan.

I swallowed, slightly scared. Actually who was I kidding? The man more than scared me - he terrified me. *I have to,* I sent back. He wouldn't understand but lying again right now was beyond me.

You don't have to just join another rural pack, Mackenzie. Come to the Brethren. Your boyfriend is joining us after all – you won't be alone.

I didn't respond. Silence hung in the mental air for just a second and his Voice appeared again. *You're not joining another pack, are you? You're going rogue.*

Again, I didn't bother to reply. My actions would be clear soon enough.

You know the consequences of this.

Way Directive No 6: All shifters must belong to a pack or they are to be considered outcasts. The Brethren put rogue shifters on their watchlist and they ended up forever looking over their shoulder, waiting to be caught. Fair enough, yeah, but I wasn't actually a shifter, was I?

I will find you, kitten, sooner or later.

Goodbye Corrigan. I slammed shut my mental gates, pushing him out and trying to ignore the little flicker of regret as I did so.

The sound of a car appeared behind me and I stuck out my thumb, half-hoping it wouldn't stop. It did. The window wound down and a ruddy face peered out. "Where to, love?"

I batted down my irrational irritation at the 'love' and bit out a smile. "As far as you're going."

"Exeter do you?"

It was a start. I smiled and walked round to the passenger side.

About the author

After teaching English literature in the UK, Japan and Malaysia, Helen Harper left behind the world of education following the worldwide success of her Blood Destiny series of books. She is a professional member of the Alliance of Independent Authors and writes full time, thanking her lucky stars every day that's she lucky enough to do so!

Helen has always been a book lover, devouring science fiction and fantasy tales when she was a child growing up in Scotland.

She currently lives in Devon in the UK with far too many cats – not to mention the dragons, fairies, demons, wizards and vampires that seem to keep appearing from nowhere.

You can find out more by visiting Helen's website: **http://helenharper.co.uk**

The entire Blood Destiny series is available now.

Bloodfire
Bloodmagic
Bloodrage
Blood Politics
Bloodlust

Made in United States
North Haven, CT
23 May 2022

19434885R00193